KISSING TESS

Tess fell straight into Zack's arms. Without even thinking about what he was doing, he closed his arms around her. The feathers in her hat bounced as Tess tilted her head back, and her gaze met his.

Damn, did the hat have to match her eyes so perfectly? he wondered, looking down into their depths.

She stared at him in silence, then nervously moistened her lips. Her chest rose with her next breath, and Zack held her tighter. Her eyes widened with a blend of dismay and perhaps pleasure, while sparks of anger still flared at him.

There it was again—that mix of innocent and temptress, and it was daring him. Tempting him beyond belief. He succumbed, hang the consequences.

Lowering his head, Zack took Tess's lips in a consuming kiss that heated him right down to his boots. Damn, she wasn't supposed to taste this good. This sweet, he thought, then drew her closer, planting his mouth more fully over hers . . .

Books by Joyce Adams

REBEL MINE

GAMBLER'S LADY

MOONLIGHT MASQUERADE

LOVING KATE

TEMPTING TESS

Published by Zebra Books

TEMPTING TESS

Joyce Adams

Zebra Books
Kensington Publishing Corp.
http://www.zebrabooks.com

ZEBRA BOOKS are published by

Kensington Publishing Corp.
850 Third Avenue
New York, NY 10022

First Printing: January, 1997
10 9 8 7 6 5 4 3 2 1

Printed in the United States of America

To *Laveta* and *Ronald*—thank you for teaching me to look forward.

Mary Laveta—thanks for all our plotting and the laughter. There'll never be another book like this one!

Acknowledgments

I'd like to offer my special thanks to the following people for assisting me in my research:

Charles Jeske
Dr. Eights—a true dispenser of medical miracles
Sterling—a gambler extraordinaire and faro teacher
Dahlia
The Silverado Wild West Company
Gunfighters of the Old West
The San Jose Historical Society
The entire McCravy "clan"

Prologue

Zack Mackinzie crushed the well-creased telegram into a wad and threw it into the dead embers of last night's campfire. The act did little to ease his pain or his anger.

The missive had come too late. He'd been a five-day ride from home the afternoon he'd received the telegram informing him of his brother's death. Although he'd saddled up and rode like hell itself was after him, it hadn't been enough. He'd arrived at the ranch a day too late for David's burial.

Not David, he wanted to shout at fate. *He'd* been the one who'd joined the Rangers, *he'd* been the one who put his life on the line every day, not David. His brother had stayed behind and saw to the running of the ranch they shared. The ranch his years as a Ranger had made possible.

Yes, David had stayed home—safe. Until she came along.

Now his brother was dead. Poisoned. And all because he'd gotten himself caught up in the treacherous web of a pretty crook and her shady father. Well, if they thought for a moment that they had gotten away clean, they were wrong. Dead wrong.

Zack swallowed down the pain and kicked his booted

heel through what remained of the campfire as memories of David rushed over him. After their parents' deaths in a Comanche raid too many years ago to recall, he and his younger brother had built a bond closer than brothers, in spite of the four years that separated them. They'd almost known what the other was thinking before they even spoke the words.

Now he'd never hear David's voice again. Perhaps if he'd been home instead of off chasing yet another outlaw this wouldn't have happened. But his involvement in the Texas Rangers was his life.

And now it was part of that job to track down the person responsible for his brother's murder. He'd spent the better half of a week doing just that. He held tight to what few leads he possessed: David's last letter and a show token.

He pulled the round token out of the breast pocket of his leather vest. It had been clutched in David's hand when the sheriff found his body. Now the small disc caught the bright sunlight, reflecting it back, shimmering like gold. The shine was as fake as the charlatan who'd sold the poison to his brother.

Zack rubbed his thumb back and forth across the metal. The raised lettering was rough beneath the pad of his thumb. By now he knew the words by heart. *Good for one admission to Fontana's Fabulous Medicine Show.*

Wrapping his fingers around the token, he curled his hand into a fist. For an instant he wished it was Tess Fontana's neck. Rage boiled within him, demanding to be set free.

The pretty, deceitful Tess, the love of his brother's life, would never walk free—he'd see to that. If it was the last thing he did, he'd bring his brother's murderer to justice.

Justice. The word seared through his chest. If he hadn't been pursuing justice last month, he'd have been here to save David. Instead he'd had to learn of his brother's infatuation for the "blond beauty with eyes the color of Texas bluebells" from his letter. His last letter.

Anger ate at him, warring with the guilt as he saddled his buckskin mount. He'd find the damned medicine show if he had to ride until hell froze over.

Zack swung into the saddle, pulled his dark hat low, and spurred his horse on. A traveling medicine show shouldn't be too hard to track. Especially not if it were leaving death in its wake.

The desperate need for vengeance rose up in him, threatening to boil under the hot Texas sun. He knew vengeance wouldn't bring his little brother back. But justice and vengeance might just help some.

When he caught up with her, Miss Tess Fontana would be sorry she ever stepped her dainty foot onto Texas soil. Or into his life.

She'd pay. She'd pay dearly.

One

Tess Fontana was on the run with a wanted man . . . her father.

She wiped her damp palms down the skirt of her sky-blue gown and straightened her spine. As the minutes ticked by, she waited in the wings of the medicine show's canvas tent, its thick, dusty flap hiding her from all prying eyes. She struggled against the overwhelming temptation to turn and run. As far and as fast as she could. However, she'd already done that once seven years ago, and look where it had gotten her.

But she'd had no other choice, she reminded herself, shutting out any guilt. She'd done the right thing.

Brushing aside the past as if it were a pesky fly and not something that possessed the power to reach out across the years and destroy her, she raised up on her slipper-clad tiptoes and peered out through the small tear in the dust-covered canvas. Not for the first time she wished for a few more added inches to her height of scarcely over five feet. Above the makeshift stage furled the battered banner proclaiming "Fontana's Fabulous Medicine Show," her father's pride and joy.

She checked over the members of the audience as she did at the beginning of each show. Experience coupled with years of living life on the run had taught her never to let her guard down.

However foolish the feeling might be, she always expected for someone to stand up from the audience, point an accusing finger at her, and shout, "There she is. That's the one."

Tess scanned the faces of the men absorbed in the performance—looking for one face that might present a danger to her father. A sigh of relief drifted past her lips as she nervously nibbled on her full lower lip. No familiar faces, and even better, no lawman badges greeted her tense survey.

She had no use for lawmen—no good use, that was—for any interfering lawman. The traveling show had been chased out of too many towns by their kind for her to foster gentle feelings for a man wearing a badge.

She began to breathe more evenly. Maybe tonight would go off without a hitch. Maybe . . .

But some vague sense of unease told her not to count on it. Time had taught her not to count on anything except her father and her own ability to keep them both safe.

And alive.

Her sense of duty demanded she turn her wayward attention back to the stage, and she scanned the platform. Kerosene lanterns lit the makeshift wood-plank floor, but it was the distinguished-looking man, arms held high, who commanded attention. Clothed in a black shirt and trousers, with a thick red cape embroidered with golden suns and moons, he held the audience of rough miners enthralled as if he were royalty commanding them.

Her smile widened into a grin of pride. Papa was a showman—pure and simple. Back in Texas he'd often helped out at visiting performances, as well as working hard at his medical practice. She wondered what would have happened if . . . No! She forced herself to cut off the thought with fierce determination. Hadn't Papa told her enough times to look forward not back.

Her throat tightened. He was right. No good came out of looking back. If she ever allowed herself to dwell on what had happened because of her, on what she'd allowed to happen . . .

Tess shook her head, sending her long silver-gold curls tumbling over her shoulder. No, if she looked back, she'd never be able to continue. And she had to. She was the only one who could keep her papa safe now. She owed it to him. She owed him more than words could ever say for what had happened seven years ago. He'd done so much for her since that night.

Blinking away the moisture clouding her vision, she shook off the haunting memories. She would not think about the past. She wouldn't.

Resolutely, she turned her full concentration back to the stage spread before her. Papa would signal for her soon.

A surge of pride caught her as she watched the man holding the audience's attention. Tall with silver-tipped hair, distinguished even in his attention-grabbing costume, her father had the people in the palm of his hand, like always.

A flicker of a smile brushed her lips again, even while her hands clenched into fists of pure nervousness. Soon it would be her turn. How she hated the waiting. The seconds stretched out into eternity for her. She swallowed down the ever-familiar surge of stage fright that arose. She'd get through this performance, even if it killed her.

She pressed her palm against the flutter of nerves that rose up in her stomach like the launch of a hundred butterflies over a field of wildflowers in springtime. The iciness of her hands seeped through the shimmery silver and blue gown, tightening the nervousness into a cold lump of near fear.

No matter how many times she'd done this over the past seven years, a hard knot of nerves always lodged in the pit of her stomach. Tonight, like always before each performance, she'd staunchly refused the bottle of laudanum Papa's partner Simon White offered her—to settle her womanly nerves, as he called it. Now she took a deep calming breath instead, dragging it into her lungs. It didn't do a whit of good. Her stomach lurched. How much longer?

The lump of nervousness grew, threatening to choke off her breathing. Then, at long last the signal came. Papa raised his right hand and beckoned. The golden symbols on his cape glittered in the lamplight as the tiny mirrors she'd sewn into the folds of red velvet turned into sparkling, bright prisms of light.

It was time.

The legion of butterflies in her stomach took flight, taking her stomach upward in their wake to snag in her throat.

"Ladies and gentlemen," her father's rich voice boomed out. "May I present to you," he paused to sweep his hand toward the corner with a grand flourish, "the Tempting Tess."

Papa bestowed a grand bow in her direction, the command for her to appear. As he waved his right arm again, the tiny mirrors reflected the light into sparkling fractions. At his quick undetected movement, a cloud of smoke, rich with the smell of sulfur, arose before her. Papa never could resist his favorite trick. Holding her breath against the pungent smell, Tess dashed into the midst of the mysterious cloud.

Flicking back her wayward curls with a defiant toss of her head, she stepped out of the cloud and onto the center planks of the stage, a smile for the audience. To the people awaiting her, it must have appeared as if she'd materialized from the smoke itself. The audience's startled oohs assured her of the trick's success.

The shimmering silver material of her ankle-length cape rippled back and forth across her legs as she dashed across the wooden planks, ending in a sassy pirouette at her father's side.

Bowing low into a curtsy, she caught a shift of movement out of the corner of her eye. Was that a person standing in the opposite wing of the canvas tent? It couldn't be, she assured herself, focusing her attention on her performance. Distraction during a magic trick could be dangerous, she reminded herself.

Zack Mackinzie leaned against the tent pole, his raised brows the only outward reaction to the mysterious feat conjured before him. He nudged his black hat back with his thumb in disgust. Likely as not, half the people in the audience believed the conjurer's trick to be real magic.

He didn't doubt for a minute that most of the people's attention had been focused completely on the beautiful blonde. Tess Fontana herself. Exactly what the charlatan had wanted them to focus on, instead of the sleight of hand trick the magician had used to produce the smoke. Magic, hell.

It was all a carefully planned scheme. Dazzle the audience, distract them with the woman's beauty, and steal the people's money. It was the way they'd operated from Texas to here, and if his suspicions were correct the Fontanas had left at least one more victim behind— dead and looted of his riches.

He'd stop them once he had the proof, but for tonight the Fontanas would have no problem peddling their potions. It was an impressive performance. In spite of his derision, the illusion of magic tenaciously clung to the very air surrounding the pair's performance. And the woman . . .

She was enough to steal any man's breath away. And likely as not his wallet right along with it. Eyes narrowing beneath his hat, Zack observed her every move. The woman wasn't what he'd expected.

She moved with the grace of a mountain cat. Zack tipped his hat back further and watched her. In fact, she wasn't at all what he'd expected.

So this was Tess Fontana. She didn't look much like a murderer. The thought chewed at his gut, daring him to deny his instincts which had been honed to razor sharpness through the hard years of chasing down cold-blooded killers and bringing them to justice.

As the cape swirled about Tess again, displaying a pretty turn of ankle, the thought repeated itself in his mind. Not at all what he'd expected.

Her hair shimmered like spun gold shot through with silver, in sharp contrast with the silvery threads of her cape. The blue gown beneath hugged her shapely body like a lover's touch. His gut churned and he reached for the anger that was never far from his mind. This was the woman who'd killed David.

However, she couldn't have looked less like a killer. In fact, she looked calm, cool, and innocent. And tempting. What a hell of a mixture. The lady had "don't touch" and "please" written across her startling pretty face in the same breath. Quite a trick for any woman to pull off. He hooked his thumb into his gun belt. Damn. The lady was most definitely tempting, even without the aid of the stage name "Tempting Tess."

He had to remind himself that in all probability she also shared the deceitful tendencies of a deadly rattle-snake. She'd likely strike with or without warning, whichever suited her purposes best.

She was a murderer, after all.

* * *

Tess felt his gaze on her long before she spotted him. Who was he? Tall, sure of himself, and ruggedly handsome, the stranger stood in the wings backstage, as if he had every right to be there. He was trouble, pure and simple; she felt it all the way through her body down to her cold toes.

She didn't have to be aware of his wide shoulders and lean body to know he was trouble. But she was aware—very much so. His dark hair beneath an even darker black Stetson and granite-set face were guaranteed to set any woman's heart racing, even hers. It wasn't only his wide stance that practically dared anyone to challenge him; it was something else about him . . . something that almost shouted danger.

This man didn't follow anyone's rules; he made his own. She should know. She'd once lived the same way. A tiny shiver rippled along her spine and she stiffened, forcing her thoughts back to the present.

No one but no one was allowed backstage at Papa's shows. It was an unwritten rule of every medicine show she'd ever known, and especially Papa's. And one rule this stranger ignored as completely as he focused his full attention on her. Tess could feel his eyes watching her every move.

It made her as jumpy as a long-tailed cat in the middle of a porch full of rocking chairs. The stranger stood so tense that his leanly muscled body looked ready to snap or lunge at her. At the least, his gaze was practically devouring her.

Why hadn't Frank urged their visitor to find a seat out front? It was part of Frank's job to keep unwanted visitors away from where they didn't belong. And this man definitely didn't belong here.

Tess forced her gaze back to her father and met his

concerned frown. She smiled to reassure him, though it was the last thing she felt like doing. She had the strangest urge to grab up her skirts and run, except she didn't know whether the urge was pushing her away from the stranger or straight toward him.

Defying the unusual impulses, she squared her shoulders and faced her father. Her dear papa smiled back at her and winked. She caught the gold coin he tossed her and held it up for the audience to see before depositing it into the gossamer-thin black scarf her father held out.

With a flick of his wrist and a swirl of his red velvet cape, Papa flung the scarf up into the air. It drifted down toward the wood plank flooring, and Tess let the scarf slide across her palm before holding it out for the people to see that the shiny gold piece had disappeared.

Applause sounded from everywhere except the side wing of the tent. It remained strangely silent. Tess couldn't resist letting her gaze stray to the side curtain again. He was still there, not moving, not giving an inch.

He was after something; she knew it for a fact. She'd bet the proceeds from this show that this stranger never gave up anything he went after. A shiver as soft as a feather brushed along her back and over her shoulders. She knew without looking that it was the stranger's gaze rippling over her. Not unpleasant, the feeling wasn't pleasant, either. Simply unfamiliar, she told herself.

The sheer intensity of the strangers' attention caught her off guard, and she almost let the black scarf slip through her fingers Only her father's whispered "Tess" stopped her in time.

She grabbed the scarf and dragged her wayward thoughts back to the performance. Flashing the audience a smile, she tossed the scarf up into the air where her father caught it deftly between his thumb and forefinger. A second later, the gold coin glittered between her father's fingers.

A flutter of nerves rose in her stomach. She could feel the stranger's gaze resting on her once again. Where was Frank Larson? As the show's bodyguard and piano player, he never strayed far from the edge of the stage. Why wasn't he urging the stranger on his way?

Tess knew the answer as soon as the thought left her mind. Not even Frank, with his large bulk, would dare to suggest *this* stranger move elsewhere. Something about the dark-haired stranger caused men to pause and women to draw nearer. Even Tess wasn't immune.

She fumbled as her father handed her back the scarf, nearly dropping it. It earned her a quizzical glance. She tried to smile to reassure her papa, but the gesture came out weak and unsteady.

Damn the stranger. His very presence made her unsure of her moves. From the corner of her eye she saw him shift his position, resettling himself more firmly against the tent pole, and her breath raced for her throat.

"Fontana's elixirous waters cover you like a scarf," her father announced, magically producing a small glass bottle from his voluminous cape.

She tuned out her father's spiel about the wondrous benefits of his elixir. She knew it by heart. In fact, she wished it could protect her from the stranger's ever-watchful eyes. Somehow, she knew the elixir didn't stand a chance.

And neither did she, an inner voice of warning whispered to her.

She shook off the feeling, mistakenly shaking her head at the same time.

"Oh, yes," her father corrected aloud. "I can make this beautiful creature beside me disappear."

Tess jerked herself up. She'd almost missed her father's signal; she had to pay closer attention. It was time for her father's most famous act.

A loud creak sounded from overhead as a large paper cone was lowered by ropes toward the wooden platform. Tess curtsied to the waiting audience and turning, dashed across the stage to take her place seated beneath the descending cone.

Positioning herself, she spread her silver cape around her ankles, at the same time feeling for the hidden trap door in the wood plank. Her fingertip snagged the corner and she rested her palm over the edge. The cone lowered, shutting out her view of the audience, and its view of her.

In the instant before the cone completely enveloped her, Tess heard footsteps from the edge of the stage. The stranger.

Her heart raced straight for her toes. Before she thought about what she was doing, she leaned back to glance over her shoulder. Her fingertips accidentally snagged the trick latch and the panel began sliding back too soon for her to prepare herself. Her gaze locked on the vacant spot where she'd last seen the stranger. The next instant the trapdoor released, and she plummeted through the opening for the hard ground beneath the stage.

Barely holding back her scream, Tess tried to right herself as she tumbled through the unexpected opening. Oh, damn, damn, damn.

An unprepared fall from the elevated stage to the hard-packed dirt below was certain to produce some painful bruises, if not worse. Not to mention that the thump of her unprepared landing would give the trick away to the entire audience. Papa's best trick would be ruined as well as their chance to bring in any proceeds from the elixir in this town.

Tess closed her eyes against the fate awaiting her. The next instant, strong arms enveloped her and she was caught close against a broad male chest.

Two

Tess bit back her startled yelp of surprise. Strong, decidedly male arms held her close against a tightly muscled chest. So tightly that her breasts were crushed against his shirt and the smooth leather vest he wore.

One firm hand clasped her midriff, his fingers pressing intimately against the soft flesh of her breast. The other hand gripped her behind tightly, where no gentleman dared touch a lady. Her face heated with embarrassment at the surprised intimacy.

Instinctively, she shoved against her rescuer with the palms of her hands. He released her a scant few inches, not moving his hands enough to please her. However, it was enough to allow her a glimpse of his face.

The dark-haired stranger.

His head tipped low over hers, his breath lightly teasing her cheeks when he exhaled. The space under the stage, while more than high enough to accommodate Tess's scarcely over five-foot frame, hadn't been designed with his six-foot height in mind.

She risked a good look at his face and wished she hadn't. What she saw held her in a tighter hold than even his strong arms. Danger emanated from this man, reaching out to envelop her as surely as his scent was doing. The strangely pleasant smell of leather, sweat, and mint wrapped itself around her as tightly as his arms about her body.

If she'd thought him impressive from a distance, up close he was devastating. Dark hair, with an errant curl that had escaped from beneath his black Stetson to lay against his wide forehead, gun-metal-gray eyes with a hint of blue, and a chin that could have been carved out of granite.

He opened his mouth to speak, and Tess knew she had to stop him. Any words overheard by the audience would ruin Papa's trick as well as his reputation. The show would likely be run out of town. Before she even thought what she was doing, she pressed her fingers against his mouth. His lips were warm beneath her fingertips, and she jerked them away with a strangled cry.

"What in . . ." the stranger asked in a deep voice with the hint of Texas drawl.

His drawl was a rumble beneath Tess's ear; deep, silky as a feather stroking her, and too enticing for her own good. She fought the dangerous allure with every fiber of her being.

Above them, Papa stomped his foot, a signal for her to remain silent. Tess clamped her lips together, shutting off any words that wanted to break free. The sharp stomp had the opposite effect on the stranger. His head snapped up, right into the wood planking. Tess heard the thunk and winced. Another stomp quickly came from above their heads.

Consternation, she muttered under her breath.

The stranger's hat tumbled to the ground in the same moment he released her. Tess hit the dirt with a hard thud that knocked the breath right out of her. The next instant, before she could even open her mouth to drag in another breath, he landed atop her.

Tess's yelp was muffled by the male chest pressed

against her face. She pushed against his shoulders, but to no avail. He didn't move a bit.

The stranger sagged against her, unconscious, or too nearly, to be of any assistance. His chest covered her face, and with each breath she inhaled his scent. The pure male elixir was more potent to her senses than any mixture Papa could devise.

She forced herself to take another breath and something cool brushed the tip of her nose. She jerked back and the same thing happened. Something downright cold, flat, and metal scraped her skin again. She pressed back against the dirt, straining for a glimpse of the object.

A dull metal badge hung less than an inch from her nose. It was firmly pinned to the man's shirt. She stared up at it while she swallowed down the first twinge of fear. Without blinking, she read the letters inscribed on the metal. *Texas Ranger.*

A second shot of pure fear coursed through her, chilling her so that she shivered beneath the warmth of the lawman atop her. Her heart would have raced straight for her toes if she'd been standing; instead, it sunk to the pit of her stomach. She was certain even the half-conscious man atop her could hear its thud as it hit.

She forced her gaze away from the badge, only to be stopped by the sight of a firm sexy mouth framed by deep dimples in cheeks covered with a day's dark stubble. Instead of unkempt, the stubble lent the impression of dark strength. Here was a man who most decidedly made his own rules. And where did she fit in with a Texas Ranger's plans?

A tremble of apprehension jolted her. What was he doing here? In Nevada. Not only at the medicine show, but at the exact spot where she'd fallen through the trapdoor?

Was he after her or Papa?

Suddenly two loud thumps sounded from above—Papa's secret signal for her to reappear on the stage. Tess smothered back her groan of dismay. It had to be now of all times.

Pushing against the lawman's chest, she eased his bulk sideways, then rolled him off her. Sucking in a deep breath, she surged to her feet and dusted off her gown and cape. She likely looked a sight, but there wasn't time to do much about it.

Smoothing a hand over her tousled locks, she glanced down at the stranger. He lay on his back, his eyes closed. His dark lashes were deep crescent slashes against his tanned skin. A twinge of guilt assailed her. Was he hurt?

Should she try to help him? Why did he have to come and interfere? She nibbled the tip of her finger, wondering what she should do. Papa needed her on stage. But what about the lawman, did he need her? She knew the wisest thing was to turn and run. A lawman boded no good. That breed of man never had in the past. Why would now be any different?

He moaned softly, and Tess took a concerned step toward him, thinking she really should check to see that he wasn't injured badly.

She knew she was courting danger, courting the unknown, and . . . Her gaze fell on the cold metal badge pinned to his broad chest. And courting jail!

Tess's heart lodged once again into a knot in the pit of her stomach. *A lawman.*

The shiny metal circle pinned to his shirt stared back at her unblinking. It accused her as surely as if the badge had spoken aloud.

The reality of the danger facing her struck Tess with the force of a blow, almost stealing her breath away for good this time.

A Texas Ranger.

She closed her eyes, drawing on whatever shield of

calmness and supposed innocence she could possibly grasp. Then she forced her eyes open and looked down at the stranger again. All the way to that pair of piercing silver gray eyes staring into her own.

Shock hit Tess like a fall from one of Papa's trick tables. She tried to blame the persistent breathlessness on her fall through the trapdoor, but knew it to be a lie. The reason for the lack of air in her lungs lay right before her.

A lone thought flashed into her mind. A Texas Ranger always got his man. Or woman. She'd heard that remark somewhere. Was this particular Ranger after her?

One look into those determined, gun-metal eyes and she had her answer. It was a resounding yes. As she continued to stare at him, she couldn't muster up a single word to say to him, or in her own defense.

Shrouded in tense silence, she tried to slow the racing of her heart. Suddenly, the loud thump of stomping thundered through the wood planking. Papa!

"Tess." She heard her father's agitated voice announcing her return. "Yes, ladies and gentlemen, your pain can disappear as surely as Tess."

The piano keys duplicated the tempo of a drum roll, evidence that Frank was on stage at the piano. A second da-da-da from the piano summoned her.

The show! How could she have forgotten it so completely?

Jerking herself away from the invisible bonds holding her in place, Tess stepped back.

The stranger raised his hand as if to detain her. It was all the impetus she needed. Tess spun about and ran for the stage.

"And once again, my dear ladies and gentlemen of Virginia City . . . the Tempting Tess."

As she reached the edge of the platform, Papa's triumphant announcement came to her as a shouted order for her to reappear in the show.

Grabbing hold of the edge of the wood platform, Tess paused a second to risk a glance back at the stranger. He sat in the dirt, knees bent, his eyes glaring across the distance at her. She knew without a doubt that he held her accountable for what had transpired beneath the stage. Gulping, she turned away from the intense gray eyes that promised—no demanded—retribution.

She swung herself up behind the curtains. Once again a cloud of smoke filled the air about her, and Tess ran across the stage to join her father. And safety.

Zack raised himself up on his elbows and stared at the spot where Tess Fontana had been standing. Hellfire and damnation.

He'd had her in his grasp, planned to ask her some very serious questions, and look what had happened. He'd ended up flat on his backside in the dirt at her dainty feet. Knocked unconscious, as a matter of fact, and when he'd come to, she'd disappeared again. The lady had the particularly irritating habit of disappearing and appearing at will. Only to turn around and disappear on him again.

Hellfire, things couldn't have gone more wrong.

Zack stood to his feet in a swift move, bumping his head against the wooden planking again. His muffled curse pierced the emptiness beneath the stage. He rubbed the back of his head. It hurt like hell. He felt like he'd been coldcocked with the butt of a Colt .45.

Pretty, tempting Tess Fontana had most assuredly won this round, or so it seemed at the moment. But wait until their next encounter, he vowed, things would end differently.

A Ranger was supposed to be the one who came out

ahead. A Ranger always got his man, he derided himself. And what had he up and done this time? He'd let
a slip of a woman best him and get away. Not only get
away, but leave him sitting in the dirt feeling like a fool.

Zack stared at the spot where Tess had disappeared.
Damned if the woman didn't manage to appear and
vanish like a sprite. Was that what had tempted his
brother to her questionable charms?

Damned if the lady wasn't a lot stronger than she
looked at first glance. What she looked like was gossamer, as if she'd float away if not held down to earth.
Did he want to be the one to hold her both down to
this earth and close to his own body?

He felt his loins stir in response to the thoughts that
question brought in its wake. A memory of Tess held
close in his arms rose before him. Without any conscious effort on his part, he recalled each and every
one of her delectable curves pressing against the palms
of his heated hands.

He clenched his right hand into a fist. He was here
for one reason—to prove she was responsible for his
brother's death. And for that reason only. He staunchly
refused to acknowledge the nagging voice in the back
of his mind that said something entirely different.

Above his head he could hear Philip Fontana's sales
pitch. He listened for a minute to the practiced words.
The conjurer's silver-tongued speech and accompanying sleight-of-hand tricks would convince many a miner
to purchase his special elixir this night.

Zack shook his head. Anger in each footfall, he strode
to the edge of the stage. Following Tess's example, he
grasped the side of the platform and swung himself up
to the side of the stage. He stood, just out of sight of the
audience, but with a clear view of the woman he sought.

Tempting Tess—the title most definitely fit. Most definitely. He shifted position, once again leaning against

the tent pole. Idly, he slid his right hand into his vest pocket and withdrew the round token. He rubbed it between his thumb and forefinger, not needing to read the inscribed wording to recall it. He knew the words by heart: *Good for one admission to Fontana's Medicine Show.*

The round token caught the lamplight, reflecting it back. The shiny metal piece condemned Tess Fontana as surely as any witness could have done. It was the token his brother David had clasped tightly in his hand with his last dying breath.

"What in heaven were you doing tonight, Tess? Whatever were you thinking about?" Philip Fontana asked, an unmistakable edge of concern in his voice.

The light from the kerosene lanterns cast a warm glow over the deserted stage. Instead of being comforting like usual, it lent an eeriness, almost a warning, to her mind.

He caught Tess's shoulders and looked into her face, angling her toward the flickering light. "You could have been badly injured tonight. Woolgathering that way."

"Papa . . ." Her voice came out tumultuous even to her own ears. She cleared her throat. She didn't want to scare him. He worried over her far too much as it was. The performance was over and the tonic sold, it was time for him to rest.

She was too late. Worry lines etched his brow as he drew her closer. "What is it? You were hurt, weren't you?"

"No, Papa." She tried to instill a laugh into her speech to reassure him all was well. "Merely my pride was bruised from my fall."

"Then what is it?"

She swallowed down the words that wanted to burst free. Instead, she forced out the well-rehearsed casual tone that sounded false even to her own ears. "I thought I saw a lawman here tonight."

Her dear father stiffened an instant, reminding her of a startled deer caught by a band of hunters.

"A lawman? Are you certain?"

She crossed the fingers of one hand behind her back. She hated lies, hated even tiny half-truths, but sometimes they couldn't be helped. Like now. She couldn't tell him the full facts of the evening. He looked too tired from the performance to burden with her fears.

"I think so."

"Tess," he insisted.

He always could see right through her fabrications, ever since she'd been a small child. The only person she could ever fool had been her mama.

"Was he one we knew?" He closed his eyes in a defeat that tore at Tess. "Who was he?"

Her heart ached for him, and the pain silenced her for the space of a moment. Unable to speak in that instant, she rested her hand on his arm. The mirrors she'd so patiently sewn on his cape twinkled with her movement as if to scold her.

"I don't know who he was." She realized with a start that this was the truth. She didn't have a clue to the strangers' name, while he might know all about her.

Tess's throat tightened with the realization. Danger became a living thing beside her.

"Perhaps you were mistaken."

Her father's voice startled her out of her reverie. "What?"

He frowned at her. "I've never known you to do so much woolgathering. Not since those days after—" He cut the sentence off and brushed at an imaginary speck on the hem of his cape. When he straightened back up, he was smiling. "Perhaps your lawman was only a curious patron."

Tess stifled the impulse to shout that the stranger wasn't *her* anything.

"I'm sure that's it." Papa's voice held a thread of hope.

Hating to break that thin thread he clung to so staunchly, she held her tongue.

"See, there's nothing to worry about, dear girl," he assured her with a winning smile.

She recognized that smile. It was the same one he used on the audience—the one that enchanted people into believing his every word. However, tonight it failed to work its usual magic. She knew she had to tell him the truth. If her fears were right and the Texas Ranger was after them, her papa had a right to know it.

Tess nibbled her lower lip in a habit of nervousness she'd thought she'd long outgrown. She'd give anything to remain silent, not to speak the damning words. But she had to. It might be the only way to keep them both safe. And alive.

Taking a breath, she plunged through the fray of emotions that swirled within her. "Papa, it was a Texas Ranger."

The words fell like rocks on a glass-still pond. His face fell.

"Are you certain?"

Most definitely. After all, she'd been nose to badge with the stranger beneath the stage, but she couldn't tell him that. Could never let him know she'd been held close in the lawman's arms. A recollection of past dealings with lawmen swept through her, erasing the softer feelings she'd been nursing. Shame washed over her at the memory of the time she'd spent under the stage.

"Tess," her father pressed, a wrinkle of concern on his brow.

She ached to reach up and smooth away the worry. It prompted her to rush to reassure him. "I'm sure the man was only riding through—"

"Texas Rangers don't simply ride through, Tess," he pointed out.

"I know."

There was only one recourse left for her. She had to follow it and keep her father safe. No matter what the cost. Grabbing up her wavering courage with both hands, she plunged in. "I'll find out what he's up to. That shouldn't be too hard, should it?"

For her father's benefit, she flashed a coquettish smile. "I'll go see him tomorrow and keep an eye on him and his dealings."

"Be careful."

If only he knew that the warning was far too late, she thought to herself. She'd already attracted far too much of the Ranger's attention for her own peace of mind, but there was nothing to be done about that now. She had to continue. She had to find out what he was up to.

It was the last thing on this earth she wanted to do right now. She didn't want those eyes trained on her and the intensity from him that followed along. Did she?

The thought sent a shiver of excitement through her body in spite of the trepidation she felt. Whatever was she thinking? she asked herself. She'd experienced first-hand the power of his scrutiny.

Whatever was she getting herself into? Tess wondered. A thought hit her with the impact of a sudden jolt. She didn't even know the stranger's name.

Three

Gathering up her skirts and the edge of her cloak in her hand, Tess stepped down off the show's platform to the hard-packed soil. Instantly, a mental picture of the mystery lawman sprawled out on that same hard dirt less than an hour ago haunted her.

Long denim-covered legs, muscular thighs, flat stomach, and a wide chest—quite an impressive picture and one that positively refused to abandon her and leave her in peace. What was it about the stranger that insisted in occupying her thoughts so much?

He was a traveling man, and even worse, a lawman. Didn't she know better? Tess sighed in disgust at the path of her wayward thoughts. Any man wearing a badge was trouble. Pure and simple.

Of all things, the stranger had to be a Texas Ranger, too. Didn't she know better than to even associate with one of them? And now necessity demanded that she pretend an interest in him to find out what he was up to. Once again she paused to ask herself what she was getting herself into.

A memory of his piercing eyes the color of a gleaming gun barrel taunted her, their intensity reaching out even now to grab her and hold her tightly. They bound her so that she had to shake her head twice to break the tenacious hold.

"Why, Tess, whatever could be the matter? Ohh, are you having second thoughts so soon?" A sly, sugar-laced voice came out of the near dark beside the tent. It reached her across the short distance separating her and the woman approaching like a snake slithering ever closer to its prey.

Tess jumped, a hand to her throat, then recognizing the voice, she groaned under her breath in frustration. Marlene Boudreaux.

If only she'd stayed talking with Papa a few more minutes, she might have missed an unpleasant encounter with Simon's lady friend.

"Ohh, did I startle you? I didn't mean to."

Liar. Tess held the accusation back with an effort of sheer will. She refused to let the woman know she got under her skin so.

"Good evening, Marlene." She smiled as sweetly as she could, and thoroughly enjoyed the disappointment that crossed the other woman's face at her outward calm.

Tess noted with satisfaction that those cheeks turned almost the same bright hue of her gaudy pink-and-black gown. The woman's lack of fashion sense never ceased to amaze her.

However, if the wicked witch, as she'd aptly nicknamed Marlene, were here the evening would prove to be far from pleasant. She hadn't a clue what the woman was up to, but sure as she stood on two feet, it boded no good.

"You didn't think anyone saw you, did you?" Marlene reached up and patted the white bow set amongst her brassy, too-tight curls almost as if she were congratulating herself on something.

Consternation, Tess thought, what was she talking about? Had the woman taken to spying on her as well as keeping her eye on Uncle Simon?

"Ohh, rolling around in the dirt with that cowboy."

A deliberately girlish giggle slipped past the woman's painted lips.

Laughing was the last thing on Tess's mind. The possibility that anyone had witnessed her near-disastrous tumble and her rescue by the stranger hadn't occurred to her. Much less, that the scene would be viewed by Marlene who would relish exposing the magic trick just for spite. At every opportunity she had ensured that Tess knew how low she viewed both her and her father.

She bit back the harsh words of defense that sprang instantly to her mind. She needn't defend either her papa or herself to this woman.

However, since Marlene was Uncle Simon's lady friend, she should at least make an attempt to be polite. Besides, Papa would be upset if he were to walk out of the show tent and overhear an argument between them, and the last thing he needed right now was anything else to trouble him. For his sake, she counted to five and held her tongue.

The news that a Texas Ranger attended their medicine show had provided more than enough of a shock to her papa for now. He needn't know just how she'd come to be aware of the fact he was a lawman. A memory of his firmly muscled body sprawled atop her brought a surge of heat to her cheeks.

Consternation, would the stranger never leave her mind? Tess wondered yet again. He seemed as firmly planted there as Marlene was in front of her.

As if totally unaware of the tension, Marlene continued, "Although I could see the temptation he presented to one of your limited experience. He was something to look at, wasn't he?"

Tess clenched her fist and reminded herself she was doing this for Papa's sake. What she wanted to do was . . . She closed off the tempting picture of the brassy ringlets hanging from an Indian's belt. Scalping was too good for the woman.

A hungry look crossed Marlene's face before her lips twisted up into a smile that forewarned of more taunts to come.

"But surely even you could have found someone more suitable to your, ah . . . station than a dusty cowpoke to roll around in the dirt with." Her voice held a strong note of censure, and her eyes glinted with malicious enjoyment as Tess's temper rose to the challenge.

This from a Virginia City prostitute, Tess fumed with a fresh surge of anger.

She hadn't liked the woman from the moment she met her almost thirteen months ago on the medicine show's last trip through Virginia City. Something about Marlene Boudreaux brought out the worst in Tess. Each confrontation—she never thought of them as chance meetings—made her feel like a kitten who'd been picked up by the scruff of the neck and shaken. Hard.

The woman always succeeded in making her fighting mad, but she usually held her tongue for Uncle Simon's sake. He was clearly smitten with Marlene, and she played him as deftly as Frank played the piano keys. When was her father's lifelong friend going to see Marlene for the greedy creature she was? Tess hoped soon, very soon, for all their sakes.

She gritted her teeth and counted to five again. The attempt at calmness wasn't working worth a whit. Anger rose up, demanding release, but she held on to her temper.

Marlene tapped her foot repeatedly, waiting for a response. The action was likely designed to add kindling to the flame of anger that already burned on the tip of Tess's tongue.

Sugar sweet and as venomous as a diamondback rattler, Marlene Boudreaux was always poised to strike at any other woman in her range of attack. She had obviously viewed Tess as a threat from the moment they'd been introduced by Uncle Simon.

Finally unable to silence her anger any longer, Tess opened her mouth intending to leave Marlene in no doubt as to what she thought of her.

"Oh, there you are," Simon's voice boomed, cutting off what she had been about to say.

The disappointment coloring the other woman's face confirmed Tess's suspicion that she'd narrowly escaped a planned setup by Marlene.

Simon dropped a quick paternal kiss on Tess's cheek, then slipped an arm around Marlene. "My two favorite girls. Having a nice chat?" he asked.

"Why, of course, darling," Marlene cooed.

Tess wondered how he could fail to notice the strain and anger simmering between her and his lady friend. It could practically singe the hair off his balding head. Love must truly be blind, at least in Uncle Simon's case.

"Ohh, darling, I was talking to the dear girl about you men. A girl must guard her reputation, you know." Sincerity edged every single word, but Marlene did it so well that only those who knew her could detect the slyness tucked beneath the outward show of concern.

Tess nearly choked on the words that trembled on her own tongue. The witch.

As Marlene giggled in a feigned show of embarrassment, Tess ground her teeth together. The woman's "reputation" was well known in Virginia City. As if to taunt her, the dim light shone on the stark white bow perched like a flag in the reddish-yellow curls.

The bow was something a woman a third Marlene's age would think twice about wearing. But not Marlene. She always displayed a pristine white bow in her hair. Trying for purity, Tess thought with a surprising burst of sarcasm. The bow made the greedy whore look even harder and harsher than she was, if possible.

"Marlene, your teasing is embarrassing the dear girl." Simon tucked Marlene's hand through the crook of his arm and patted it in rebuke.

Tess found herself stifling a groan at the tender gesture. Sometimes she wished she could reach out and shake Uncle Simon until he saw reason.

He turned his smile on her. "Isn't she something?" he asked.

Tess barely stopped herself from answering him aloud. Her father's partner most assuredly would not appreciate her opinion of what his lady friend truly was in fact.

How on earth could she say the damning words that begged to be released when he so obviously doted on the witch?

"Ohh, I was only cautioning the motherless girl that she really should find someone better than a dusty cowboy, but . . ." Marlene let the words trail off and lifted one shoulder in a careless shrug.

"Marlene." Simon caught her hand in his and squeezed.

For the flash of an instant Tess thought she saw a flicker of fear in the woman's eyes. However, she knew she'd been mistaken as Marlene tilted her head back to smile up at Simon and snuggled close against his side.

"Of, course, Sy, you're right. How rude of me."

This was the first time Tess had ever witnessed the woman yield to Simon's urging. Or abide by his wishes. Perhaps she did have feelings for him— No, Tess instantly revised her opinion. She knew that the only thing Marlene had fond feelings for was any man's money.

He patted her hand again. "Shall we go, my dear?"

"You go ahead, I'll be along in a moment."

After giving her a warning glance, Simon bid them both good night. The second he was out of earshot, Marlene turned back to Tess. She looked her up and down and smiled a smile as fake as the woman herself. Tess tried counting backward this time from ten and waited.

"Really, dear girl, you should *try* and do better. Tsk. A shiftless cowpoke."

How Uncle Simon could stand this wicked witch she'd never understand, much less how he could be attracted to her. In spite of her good intentions to keep peace, the words burst free, unable to be restrained any longer.

"He wasn't a shiftless cowpoke. He was a lawman." Tess snapped her lips closed, wishing she could snatch the words back. But it was too late.

Any possible hope that Marlene hadn't heard her was squashed the instant Tess spotted the gleam in those dark eyes.

"Ohh, my, my." Marlene raised a long, tapered hand, rings glittering, to tuck in a loose strand of reddish-yellow hair. The perky little white bow bounced with her movement.

"I'm sure Sy will be delighted to hear the little tidbit you dropped me."

Tess scarcely bit back the gasp of shock. Surely Uncle Simon hadn't told this . . . this . . . *woman* about the past. No, he wouldn't have done that. She knew he shared her fears for her father's safety. Simon and Papa had been friends since first meeting in the War between the States when Papa had saved Simon's life. Only he and Tess knew the whole of their past.

Surely he hadn't told . . .

The satisfied gleam in Marlene's glance told her that he had. Giving her a knowing smile, Marlene turned away and sauntered off to join Simon without another word.

Tess replayed the conversation over and over in her mind, hoping she'd misunderstood, but she knew with a certainty that she had understood exactly what Marlene intended. The woman knew about everything.

Now the question remained, what was Marlene going to do with that information?

The next morning dawned bright and clear in sharp contrast to Tess's mood. By midmorning she'd already been to three places trying to find out the identity of her mystery lawman, but to no avail.

Determination drove her on. She *had* to find out exactly who he was and why he'd visited Virginia City. And paid a call to Fontana's Medicine Show. Her casually cloaked questions netted her nothing but equally casual chitchat. Obviously subtlety must be the wrong approach. Exactly how did a lady go about finding out about a certain man?

She strode down the uneven wooden boardwalk in front of the bustling shops, her mind running over any number of possible ideas and discarding each one. The obvious solution presented itself as she neared the local jail, but she just as quickly threw the very possibility of going in and asking the sheriff questions to the winds. The last place she'd go willingly was to a jail.

She did a sharp about-face. First, she'd go talk with Ella. The show's cook and costume caretaker was always a fountain of information. If Ella didn't have the answers, she'd simply have to get more bold in her quest. However, no amount of boldness could entice her to enter the local jail.

Zack Mackinzie stepped out of the sheriff's office in time to spot Tess walking down the boardwalk. She strolled along the uneven planks with amazing grace. He determined that she must do everything with that same polish and refinement. Didn't anything ever ruffle the beauty?

For the flash of an instant the question of whether she made love with that same grace hit his mind with the force of a Washoe wind. The image it brought along in its wake staggered him. He sucked his breath in through clenched teeth. As he observed the smooth back and forth sway of her bustle, his gut tightened in response.

No wonder David had been so taken with her. The memory of the words of his brother's letter extolling the wonders of the beautiful blonde with eyes the color of Texas bluebells pulled him back from the precipice of desire. This was the woman his brother wrote him about—the woman who was traveling through town shortly before his death. The woman responsible for David's death.

Cold vengeance filled Zack, coursing through his veins and turning his earlier unexpected desire into anger. It tightened and twisted his gut, churning inside of him.

Conflicting emotions tore at Zack before duty won out. Tess Fontana was only a suspect for now. He didn't have near enough evidence to arrest her. And it was past time he started gathering that evidence.

Tugging his hat lower, he strode down the boardwalk after her. Once again the gently seductive sway of her hips enthralled him. Damn, but she was the prettiest suspect he'd ever encountered.

Zack's long legs ate up the distance separating him from his quarry. As he drew even with her, he slowed his pace to match her dainty steps.

"Morning, Miss Fontana." He eased around in front of her, effectively cutting off any escape.

Bright blue eyes met his gaze, and he recognized the look of a startled doe. Quickly the shock turned to the faintest hint of fear, then welcome. The last surprised him. He hadn't expected the lady in question to be particularly pleased to see him. At least not before he'd had the chance to turn on the Mackinzie charm.

Tipping his hat, he bent closer to her, noting the flecks of darker blue set amongst her incredible eyes. Once again, she had "don't touch" and "please" written across her pretty heart-shaped face. The combination practically tempted a normal man beyond control. And he was as normal as any man.

As he continued to take in every nuance of her face, her cheeks turned a becoming shade of pink. Her flawless, smooth skin tempted him to reach out and touch it to see if it was truly as silken soft as it appeared.

He purposely lowered his gaze, intending to settle on something a little less tempting. The moment his eyes brushed her lips, though, he was lost. She had soft, full lips that were made to be kissed. Thoroughly and often. Those tempting lips parted slightly as she drew in a breath, and it took all his control not to crush her mouth beneath his and fill himself with the taste of her.

Hellfire, what was he doing? Letting his mind be overrun by the lower half of his body, he answered in derision. She was doing it again—muddling his brain and diverting his professional control. Here he stood, a seasoned Texas Ranger, on the town street in broad daylight lusting after her like a wet-behind-the-ears cowhand who'd been out on the range too long.

Yup, the stage name Tempting Tess fit her perfectly. About as perfectly as the ivory gown fit her luscious body, the enticing bustle above her finely shaped behind causing him to ache to hold her close. However, the pearly color managed to offset her delicate features and make her look every inch the fine lady one would find in a fancy drawing room.

The thought recalled to mind his own manners which had been sorely lacking. How long had he been standing there admiring the view?

Too damn long.

He resettled his hat back on his head and flashed her

the Mackinzie smile that had always worked on women in the past. "Ma'am, pardon my manners. Name's Zack Mackinzie, and may I buy you a cup of coffee and piece of pie for keeping you standing out here in the sun?"

She stared back at him, a look of amazement on her pretty face.

His smile widened. "Or perhaps a cool glass of lemonade would be more appealing?"

When she hesitated for the space of a heartbeat, he added, "An old family custom says that if a man saves another's life, that life then belongs to him."

He watched her mouth drop open in surprise. Before she could deny him, he caught her arm with his hand.

"All I'm asking for is a cup of coffee." He lowered his voice into a persuasive purr. "Can I tempt you into saying yes, Tempting Tess Fontana?"

The way he said her name shook her out of the languid spell he'd woven about her. Suddenly she noticed they were standing in the middle of the wooden boardwalk, while passersby had to step around them. Tess closed her eyes in embarrassment as a group of three miners sidestepped, dodging Zack's broad frame.

Consternation, whatever had come over her? She'd stood there, gawking up at the tall too-handsome man leaning over her, letting him weave his seductive spell about her without offering a single whit of resistance. Where was that steel backbone she was known for? Not to mention the sharp mind.

Both came to life, and she straightened to her full height. It didn't do much to counter the overwhelming presence of the man beside her, but it made her feel more in control of her own self.

She opened her mouth to refuse in spite of the temptation he offered. Just as quickly, she snapped her lips closed on the words. Whatever was she thinking? He'd just provided her with exactly what she wanted—an opportunity to find out what he was doing in Virginia City. And more importantly, what his interest was in the Fontanas' Medicine Show. Not only that, he'd also supplied the answer to the question she'd been seeking since last night—his name.

Never one to pass up a choice opportunity when it presented itself, Tess smiled her sweetest smile at him. "Mr. Mackinzie, I do believe that's an offer I can't say no to."

Nor did she want to say no. This was exactly what she wanted.

"Zack," he corrected her in a low drawl that sent her heart skittering for safety.

If she weren't careful this man could present more of a danger than she wanted to deal with right now. Or maybe ever.

She smiled up at him sweetly, trying to get in all the practice she could. She'd have to give the best performance of her life if she were to get the answers to her question without him realizing what he'd given away. Could she do it? a little twinge of doubt asked.

Tilting her head to get a better look at Zack Mackinzie, Texas Ranger, she vowed she'd succeed. She had to.

Taking her look for acquiescence, he motioned toward a storefront boasting the name MAGGIE's in big block letters across the street. "Best pie in Virginia City."

Tess couldn't stop the smile. He was a charmer. "And how would you know?" she challenged.

"You'd be surprised what I know, Tess Fontana," he answered in a low voice.

Tess found it hard to swallow the sudden knot that lodged in her throat at his words. Was he only teasing? Or did his remark hold a more dangerous meaning?

The way he'd said her name sent a flash of trepidation skittering through her, all the way to her toes, which curled against the wooden plank beneath her slippers.

It was almost as if he doubted her, suspected her. But he couldn't. Could he?

There was no way he could know the name Fontana was as false as the gold-colored brass tokens they handed out in the towns before each performance. No way he could know, she reassured herself silently. Papa had changed their name at the first town they'd come to after their flight. Fontana—after the stone fountain in the center of the little town. Had it really been all of seven years ago?

Tess shook off the sudden melancholy that permeated the air about her. It was as if the bright sunshine had suddenly disappeared to be swallowed up by a dark cloud threatening a coming storm. But no, the sun shone as bright as ever, glinting off the glass-fronted stores, reminding her to look forward, not backward. And forward meant facing Zack Mackinzie's questions and deflecting any suspicions he might possibly have about her papa.

She turned to Zack with a bright smile as false as her name. Stepping closer to him, she linked her arm with his. The sudden tensing of the corded muscles beneath her fingertips told her more than any words he might utter at that moment.

Texas Ranger Zack Mackinzie was attracted to her.

Tess's smile turned genuine. The day was looking up. Just perhaps she could handle this lawman.

One quick glimpse from beneath her lowered lashes at his face put an end to that assurance. No one "handled" this man.

Well, she'd just have to settle with distracting his attention away from the medicine show and away from her beloved papa. A little whisper of doubt surfaced in the back of her mind. Could she do it? Self-doubt assailed her, clouding the beautiful day about her. Tess stiffened her resolve and her back at the same time.

She could do anything she had to do—if it meant keeping her father safe and alive.

She rested her hand more firmly on Zack's arm and almost gasped when his muscles flinched and bunched under her palm. She glanced up to witness a self-satisfied expression cross his face. Anger surged in her at that. Well pleased with himself, was he?

She'd love to inform him that she was only accompanying him because it suited her purpose, not because of any masculine charm he'd exuded. He hadn't won this round, not by a long shot, she vowed.

His reaction was merely further proof that he was definitely susceptible to distraction by her. That was all, nothing more, she assured herself with confidence.

As he clasped his broad, calloused hand over hers, warmth stole through her, nearly stealing her very breath away. Along in its wake, a thought jabbed her. Just how susceptible was *she* to *him*?

Four

Not a whit, Tess thought in defiance. She wasn't susceptible to Zack Mackinzie one bit. No, not a whit. Tess raised her chin in determination, ignoring the possibility that perhaps she was protesting this too much.

Remember. The nagging voice of her conscience arose like a scepter. Remember what caring had gotten her once before.

The warmth in her body cooled, turning colder than a Virginia City night in wintertime. It calmed her turbulent emotions faster than anything else could have done. All she needed to do was distract the Texas Ranger's attention onto something else besides the medicine show and Papa. Nothing else. Relief flooded over her.

As Zack led her across the street, she risked a look at him. Sunlight shimmered in waves off the badge pinned so prominently to his wide chest. Why oh why did he have to be a blasted lawman? she wondered.

Not that she'd be interested anyway. Tess raised her chin a notch in silent determination. She wasn't interested in Zack Mackinzie, lawman or not.

No, not one little whit.

She felt her cheeks heating at the lie as she saw him glance down at her again.

He had to be out of his mind, Zack derided himself. Certain of that fact, he questioned the intelligence of his former plan as he slowed his stride to match Tess's much smaller steps. In the past he'd always steered clear of small, dainty women, preferring to match his height to a female closer to his own stature. For the first time, he found himself liking to have to slow his steps, liking the feel of a tiny, delicate hand nestled in the crook of his arm, and liking the feel of Tess Fontana walking next to him.

He found his body taking a fancy to a few other things about her as well, such as the pleasing smell of the hint of roses that clung to her silken skin and soft hair. Not to mention the surge of awareness jolting through his body each time her delicate shoulder brushed against him.

She remained silent as they crossed the street, exuding a shyness that was strangely appealing. No doubt about it, Tess Fontana was getting under his skin. And he didn't like it one little bit.

The short walk to Maggie's establishment seemed endless and yet ended way too soon for him. He knew he should be spending these minutes laying out his questions, but all he could do was notice the graceful way Tess moved and how damn good she felt next to him.

What was it about this temptress that sent his thoughts and intentions into a tailspin? he wondered in growing irritation.

As he took her arm to help her up onto the next boardwalk, he noticed for the first time how finely boned she was, how tiny she felt beneath his hand. A heated vision of how she would fit beneath him in bed flooded his mind with the intensity of one of the fierce zephyr winds racing through the canyon.

When they made love, he'd have to . . . Jerking his body away as if he'd been scalded, Zack put a firm halt to the path his mind had been taking. There wouldn't be any lovemaking with Tess Fontana. There wouldn't be anything between them.

Damn, what was it about being around her that fired him so? The more time he spent with her, the more he had to remind himself that he was a sworn lawman doing a job.

Determined to concentrate on that job, Zack led Tess to a table by the window of the crowded little cafe. Like everything else in Virginia City, the restaurant was bustling with the activity of miners eager to spend their money in one of the city's best eateries.

The busy establishment wasn't conducive to much conversation, while the very air between them remained fraught with unspoken words. Zack held out Tess's chair, careful not to let his fingers brush against her shoulder or the delicate nape of her neck. He'd already learned what havoc a mere touch of her could do to his senses, and right now he needed his head clear.

Their order was taken in a short amount of time, in spite of the crowd of miners and businessmen filling the restaurant. Before they could do much more than exchange the normal pleasantries about the unusually warm, sunny day their two slices of apple pie were delivered.

Tess didn't think she could hold out much longer. While she wanted to come right out and ask him what he was up to, she knew that her search for answers demanded some subtlety. Something she'd never been too good at.

Watching him from beneath lowered lashes, she toyed with her fork, tracing the handle back and forth across the gaily checked tablecloth pattern, searching for how to begin. The shiny metal of the badge pinned to his shirt glinted at her, as if daring her to proceed with her plan.

She'd thought the blasted thing had been intimidating when she'd been nose-to-nose with it last evening, but today in the bright light of a sunny day, it was worse. Staring at the badge, the answer suddenly presented itself to her and she questioned why ever she hadn't thought of the solution sooner. A smile tipped the corners of her mouth, and she felt a little like a cat given a bowl of fresh cream.

She owed him a thank-you for his opportune rescue during last night's performance. What a perfect place to start.

"Mr. Mackinzie—"

"Zack," he corrected almost the moment the words left her mouth.

Tess swallowed at the suddenness of his response. He had a quick mind, something she should have anticipated, but instead she'd allowed herself to be caught up by the very presence of the man himself. Not to mention her premature satisfaction with finding a suitable question and place to enact her plan.

"Zack . . ." She paused. The name felt strangely right on her tongue.

He smiled across at her, showing even, white teeth framed by those two alluring dimples, and her heart did a most peculiar flip-flop. She found she had to clear her throat before she could speak again.

"I wanted to thank you for your rescue last night." She closed her lips on the words.

Consternation, the words sounded as stilted and phony as she felt right now. She gathered up her scattered wits to try again, but he forestalled her.

"I have a few ideas on how you can do that."

"What?"

"Thank me."

"What?" she repeated, her voice rising.

He smiled disarmingly, and two dimples flashed at her, tempting, teasing.

"You could show me around Virginia City."

Tess stared at him blankly, the patterned silver fork in her hand forgotten.

"This is my first visit. I assumed that you knew the town well . . ." He let the rest trail off, enticing her to respond.

Tess drew in a deep calming breath. His ploy for information was almost too obvious to believe. He clearly expected her to blithely provide him with all the answers as to how long and how often the show had been in Virginia City.

Not on your life, she answered silently, flashing him a smile full of innocence.

"Why ever would you think that?" she posed the question to him. Turning her attention to the flaky-crusted apple pie, she took a small bite, pretending to savor it. "You were right, it is delicious."

Tess eyed him over another forkful of cinnamon-laden apples. She hadn't lied, the pie was good—as mouth-watering as always. In truth, much better than what they served at Cora's larger eating place, situated farther down the street. Maggie's had long been a favorite of her own. However, she'd wisely kept that fact to herself.

She wasn't particularly eager for the lawman part of Zack Mackinzie to be aware of how well she knew Virginia City, nor of how many times over the past few years the traveling medicine show had passed through the mining town perched on the side of a mountain. No, the less he knew about her, the better.

A flash of frustration darkened his face before he smiled at her and continued, "So, tell me, how do you like Virginia City?"

"It's pretty in its own way."

He gave her a startled look. "But don't you think it's desolate, after the other places you've been?"

Tess recognized the real question behind his words and dodged it. She wasn't about to blithely tell any lawman a list of the towns they'd visited. She wasn't anybody's fool.

"Oh, no," she answered in a rush of words. "That's what I like about Virginia City. It's open and beautiful. You have to admire a place that can survive, and even flourish on the side of a mountain. Don't you?"

He nodded in agreement, encouraging her to talk on more.

"And it is flourishing. Even more so since all the rebuilding after last year's fire." Tess wished she could bite her tongue and call back the burst of words she'd loosed. She'd given away far too much. She might as well have come right out and admitted that Fontana's Medicine Show had been here last year and performed before the devastating fire. In fact, the show had even played in the famed Piper's Opera House—quite a feat for her papa to have pulled off. Now she had to distract the lawman seated across from her from thinking over the information she'd so freely given him.

"I just love these wide-open spaces, don't you?" she asked, injecting a hint of awe into her voice. She tried to bat her eyes at him the way she'd seen Marlene do so successfully yesterday.

He looked taken aback for a moment, and Tess dared to hope her ploy had worked.

"You surprise me. I'd take you for a city woman." Zack leaned back in his chair and studied her.

His action made her decidedly uncomfortable. The last thing she needed was those intense gray eyes of his fixing their full attention and powers of observation on her.

"Me?" Tess answered before she thought. "Not likely." She scarcely bit back the admission that she'd grown up on a small homestead in Texas.

If she didn't watch herself, next she'd be telling him that what she really wanted in life was a home to call her own. One with walls and a real roof, not a traveling show wagon or even a hotel room—a home. And a husband and children to go along with it. However, wishing for the impossible was like building dreams on the dust blown by the wind.

Most assuredly she'd thrown away any chance at that dream seven years ago. She swallowed down the sudden tightness in her throat.

She was here to find out what he was up to, not let him investigate her. She always figured the way to confront a problem was usually best done head on. So she proceeded to do just that.

"So, tell me," Tess smiled at him with all the innocence she could muster, "what brings a Texas Ranger all the way to Virginia City?" She scooped up another forkful of pie and concentrated on the lush apple mixture, pretending only mild interest in his answer.

Zack almost choked on his swallow of coffee at her bluntness. Would she ever cease to amaze him?

He made the mistake of watching her lift the fork to her mouth, and couldn't for the life of himself pull his gaze away. As he saw her lips close over the tines of the fork, he was as enthralled with her actions as the miners watching the show last night.

"Business." He answered her question without a thought as to anything but her mouth.

As soon as the words left his mouth he realized his blunder. Hellfire, what was it about Tess Fontana that sent his sense scattering to the winds? Yet again he felt like a callous cowhand. Damn.

Every time he was around this woman she managed to do that to him. At his age he should know better. How did he constantly come out on the losing end where Tess was concerned? That answer was simple enough for any fool to see. All he had to do was look at her lips or touch her and his mind traveled only one place.

"Ma'am?" A miner approached the table, hat in his hand. He shuffled from one foot to the other before he spoke again. "I had to stop and tell you I surely did enjoy your show."

"Why, thank you." Tess flashed him a genuine smile with a hint of embarrassment. "Mister?"

"Foster, ma'am. Charlie Foster." He extended his work-worn hand.

Tess slipped her hand in his, and he pumped it up and down several times, then released it.

"Why, thank you, Mr. Foster."

He flushed and scuffed his foot, then added in a rush. "And that tonic your father talked about, well, I'm right glad I bought that, too. Why, today I'm feeling right spritely." He nodded his head vigorously as if to reaffirm the fact.

As soon as the man turned away to leave, Tess dabbed at her lips with the edge of her napkin.

"That reminds me I really must be getting back to the hotel." She began to scoot her chair back.

Zack stared at her, suspicion mounting at the quick change in her. She seemed strangely uneasy all of a sudden; she'd been fine until the miner's enthusiastic visit. His eyes narrowed in thought.

Tess dropped her napkin atop her plate and stood in a movement of pure grace. Gathering her reticule, she stepped back from the table.

Now what had sent her skittering off that way? Zack wondered.

"I'll walk you back to your hotel," he told her.

"No, really, that's fine. I need to get ready for this evening's show." She took another step back.

Zack's instinct to pursue came to the forefront. The lady was definitely hiding something. And he intended to find out what that was, too.

"I insist. A lady shouldn't be on the streets alone."

He pushed his chair back in a swift movement, dropped bills on the table, and caught her arm.

"Shall we?" he asked in a low voice that brooked no argument or escape.

Once outside, Tess eased her arm from his hold. Her eyes took on the look of a startled doe again. He was beginning to get accustomed to that look.

Zack noted that she couldn't seem to get away fast enough. She took two quick steps away from him that carried her to the edge of the boardwalk.

"Tess—"

She spun around at his voice, teetered on the edge of the wooden plank, and promptly lost her balance. Arms flailing, she slipped off the raised platform and landed in a tumbled heap on the rock-hard street.

"Tess?" Zack was at her side in seconds. "Are you hurt?"

Pushing herself upward, she gave him an embarrassed smile. "Only my pride."

Before she could stand, he reached down and helped her to her feet. His hands were strong and sure beneath her arm and made her want to stay right were she stood, close beside him.

This was folly, she chided herself. Pushing herself away from his tempting strength, she took a step and crumpled against him with a cry of pain.

Calling herself ten kinds of a fool, she bit down on her lower lip and straightened away from the heat of his body. Sharp shards of pain raced upward from her ankle almost to her knee, practically stealing her breath in their wake.

She attempted to cut off the outcry, but couldn't stop the wince of pain that crossed her face. Zack saw it immediately.

"You are hurt."

Tess shook her head. No, she couldn't be hurt. If she

just stood still for a minute everything would be all right. It had to be. She had a show to do tonight. Papa depended on her. So did the rest of the members of the show—Uncle Simon, Frank, Ella.

She'd be fine. All she had to do was set her mind to it. The pain had eased from the first shocking jabs that had stolen her breath. She was fine now. All she'd needed was to catch her breath, she assured herself.

"No, really, I'm quite all right."

Tess attempted to ease back away from Zack at the same moment he stepped forward. His counter movement startled her, and she jerked her head up, the top of her head connecting solidly with the bottom of his chin. Once again, she heard a loud thunk. The force of the impact snapped her teeth together.

"Ouch, hellfire," Zack swore.

Tess flinched and gritted her teeth. Not again. Why did Zack end up getting whacked on the head whenever the two of them were together?

She closed her eyes. God must have a real doozy of a sense of humor. Suddenly the corner of her lips twitched. It was funny. She caught back the giggle that dared to tickle the tip of her tongue.

Beyond a doubt, she knew that Zack Mackinzie, upstanding Texas Ranger, proud and tall, would not cotton to being laughed at. Not in the slightest.

That thought managed to smother the laughter that had been threatening to bubble forth. It seemed that when they spent any amount of time in close proximity, disaster struck. Usually at Zack.

"Lady, you're a walking accident," he muttered low under his breath.

She opened her mouth to retort, then thought better of it.

"We need to get you to a doctor," he announced.

Tess barely stopped herself from blurting out the fact

that her papa was a doctor. That fact wasn't for public knowledge, especially not for a lawman, she reminded herself.

"No, really, I'm fine," she insisted.

Zack took a step closer, and she swallowed the sudden lump that rose in her throat. "No, I—"

He took another step closer. Tess quelled the urge to turn and run. Not that it mattered, she knew she wouldn't get far even without her injured ankle. Something told her Zack Mackinzie was a man who enjoyed the chase. And who always won.

Not this time, she told herself.

Stiffening her spine, she raised her chin to meet his eyes. She wished she could kick him for the smug self-assurance written on his face.

"I said I'm fine. I—"

Over her protests, Zack suddenly swung her up into his arms, cradling her close against his chest. Surprising her with his lightning-fast move, it took her a moment to realize what he'd done. Her words sputtered to a halt on her lips.

In spite of the speed of his movement, he'd been gentle, handling her as if she were a fragile piece of priceless porcelain he feared would break. Tess realized it was a very pleasant feeling.

"Which way's the doctor?" he asked.

She pointed over her shoulder.

Zack strode down the street, his long legs devouring the distance to the doctor's office. Goodness, Tess thought, he wasn't even breathing hard. He carried her as if she weighed nothing at all.

Daring a glance up into his set face, she wished she hadn't. Worry creased his brow into a deep frown of concern. It tugged at her, and she forced herself to look away. Anywhere but at his face.

Her gaze settled on his broad chest and the sprinkling

of hair peeping through the open neck of his shirt where he'd unbuttoned the top button. Her pulse sped up, her heart nearly skipping a beat. No, that definitely wasn't any better.

"Zack, no," Tess argued. "Put me down. I'm perfectly capable of walking."

Ignoring her request, he continued down the street, his arms braced firmly around her body.

"Zack . . ." Tess began again, but it did no good. If anything, he only held her tighter.

His breath stirred the hair at her temples and she shivered in delicious agony. She had to put a stop to this. But it felt so good. So right.

"You can't keep carrying me—"

"Why not?"

She opened her mouth to answer and shut it. How was she supposed to answer that one?

"You don't weigh more than a wet kitten." There was the hint of a smile beneath his drawl.

She didn't know whether to thank him or hit him. A wet kitten? She tried another tactic.

"What about what people will say?"

"They'll say how lucky you are to have such a strong man to tote you around," he teased.

Tess sighed and shut her lips on her next argument. It did absolutely no good to reason with the man, she fumed. It was like arguing an issue with a slab of granite. However, a tiny part of her dared to blossom under his firm yet gentle care. And it scared the daylights out of her.

"Dammit, Zack," she snapped.

He faltered a step and threw her a look of surprise, but didn't stop or release his hold on her. Outside of that, he continued to ignore her words, simply striding straight down the streets of town.

Tess was still arguing with him to no avail as he car-

ried her through the door of Doc Taylor's office. As
Zack yelled for the doctor, his booming voice overly
loud beneath her ear, she winced.

"Is the pain worse?" he asked immediately.

"Only in my head," she muttered.

"Doc!" he yelled again.

"Coming. What's the rush?" A bespectacled man of
medium build with a kind smile walked into the room
from the back room.

Tess met his concern while Zack pulled up a chair
with his foot and lowered her onto the cushion.

"I fell," she admitted. "Really, it's nothing."

"Let me be the judge of that," the doctor ordered.

He sounded just like her father. Did all doctors use
the same standard book of phrases when speaking to
patients, she wondered, then winced in pain as he
probed her ankle with his fingers. He moved her foot
to the side and a cry escaped her lips.

"Doesn't seem to me that you broke anything. But
you'd best stay off it for a while."

"A while?" Tess questioned, She couldn't.

"Um huh." The doctor turned to get his supplies.

After binding her foot and ankle, he ordered her
again to stay off her feet for the duration of three days.

"But—"

"No buts, young lady. I don't want you putting any
weight on that foot for at least two days. Better three."

When Zack added his own instructions to the doctor's, Tess decided it would be wisest to remain quiet.
She had no intention of staying abed that long. Papa
needed her help. She also knew better than to tell the
two men standing over her of her decision.

She'd wait and send word to Ella. Between the two
of them they would surely come up with a solution.

Zack drew her out of her thoughts when he scooped
her up into his arms again.

"Oh, no." Tess shook her head in vehement denial. Zack merely smiled and turned to the door.

"No," she stated firmly. "You're not carrying me all the way through town to my hotel."

Her only answer was another irritatingly sexy smile. Consternation.

He held her close against his chest, his heartbeat strong and sure beneath her ear. Tess attempted to stiffen in his arms, but found it an impossible feat. Her body deserted to the enemy, relaxing against the strong assurance of his broad chest in spite of her efforts to remain stiff and unrelenting.

Traitor, she chided herself.

How was she supposed to resist this man when even her own body betrayed her?

Only later did she recall that he hadn't frightened her in the least.

It seemed like only moments had passed when they reached her hotel. She held back her sigh of disappointment and blamed it on her fall. It had upset her emotions, that's all it was, nothing more.

Zack asked the room number, and she gave it in a quiet voice. One look at his face told her he would carry her to her room no matter what she said or did. The man was as solid as the mountains when he set his mind to it.

He drew to a stop outside her door and eased her gently to her feet. The force of weight on her bruised ankle sent a jolt of pain. Doc Taylor was right; it was worse than she'd let on. However was she going to perform tonight?

Facing Zack, she shifted her weight and reached for the doorknob as if it were a lifeline. The pain in her ankle worsened, but she blinked away the tears building behind her eyes. She'd been hurt far worse than this and never cried.

A long-dead memory of the beating that had set the

past seven years of events into motion assailed her, and for an instant she felt the old pains again. Clamping down on her fragile emotions, she concentrated on the present. The pain in her ankle was nothing compared to the other. Nothing.

For now she had to get through tonight's show. She owed it to Papa. She'd get through tonight, and find a way not to let Papa down. He hadn't let her down that awful night . . .

"Tess?"

Zack brushed a roughened fingertip at her temple, tucking a wayward tendril of hair behind her ear. The gentle caring was her undoing. A tear spilled over to trail across her cheekbone.

He rubbed it away with the pad of his thumb. "Ah, honey," he whispered.

She tilted her head back to meet his eyes. They'd darkened to the shade of storm clouds, intense and turbulent. The corner of his mouth tipped upward and one dimple set in the side of his cheek. His face lowered ever so slightly, closer to hers.

He was going to kiss her. She knew it as sure as she breathed the fresh mountain air surrounding them. And she knew there wasn't a thing she could do to stop him, not that she honestly wanted to.

What she wanted was for him to hold her tight and make her forget. She wanted him to kiss her until her toes curled. The admission startled her.

In the instant before his warm, firm lips touched hers, Tess questioned her very sanity.

Five

Zack's lips brushed hers ever so gently, at first offering her comfort. The kiss was pleasant to Tess. Very pleasant.

Of their own accord, Tess's lips softened beneath his. A part of her noted that his kiss didn't intend to subdue or frighten. The warmth of his lips soothed, tingled, and seduced.

He cupped the back of her head with the palm of his strong hand, but he didn't use that same strength against her. A strange sensation of liquid warmth flowed through Tess, as if it were touching every portion of her body. It was the most pleasant feeling she'd ever remembered having in her entire life.

Whatever it was, it went far beyond mere comfort. In fact, it excited her, wrapping around her and holding her as tightly as his arms held her body against his.

In fact, Zack was granting her unspoken wish—his kiss was curling her toes. It also turned her insides into butter. She nestled closer in his arms.

Zack didn't know when his intention had changed from one of providing solace, but it had. And it was too late to go back now. Neither his mind nor his body would allow it.

He drew her more tightly into his embrace, crushing her body against his, enfolding her thoroughly into his arms. And his heart, a little voice of warning tried to whisper. He silenced it with a deepening of the kiss.

The slamming of a door down the hall and the sound of booted footsteps jolted Tess back to reality. Realization struck her with the force of a bucket of cold water in her face. Here she stood in broad daylight, in front of her hotel room, kissing a man like a common—

She pulled back out of Zack's embrace, and he let her go, except that he kept one arm around her shoulder. Shaking her head in disbelief at her actions, Tess eased back farther, attempting to put sufficient distance between herself and his overwhelming presence.

She suddenly knew with startling clarity that she couldn't allow Zack to carry her into her room, couldn't allow him to enter her room. It would be absolute insanity. There was no way she was getting anywhere in the immediate vicinity of anything resembling a bed with Zack Mackinzie nearby. No, absolutely not.

The expression on his face told her she was going to have one heck of an argument on her hands.

"Tess?" Zack began. His low drawl deepened, stroking her like a feather brushing across her cheek.

She felt her firm resolve weakening.

"Tess?" another male voice echoed from the hallway, this one frustratingly familiar.

Oh, no. Embarrassment and shame flooded over her in silent waves. Someone from Papa's show.

"Tess, is this man bothering you?" Frank Larson rushed forward, forcing Zack to step aside.

Tess recognized an opportunity when one walked up. She grabbed the distraction of Frank's presence like a drowning man grabbing a lifeline thrown to him. She not only grabbed, she held on tight.

"Frank, I'm so happy to see you." She tried to inject some semblance of sincerity into her voice. The show's piano player had been making a pest of himself lately, but right now she'd welcome any distraction from that kiss. Turning toward the man, she added, "I hurt my ankle. Now that you're here, Mr. Mackinzie has some help."

"Zack," he practically growled in her ear.

She smiled sweetly, first at Zack, then at Frank. The two men sized each other up, dislike arising immediately. The unexpected animosity surprised her, although she told herself she should have expected it. Frank had been increasingly insistent on accompanying her over the past few months. The enmity between him and Zack crackled in the very air surrounding them.

She felt like that kitten again between two angry dogs. Two territorial ones at that. And they were becoming less patient by the minute.

As much as she hated subterfuge, the situation called for a drastic measure to diffuse it. Cringing inwardly at what she was about to do, she gathered up her resolve and put her plan into motion.

"Oh, oh," she cried out in a pretense of pain.

As she'd expected, both men turned their attention toward her. Shifting her weight caused her to moan for real this time. She'd received her punishment for lying already.

"Tess—" Zack reached for her.

"Tess?" Frank pushed his bulk up on her other side, placing a proprietary hand on her arm.

The animosity increased even more than before her act, and she realized she didn't like two men readying to fight over her in the least. She wasn't a bone tossed out between two dogs. She was tired, her ankle ached, and her temper threatened to soar.

"Please . . ." she began, only to snap her mouth shut the second she realized neither man was listening to her. They faced each other, squared off in a fighting pose.

Taking a deep breath against the coming pain, she

reached out and grabbed each man's forearm. It worked; both men turned their attention on her.

"Would you two please help me inside before I do something to embarrass myself?"

Like slap you both, she thought in mounting irritation.

"Don't faint," Frank ordered.

Tess threw him a look that clearly said she'd never fainted in her life and wasn't about to start now.

As both men reached for her at the same time, she rushed to add, "I'll just take each of your arms, and you *both* can help me inside."

"Like hell," Zack muttered, then swung Tess up into his arms. "Frank, get the door," he ordered.

Zack's wide-legged stance practically dared the other man to challenge, but that undeniable power that was a part of Zack suggested that he not do it. Tess tensed, waiting for what was to come.

Surprisingly, Frank turned to the door, opened it, and held it back with one large hand. Tess realized not even Frank could ignore the stamp of authority in Zack's voice, or the barely leashed power behind the order.

Zack strode through the doorway and straight to the bed. He deposited her on the center of the mattress with a gentleness that almost took her breath away. The look in his eyes warned her of more to come. Much more.

Tess panicked. She knew that the last thing on this earth she needed right now was to be left alone with Zack Mackinzie.

"Thank you both—"

"No thanks needed, Tess," Frank proclaimed, rushing to grab up the decorative pillow on a nearby chair.

Before she could protest, he slid it under her foot. Although he was gentle, he touched her with nowhere near the tenderness Zack demonstrated.

She could feel his gaze on her and knew even before she turned her head that she would find him staring into her own eyes. Dear heavens, she thought. She'd succeeded in distracting him from the show all right, now what was going to distract him from her?

Nothing, a little voice of caution warned.

Zack took a step closer to the side of the bed, and Tess's stomach clenched. He had the look of a man who was preparing to settle in for a long stay. A very long stay.

Licking her lips in pure nervousness much worse than her usual dose of stage fright, she forced her gaze away from him and over to Frank. He stood at the foot of the bed, waiting for her slightest command.

"Frank, would you please find Ella for me?"

At Zack's suspicious look, she rushed to add, "I could use her help."

Zack continued to watch her closely. Consternation!

"With ah . . . with some womanly things." She lowered her gaze to the dirt stains on her skirt, pretending embarrassment.

This had to work. She needed her friend as a buffer against these unknown feelings that were eating her up inside. She couldn't allow this to continue. At least not until she was feeling stronger and better able to handle her own where Zack was concerned.

Ella was also her only chance of getting out of this blasted bed and performing tonight's show. And nothing was going to stop her from doing just that. Not Frank's overly solicitous attitude. Nor one particular Texas Ranger's intense, all-knowing gaze.

"Anything you want, Tess," Frank answered with a wide grin.

"Thank you."

Frank turned and took a step toward the door. Tess felt her heart skip a beat. Zack hadn't moved a fraction of an inch from the side of her bed.

"I think I'd like to take a nap now." She hid a pretend yawn behind her palm.

Zack remained beside her bed like the slab of granite she'd mentally compared him to once before. Tess swallowed down a knot of nervousness.

"Ah," she began. Both men stared at her. "Ah, I want to thank you for your help, Mr. Mackinzie—"

"Zack," he growled under his breath.

"Would you both close the door behind you?" she asked sweetly in a voice that held a hint of steel beneath it.

Zack stared down at her for the space of a heartbeat, then added, "I'll be back to check in on you later."

With this parting shot, he rammed his hat on his head, then strode to the door without another word. He paused to glance back suggestively at Frank. The other man mumbled his good-byes and hurried out the door first. Zack sent her one last intense glance, then the door slammed, echoing in the small room and causing Tess to flinch.

She had no intention of being here when Zack returned to "check on her," and she would find some way to do the show tonight in spite of him.

Ella's arrival thirty minutes later solved Tess's dilemma. She breezed into the hotel room, taking charge of everything in sight. Within another half hour, Tess wore a soft nightgown of fine lawn, and Ella's cold compresses had taken much of the swelling down from the injured ankle.

"Ella, what would I do without you?" Tess asked, sincerity filling the question.

Not what anyone would call pretty, Ella brightened a place just by entering it. She had a ready smile and a laugh for everyone. Reaching up, she tucked a stray wisp of dark blond hair back into the bun she always wore. Somehow the style managed to make her look many years younger than the thirty she admitted to.

"You'd do fine." Ella pulled a chair up to the side of the bed and dropped into it.

"Well, thanks to you I might be able to do tonight's show." Tess wiggled her toes and then bit back a cry as the movement sent a shaft of fiery pain upward.

"Not if you have to put any weight on that foot you won't," Ella informed her.

Tess sighed in disgust. "But I have to do the show. Papa is depending on me. And I won't let him down." In a voice almost too low to make out, she added, "I can't let him down again."

"Honey," Ella's voice pulled her back. "If you're that certain, then between us we can surely think up something. It wouldn't be the first time we've had to."

A smile tugged at the corner of Tess's lips. Trust Ella to put everything into such simple perspective. She watched her friend tap a finger to her lips and squint her eyes, deep in thought.

Tall and slim where Tess was short and shapely, both had blond hair, but Tess's was a mixture of silver and gold while Ella's bun showed only wisps of blondish brown. The two women appeared as different as night and day, but deep down they shared a common shame.

Suddenly Ella sat up straight in the chair and snapped her fingers. "I've got it."

Tess leaned forward, almost falling out of bed in the process. Ella's quick action saved her and pushed her back several safe inches from the edge of the mattress.

"My idea isn't going to work if you fall off and hurt yourself worse."

Tess brushed her concern aside. "Well?" she asked, eager to hear her friend's solution.

"Remember that fancy hand-carved cane your papa used a while back in his act?"

Tess nodded, and her smile widened with each word Ella spoke.

"I recall packing it away in that large trunk beneath the old costumes. It would be perfect. If you're careful, you could lean most of your weight on the cane and not on your foot. But, mind you, it's still going to hurt like the devil."

"I'll do it." Tess's voice clearly said there wasn't any use in trying to argue her out of it, and Ella complied, instead turning her attention to the slight change she'd noted in Tess when she'd entered her room.

Tess's cheeks held a rosy glow in spite of the occasional flickers of pain that dulled her bright eyes. But more evident to see, Tess's usual composure was missing. Shattered, Ella thought to herself. Only one thing could cause that in such a woman. A man.

"Tell me about him."

Tess jumped at the sudden order. How could Ella know . . . One glance into her friend's eyes and she changed the question to how could Ella not know.

She and Ella had formed an instant bond the evening she'd found the woman hiding in one of the tents, bruised and battered. Tess had taken Ella into the show and into her heart immediately. The two shared a bond deeper than friendship, born out of shared pain and memories that haunted each woman's sleep.

Ella was the only other person besides Papa who knew everything that had happened to her. Not even Uncle Simon knew all the events. More than anyone else, Ella understood the terrors that stalked Tess in her sleep. It had been Ella who'd sat with her when the nightmares left her weak and shaken, her nightclothes soaked with sweat.

"Him? Whoever do you mean?" Tess tried to dodge the coming inquisition, toying with the satin bow of her nightgown in sudden nervousness.

"That's what I want to know. Who? And exactly how did you hurt that ankle of yours?"

"I fell." Tess wrinkled her nose in embarrassment at the admission.

Across from her, Ella crossed her arms over her chest. "Um hum. Tess, you're the most graceful person I've ever seen. You never simply fall."

"I did this time."

"What caused it? And from the looks of you, I'm betting it was a man."

"How could you know?" The instant the words left her mouth, Tess wished she could snatch them back. The self-satisfied expression on Ella's face told her she'd revealed far too much.

"I'd rather not talk about it." Tess raised her chin and sniffed.

One glance at the set, determined expression in her friend's eyes and Tess knew she'd lost the battle. Part sister, part mother, and all friend, Ella could read her moods like no one else had ever been able to do. Not even her own mama had been able to do it the way Ella did simply and naturally.

At the unbidden thought of her mother, a flicker of pain crossed Tess's face. She still missed her so much. But her mama's death seemed a lifetime away. Tess had only been fifteen when the woman died in the flash flood that had swept through their land, overflowing the creek they'd been wading in less than an hour before. The waters washed away the remnants of the picnic, and Tess's heart along with her precious mother.

Afterward Papa had withdrawn, devoting himself to his medical practice and traveling the countryside as the only doctor willing to go so far away from home. Left alone too much, Tess longed for the love she'd seemingly lost from both parents.

As the memories swamped her, much like the flood she'd barely escaped, she couldn't escape the pain they brought. Or the shame. Desperate for love, she'd been such an easy target. Naive, vulnerable, and needing someone to love her. Shame, and then the guilt that always followed the memories, whitened her face. She tightened her fist around the edge of the material rumpled across her lap.

Ella reached out and took Tess's hand in hers. "Not all men are like Joel."

Tess's face blanched at the name. Ella's words sent her mind reeling into the past. She could still hear his shouts of condemnation, feel the blows he rained on her. What had happened to the man who'd promised before her papa to love and honor her?

She learned she hadn't really known him at all. In fact, she'd never even met any of his family. He'd told her they disapproved of his marriage, but now she realized it may well have been his way of keeping her away from all family—his as well as hers.

Shortly after the wedding he'd taken to ignoring her whenever she did anything to displease him. It wasn't until later, much later, that she recognized the act for what it was—his way of controlling her, of bringing her back in line.

Then, not long after their wedding day, the beatings started. At first they had been mere accidents. She hadn't seen his actions for what they were in the beginning; she hadn't wanted to believe it. She'd been clumsy; after all, she had been the one who'd tripped and fallen over his feet. It had been a simple accident—nothing more. Except that the accidents increased. Until finally, the beatings themselves had started. But by then she'd been too much under his control to break free.

She'd tried to fight back at first, but that only made things worse. Any show of independence on her part was punished thoroughly and completely. Ice flowed through her at the humiliating memories. The band of control he'd woven around her kept her from leaving him sooner.

After the last beating, she'd managed to escape the small house. An inner strength she didn't know she'd had surfaced, propelling her. She'd run to the only place she'd known that provided any measure of safety without condemnation. To her papa.

And the nightmare had ended, only to have another one even worse take its place.

"Tess." Ella caught her cold hands in hers, rubbing warmth back into them, and into her.

Drawing in a deep, cleansing breath, Tess let go of the past, tucking it back away. She mustered up a smile for her friend. As she opened her mouth to speak, Ella stopped her.

"Tess, not all men are like Joel," she repeated.

"I know that."

"Your mind may know, but your heart hasn't realized it yet. Only then will you be free of the past."

Ella's words stayed with her long after Ella had left, and even after she'd returned with the cane. After propping it next to the bed, she brushed a hand across Tess's cheek and left her with an order to take a nap.

An hour later Tess glanced around the room. She could swear the space had shrunken since the last time she'd looked about. Her brief nap had left her eager to be out of bed and about. She knew she couldn't make it through the afternoon if she had to stay here abed a minute longer. Her gaze fell on the cane propped beside the bed, and a smile lit her face. The perfect answer.

She'd show Mr. Zack Mackinzie he couldn't dictate to her.

* * *

It had been over three hours since he'd kissed Tess and been shaken all the way to his boots. No matter what he'd done during that time, Zack couldn't get her out of his mind. Nor could he purge the image of the showman Frank Larson bending over her, concern written on his hard features.

Something about the man bothered him. Zack told himself it was more than the fact that Frank was obviously enamored of Tess. He knew trouble when he met it, and trouble was brewing with Larson. He felt it in his gut.

However, the local sheriff had nothing on Frank Larson. Absolutely nothing. So all Zack had to go on was a gut instinct. And a growing concern for Tess Fontana.

Damn. As if that wasn't the last thing he needed right now.

Good job, Mackinzie, he muttered under his breath, pulling his hat lower against the sun as he stepped down off the boardwalk. He'd set out to question the woman and ended up nearly taking her to bed.

This time would be different. Tess Fontana would answer some carefully worded questions before he left her hotel. He fully intended to be the only one asking the questions this time.

He refused to be distracted by her again. Neither her silken skin, soft shimmering curls, or luscious lips would deter him.

Liar, his memory taunted.

Heat surged through his body at his recollection of the kiss they'd shared. And it had been a sharing. She had responded, giving herself in that searing kiss with an irresistible mixture of innocence and awakened temptress. Even now, that combination had him increasing the stride of his steps in the direction of her hotel.

He told himself it was only professional interest in getting him some answers. Nothing was urging him to check on her condition. He told the nagging voice in the back of his mind it was purely business, simply doing his job, nothing more. Then he told his conscience to go to hell and strode through the open door of the hotel.

As soon as he entered the lobby, the hairs on the back of his neck prickled. Out of habit, he slipped his right hand down to rest it on the butt of his Colt, easing it from his holster.

A crowd of men clustered around a table in the corner to his right, drawing his attention. Trouble clung to the very air around the group.

Suddenly, a man surged to his feet, and Zack drew his pistol, readying himself. The soft tinkle of a woman's husky laughter froze him in mid-step.

Tess? It couldn't be.

No, she was upstairs resting. He should know; he put her into that tempting bed himself. And had to practically force himself to leave her.

A dusty miner brushed against his left side, a brimming glass of lemonade in his outstretched hand. The man pushed his way through the crowd with a wide grin of satisfaction on his face.

As the men surrounding the table shifted, Zack caught a glimpse of long silver-gold curls tumbling over a slim shoulder and curling under a stubborn chin. Holstering his gun, he stifled a groan of dismay. Seated at the table, her foot propped up on a chair cushion, Tess Fontana held court.

He should have known.

He watched in growing disbelief as one man plumped the pillow propped behind her back, while another man adjusted the cushion beneath her foot. The miner handed her the tall glass of lemonade as if he were serving royalty. Seated around the felt-covered table was a mixture of more miners and businessmen. A game of faro was in full swing, and from the looks of the money piled in front of her, Tess was winning.

Hellfire, how had the woman created such a commotion in such a short amount of time? Time when she was supposedly resting upstairs in bed not down here playing faro, he added in a flash of irritation. And likely as not, cheating at it.

As another man attempted to catch Tess's hand in his, the irritation turned to burning anger. He'd seen enough. More than enough. What did she think she was doing?

Zack watched her deftly handle the cards, winning easily over the miners around the table. He amended his thoughts. The lady definitely knew what she was doing.

And it was time someone took her down.

Smiling, he stepped forward and sank into the chair vacated by a miner. He casually dropped his hat on the green felt, and watched as Tess glanced his way. Her eyes widened to deep seas of blue. Shock, disbelief, and trepidation flashed one after the other.

"Your deal," he said in a low drawl.

Nervously, she licked her lips and dealt the cards. She won the first, then the second, and the third. Zack won the fourth, but quickly lost the fifth and sixth hands. By the time she'd won a chunk of his money and most of his pride, he was willing to concede this one to her. However, he swore Tess Fontana was going to lose to him for certain next encounter.

He'd never been broadsided this way in his life, and he didn't like it one little bit.

"Tess, you cannot do it," Philip Fontana insisted in a firm fatherly voice. "I won't let you be hurt more."

She noted he was too upset at the news of her accident to try and use his showman voice to persuade her. He'd resorted to simply proclaiming an order.

"I scarcely feel it," she lied, intent on reassuring him. "Someone needs to help with the performance—"

"Simon—"

Tess interrupted him with a laugh. "He'd never be able to pull it off. We both know the show needs a woman's touch."

"Ella would be willing to do it," he said, then smiled at the obvious brilliance of his solution.

Once again, laughter edged Tess's voice. "Papa, you know she's much too tall to ever fit under the cone."

"But, dear girl, you cannot—"

"Of course I can."

"But your ankle—"

Tess raised the cane with a flourish worthy of her father and twirled it around. Smiling, she walked across the stage using the cane with deliberate finesse and milking her performance for all she could.

Behind her she heard a chuckle of laughter from her father. Her scheme was working. Before she whirled to face him, she carefully steeled her features so that not a trace of the pain she felt showed on her face.

"See, Papa. I'm perfectly capable of doing the show tonight."

"But you can't walk on that ankle."

"I'll use the cane." She waved aside his concern.

"And the cane—"

She answered his every objection with assurance. "We'll simply work it into the performance." Then she tossed her head and offered him a smile of pure self-assurance. "It will work perfectly. In fact, it will likely as not even increase sales tonight."

At her action, the wind ruffled the hair at her temple, lifting the curls away from her face for the space of a second. But in that moment the jagged white scar that traced the edge of her right temple and disappeared into her hair glistened in the lantern's glow.

Pain raced across her father's face, changing his expression, hardening it. "Tess, I'm sorry." He touched a fingertip to the scar.

At the change in his voice she knew he wasn't talking about her ankle. He was lost in the past, returning to that horrible night that neither of them could forget. The night that had changed both their lives forever.

She swallowed down the tightness in her throat. "Papa, it's over and in the past."

"But if only I'd stopped you from marrying." His strong, vibrant voice trembled.

He'd been against the marriage, but by then it didn't matter to Tess. Her father's love and attention came too late. She was in love or so she'd assumed, mistaking manipulation and control for love.

"You did what you could." She rested her hand on his arm, then admitted in a soft voice, "I wasn't willing to listen."

His face tightened into a mask of pain. "Oh, dear girl, if only I'd done something sooner."

"Don't blame yourself, Papa."

He brushed another feather-light touch across the tiny scar hidden by the curls at her temple. "Whenever I recall how he nearly killed you that time, I know I'd do it all over again."

"Papa—"

"Except this time I'd kill him sooner."

Six

Tess swallowed down the guilt and the rising bile that accompanied it. That night so long ago arose like a specter before her. Joel had nearly killed her father that night when he came to drag her home.

Papa had "interfered," as Joel had called it. A terrible fight ensued, but her father had been the victor. Joel couldn't leave it; instead, he'd tried to kill her father. He would have succeeded, plunging the knife into her father's back, except that she'd screamed out a warning that Joel was charging with a knife, and Papa had dodged.

After that it had happened in a blur. His momentum carrying him forward, Joel stumbled and fell. He'd lain so still. When Papa turned him over; they saw he'd fallen on the knife. There had been so much blood.

Tess shoved back the nightmare. She would not let her father suffer because of her misjudgment. It wasn't his fault.

"Papa." Tess caught her father's hand and laid it against her cheek. "Don't say that. You didn't kill him. You acted in self-defense."

"Dear girl, dead is dead. And no court is going to believe us now."

"Papa—"

"As far as the Texas law is concerned, I murdered him."

"But you didn't," she argued.

"Remember the sheriff said they had an eyewitness."

"But they couldn't, Papa. There were only the three of us that night. Whoever could it be?"

"Someone who means to see me hang."

Fear and guilt swamped her, nearly staggering in their intensity. She wavered on her feet, then used the cane to steady herself. He was right, and if he were taken back to Texas, they'd likely hang him. She would not let her papa be taken back to Texas. No matter what she had to do to stop it.

"That will *never* happen," she vowed, clutching his hand in hers.

The sound of heavy footsteps caused both Tess and her father to turn, prepared to face whoever it was together. The familiar balding head of Simon White could be seen near the edge of the stage. He climbed the last step and walked toward them.

"Uncle Simon!" Tess called out, joy and relief evident in her strained voice.

The tall, balding gentleman caught her close for a hug. She hugged him back and lifted her head for the kiss he always deposited on her cheek.

He wasn't actually a relative, but he felt like one, she'd known him so long. Besides, she and Papa were the only real family he had to count on. The only blood relations he possessed were one sister and her son, whom he hadn't spoken with since the war began, due to some disagreement he refused to discuss with anyone. Tess frowned at the thought. Family was too important to let anything stand in the way.

Simon tapped her under the chin. "Why so grim?"

"Reminiscing."

A cloud of pain crossed over Simon's face before he

smiled at her. Tess tried to return his smile, but hers came out strained.

"We need to discuss the arrival of an unwanted lawman. A Texas Ranger," Papa informed his partner. "It's time to look forward."

"Marlene told me about him last night. What are we going to do about him sniffing around?"

Papa smiled in pride. "Our Tess is taking care of that."

"How?" Simon's eyes narrowed in suspicion. He glanced from his partner to Tess and back to Philip.

"She's . . . ah . . ." Papa paused delicately, "distracting his attention from the show."

Simon laughed a hearty burst of surprised enjoyment. "Good job, girl." He slapped his knee and chuckled. "Didn't know for sure you had it in you."

Tess stiffened at his words, feeling as if she'd been slapped.

"Ah, Tess, you know I didn't mean anything hurtful by that. It's only that you usually shy away from the fellas that flock around our performances."

"I'm doing this to save Papa and the show," she said in a voice that sounded stiff to her own ears.

Simon smiled at her and dropped another kiss on her cheek. "Am I forgiven?"

Tess couldn't remain angry with him. He'd been a part of their little family for many years. He and Papa had known each other way before Simon joined the show almost six years ago. "Of course you are." She hugged him around his thickening waist. She'd show him she could so distract a lawman if she set her mind to it.

After she released him, Simon stepped back. "So, what's a Ranger doing around these parts? We're a long ways from Texas."

"Business," Tess quoted Zack's one-word answer.

"What kind of business?" Simon asked, his brows drawing into a frown of concern.

Tess shrugged and crossed her arms, leaning her weight on the sturdy cane. "I don't know. That's what I'm trying to find out."

"Well, be careful, girl. You know how much is at stake."

Yes, she did.

Simon patted her hand in consolation and encouragement. "How's the ankle?" he asked.

She didn't wonder how he knew. Word about any of the show's members always spread like a prairie wildfire amongst the traveling show.

"I'll be fine," she answered, dodging his question. Truth be told, her ankle hurt like the devil, just like Ella predicted it would. She shifted position and leaned a little more weight on the fancy wooden cane.

"Marlene has been expressing some interest in the show these past few months. Perhaps she could perform tonight in Tess's place," Simon suggested, turning his attention to his partner.

Not on your life, Tess thought in a rush of anger. She barely kept the words from bursting free.

The woman had taken part in one show in west Texas, months back when she'd visited Simon, and she'd almost ruined the performance beyond repair.

"There's no need for her to trouble herself," Tess replied in a firm voice. "I'm going on tonight. Like always."

"But your ankle?" Simon asked.

"It's all arranged. I'll use Papa's old cane. See?" Tess performed a fancy pirouette for Simon's benefit, twirling the cane in the process.

"Very good." Simon applauded her. "Do you want me to get you a bottle of laudanum for tonight? Just in case?" he offered, kindness edging his voice.

Tess shook her head. "No. My ankle's not that bad. I'll make it."

It wasn't that she didn't trust Simon's doctoring. After all, he was *almost* a doctor, except that due to some family argument, he hadn't been able to finish his schooling. However, she trusted his vast knowledge of herbs and remedies. She just hated the thought of using laudanum for any reason.

She'd make it through the show without any assistance from a bottle. Or anything else.

Two hours later, Tess stood on the stage and regretted her earlier assurances. She'd stepped out onto the show's platform, limped through Papa's cloud of smoke, and come face-to-face with Zack Mackinzie.

He sat, proud as you please, in the very center of the front row. Tess felt those old butterflies race for her throat, taking her heart soaring with them. For an instant she wished for a sip of the laudanum to dull her senses so that she wouldn't be quite so aware of him.

How could any female not be aware of Zack? He sat on the makeshift wooden bench, one long leg crossed over the other at his ankle. His black Stetson was drawn low over his forehead, but when he nudged it back with his thumb, his eyes met hers.

Tess knew she was rooted to the spot. She couldn't have moved even if someone had yelled "fire."

The Texas lawman was mad as hell. She could see it in the set expression on his handsome face, in the dark, stormy gray of his eyes. Well, he had no right to assume she'd follow his orders, she thought. She'd vowed no man would ever control her again. And Zack Mackinzie was not the exception to that vow. Not now. Not ever.

With renewed determination, she turned her attention to the show. Papa tossed the filmy black scarf toward her, and she scarcely caught it before it landed on the wooden platform. It was time for her father's disappearing and reappearing coin trick, she reminded herself, and he needed her assistance if he were to pull it off successfully. She'd do better to concentrate on him and not on Zack.

Although she tried to focus on her father's performance, she could still feel Zack's gaze on her. Hot, and powerful, and reminding her that so much remained unfinished between them.

No matter how hard she tried, she couldn't keep her gaze from returning to him, time and time again. Even sitting in his seemingly casual pose one could tell he was tall and leanly muscled, and a man accustomed to dealing with trouble.

As the show's lanterns shone on the glint of the badge on his shirt, her racing heart nearly stopped. At the very least it plummeted straight for her toes. If she weren't careful, he could pose more trouble than she could handle. Zack held the power to bring their life crashing down around them, destroying her father in the process.

It took every bit of Tess's willpower to make it through the night's show. She disappeared from beneath the cone, reappeared back on stage in a puff of smoke, and strutted around the wooden platform using the cane to its utmost. The miners applauded fiercely, guaranteeing the show's success. However, with Zack's eyes following her every move, it was the longest, most trying performance of her life.

And when it was over, he was still waiting, sitting right in the center of the front row. Tess took her bow, and when her eyes met his, she knew there was nothing final about the evening.

Performing a pirouette, she turned and slipped through the curtain. She stood a moment, trying to get her ragged breathing to return to normal. She knew without a doubt that he was waiting for her.

Tess took in several deep, calming breaths. Surely, Zack would realize she had left. Surely he wouldn't stay behind. Surely . . .

She turned and, standing on tiptoe, peered through a tiny hole in the velvet curtain. Zack sat, still as a block of granite, right in the center of the front row . . . waiting for her.

Glancing at the people milling around, she made her decision. She caught her cloak tight about her with one hand, gripped the cane in her other hand, and slipped into the departing crowd. A tiny voice accused her of running away.

She answered that she was regrouping her defenses to fight another day. For she knew without a doubt that one heck of a fight was brewing to a boil where Zack Mackinzie was concerned. She couldn't handle anymore tonight. Her ankle hurt, her spirits flagged in spite of the show's success, and she didn't particularly care to hear what angry words Zack might have to say.

Zack Mackinzie had plenty to say to Tess, and he waited for her to reappear back on stage. The stragglers remaining in the audience clapped, shouted, and whistled their approval of her and the performance. His gut clenched, and he tightened his jaw. He had plenty to say to her all right. And she would listen to him this time.

Unlike this afternoon, she wouldn't merely thumb her pretty little nose at him and do as she pleased. She would listen.

She'd been a fool to perform tonight. Why hadn't she stayed in bed where he had placed her? Where the doctor had told her to stay?

Oh, no. She couldn't do that. First, she'd had to traipse downstairs to the hotel lobby, enthrall every man in sight, and proceed to beat them at faro. As if that hadn't been enough, she'd had to find that damned fancy-carved cane and prance around on the stage for the men to admire and desire.

The whistles and stomping feet attested to the male admiration from her audience. Even now, a few of those same men still stood around, waiting for her to come back out onstage. Didn't the fool woman know what danger she might be putting herself in? Virginia City did not exactly have a reputation for being the safest place for any lady. Much less one who looked like Tess.

Once again the fact hit him that she was innocence and temptation blended together into one hell of a package. One no sane man could resist. Although, about now, sitting here waiting for her, he began to question his own mental condition.

While he told himself that he only wanted to see her and talk to her in order to question her, a part of him knew it was a bald-faced lie. He wanted to ensure for himself that she was all right, that she wasn't in as much pain as he suspected.

He suspected right now her ankle hurt like hell. She'd likely injured it worse with all her fancy walking around the stage and her performance. And for what? All for the damned show.

Damn her stubborn pride anyway.

More than mere pride stood between them, and he knew it. The brass token found in his brother's hand and the letter both pointed to Tess as David's killer. Logic told him to pay attention to the facts, but his body gave another message entirely.

That left gut instinct, which was in a turmoil as well. His years as a lawman tracking down killers told him to tread lightly and watch his back where any beautiful woman was concerned, especially one like Tess. However, his gut told him that things didn't add up right.

Every time he saw Tess or talked with her, he came away with far more questions than answers. One thing he was certain of was that the lady was afraid. Sometimes her fear ran soul deep. He felt it in the way her hands trembled, in the startled-doe look in her clear blue eyes. Those weren't the eyes of a killer.

He intended to find out exactly what lay behind that fear. And behind those eyes.

Where was she? He pulled out his pocket watch, flipped it open, and read the dial in the lamplight given off from a nearby kerosene lantern.

Too much time had passed since Tess had slipped through the faded velvet curtain. Entirely too much time. She wasn't coming back. He snapped the watch closed. Walking around more on that ankle was the last thing she needed.

He refused to sit here like a lovestruck fool waiting for her any longer. She'd disappeared like a puff of smoke, and he'd bet his badge she was running. He stood to his feet in an angry move, pulled his hat lower, and strode from the empty performance. Gut instinct told him Tess had run from more than his anger. And he fully intended to find out what that something might be.

He had plenty of questions about Tess and the traveling show, and he intended to get them answered as well. His search so far had provided more questions than answers. No record could be found of the Fontana's Fabulous Show prior to just under seven years ago. Even odder, no record of a Philip or Tess Fontana could be found before that time, either.

A lot of traveling shows like this one started up and disappeared, only to resurface under another name. But he found it damned peculiar all the same.

Perhaps he'd better pay the sheriff another visit.

* * *

Tess slept fitfully that night. For the first time in a long time, nightmares plagued her sleep. She awoke tired and irritable with a vague sense of restlessness. She had no doubt of the cause for her disturbing night, and she laid the blame right where it belonged—on Zack Mackinzie and her unwanted reaction to him.

She didn't want to react to him, to his nearness, but her body seemed to possess an independence from her senses where the Texas lawman was concerned. Even now, a warmth stole through her as she recalled him sitting in the audience last night. However, a chill followed right along on the heels of that tempting warmth.

The fact remained unchanged that he was a lawman. And he could well be here in Virginia City in pursuit of her father and her. She had to find out.

How was she ever going to try and get close to him to find out what he was up to when every instinct of survival told her to flee?

The answer stared back at her, plain as the sun shining through the hotel room's dust-laden window. It was her turn to pursue him.

Consternation, she lacked experience in that area for certain. She hadn't a single idea of where, or how, to start her new endeavor. She, who'd made a practice of avoiding men since Joel's death, now had to set out to attract one particular man's attention. And entice the answers she sought from him. Heavens.

Perplexed, but with a light of determination in her eyes, she reached for the cane. A visit to Ella might solve the first of her problems. Ella never had a problem attracting a man's attention. Maybe, just maybe, she could give her a tip or two.

Ella answered on the second knock, and after one

startled look, pulled Tess inside and shut the door firmly behind her.

"Whatever are you doing walking the halls of this hotel in the early morning hours?"

"Ella, I need your help."

Tess's plea silenced any further tirade from her friend.

"What's wrong?" The question held a tinge of fear attached to it.

"I need to know how to attract a man."

Ella's eyes widened at the statement, and she nearly choked on her next breath.

"You what?"

"I need to know how to attract a man," Tess repeated in a voice that clearly said she might as well be talking to a child for all the understanding she was receiving. As Ella merely blinked in disbelief, Tess added, "Not just any man. A lawman."

"Oh, my stars," Ella murmured and sank onto the edge of the mattress.

"Maybe I'd better explain—"

"That might be a good idea." Ella pulled her wrapper closer about her in the chilly early-morning air.

"Well, Zack Mackinzie, the Texas Ranger, attended last night's show, and . . ." she paused and took a long breath.

"I should have known," her friend cut in.

"What?"

"Not what, who. I saw him for myself last night. Sitting smack center of the audience. And watching every move you made, too."

Tess felt her cheeks warm with an unwanted heat at the observation. She brushed an imaginary speck of lint from the skirt of her soft green gown.

"Well, we'd best get started." Ella informed her in a no-nonsense voice.

At Tess's startled look, she added, "Might as well sit down. This could take a while."

Tess snapped her mouth shut on the sharp retort that rose to her lips. Ella meant well.

"First off, you got to start meeting a man's eyes when he looks at you. Instead of looking away with that manner that tells him you're off limits."

"But I—"

"Yes, you do," Ella corrected her outburst, then continued, "and for heaven's sakes, smile at him."

For the next half hour Ella instructed Tess on one thing after another. When she'd finally fallen silent, Tess dared to ask, "Do you really think this will work?"

"Let's just say, you better make certain this next meeting isn't in your hotel room." Ella's laughter brought a smile to Tess's lips.

That smile and Ella's words stayed with her on her slow walk to Maggie's. She hoped that since it was the restaurant Zack took her to before, he might be there.

Tess stepped into the restaurant and collided right into the rock-hard body of Zack Mackinzie. He caught her by the shoulders barely in time to keep her from tumbling backward from the impact of their collision.

He looked down at her and his hands tightened on her arms. "Tess? Are you all right?"

She nodded, not trusting her voice. This morning, his eyes were the softest gray she'd ever seen, the color of a beautiful mourning dove. All of Ella's carefully learned instructions flew right out the open door of the restaurant.

"Tess?"

Zack's low drawl caused tiny goose bumps to break out on her arms. His breath brushed the hair at her temples, and she was afraid her heart was going to race right out the door after those forgotten instructions.

She looked up into his face, recalled Ella's advice,

and smiled. When he returned her smile, his dimples set deep in his cheeks, what she wanted to do was turn and run from whatever she'd started.

Instead, she forced herself to glance down at his chest and the V made by the unbuttoned top of his blue shirt. As if following Ella's advice out of instinct, she glanced back up at his face, then away again. Her heart pounded in her chest, and she feared he'd hear it. When he smoothed the palm of one hand against her arm, coherent thought abandoned her nearly completely.

"Hmmm," she answered his question, unable to get more past her suddenly numbed lips.

The way he stared down at her sent her stomach dipping to her toes and surging back up to land in her throat. She swallowed and moistened her lips with her tongue.

"Tess." Her name was a groan of near pain from him. "Um huh?"

She leaned closer, not having the slightest idea why her legs felt like the stuffing had leaked out of them. All she knew was that she didn't know how much longer she could stand there with him looking at her the way he was doing. He reminded her of a mountain lion. A very hungry one.

A tiny shiver of awareness coasted down her back. Zack's fingers followed it, lightly tracing her backbone. She sucked in her breath in a startled gasp—half surprise, half pleasure.

"I think you need some air," he chuckled softly in a voice that did the strangest things to her insides.

In a swift move that startled her with its speed, he turned her about, and had them both outside on the boardwalk before she could utter a single word of agreement or disagreement. She hadn't the slightest notion which one it would have been.

He walked her to the end of the wooden boardwalk,

lifted her down the single step, and gently sat her back on her feet. His action made her feel as if she weighed nothing at all.

Then, unexpectedly, Zack sidestepped and pulled her into the alleyway with him. His quick movement left her staring at him in disbelief.

He towered over her, then leaned down slightly, his eyes meeting hers. Tess inched backward a step, and her back brushed against the wooden wall.

"Now, do you want to tell me what that little performance back there was all about?" he asked in a low voice that demanded an answer better than a shout could have done.

"What?" Tess squeaked out the question.

Maybe she'd taken Ella's tips a little too far. Just maybe she'd started something, but she didn't know what she was supposed to do now.

"I'm waiting," he reminded her.

Suddenly her friend's instruction to smile and flatter him sprang unbidden to her mind. Without pausing to think of the possible consequences, Tess blindly followed those directions.

She let a tentative smile peek out at him, then lowered her eyes. "I was trying to attract your attention."

"You got it all right," Zack muttered.

As Tess batted her lashes at him and glanced up, she heard him swear. The next instant he pulled her against his chest, his arms closing around her. He was so close she could feel the rapid beat of his heart against her own chest.

Consternation. Whatever had she done?

His head lowered, coming closer and closer. Still she couldn't manage to force out a single word. Especially not the word "no."

Zack's lips settled over hers surely and completely. He kissed her with an intensity that was devastating. His hand slid up to frame her face, and Tess practically melted against him. As she did, he tilted her head up, slanting his mouth over hers and his kiss deepened.

His kisses were as different as night from day, she thought in an instant of rationality. This time his kiss was long and hard and so thorough it curled every one of her ten toes.

And his touch made her heart race beyond anything she'd ever felt before. She didn't know if her lungs could even draw another breath, and she didn't care.

Seven

Tess's legs weakened beneath the sensual onslaught of Zack's soul-shattering kisses.

That first long thorough kiss turned into a second kiss, then a third. As he melded his mouth to hers, she thought she'd surely passed on in this world into heaven itself.

Her knees trembled, leaving her with a quivering feeling she'd never in her life experienced before this moment. She wanted it to go on forever. And forever.

Tess tightened her hands on Zack's broad shoulders, reveling in the feel of his bunched muscles beneath her fingertips. She never paused to question how her arms had come to be wrapped around him in the first place. It felt so right.

Zack eased back slightly, gazing down at her upturned face, and drew in a ragged breath. Need itself reached out from him so intense she felt she could almost touch it.

"Come back with me," Zack murmured against her ear.

His words tempted, cajoled, enticed. Right that moment she was ready to agree to almost anything. Her senses had abandoned her, shooed away by his loving touch.

"Hmmm," she sighed against his neck as he leaned over her, holding her close again.

Tess leaned closer against him, feeling treasured and protected. Zack would never let anything happen to her. Her heart told her so.

"Tess?" he whispered, his breath ruffling the hair at her cheek.

"Hmmm?" Her eyes drifted closed. It felt so nice in his strong arms.

She'd never in all her days felt anything quite like this. She didn't know being held by a man could feel this way.

"Come back with me to my room. I'll show you how good it can be between us.

Zack nuzzled the sensitive spot beneath her ear. It half tickled, half heated her.

Without thinking of anything else but the sensations he was awakening in her, she asked, "What?"

"How good it could be in bed," he sighed, his lips brushing her temple and the seven-year-old scar.

Alarms sounded in Tess's mind at the combination of his words and and the feel of his lips. Harsh memories came flooding back over her, threatening to sweep her away into the nightmare her past had once been. She shivered against the sudden chill that arose. It seeped into every part of her.

She couldn't do this. She couldn't!

Gasping, she drew away from Zack, then forced herself to swallow deeply. Tilting her head back, she looked up into his face. Her fear-filled eyes begged his for understanding.

Her response was a whisper so low it couldn't be heard above her uneven breathing.

"What?" he asked, brushing his thumb over her lower lip.

Tess shivered under his ministrations. Her lower lip

trembled, then she steadied it with an act of sheer willpower.

"No thank you," she answered stiffly and politely through lips that had been almost frozen in a forced smile.

Zack opened his mouth to question her unexpected reaction.

She shook her head. "I've seen firsthand how 'good' that can be."

Her chin trembled as she pulled out of his embrace. When he reached for her, she flinched and dodged his arms as if he were preparing to strike her.

Spinning away, she dashed across the street, not caring a whit about her ankle. A wagon passing stopped him from pursuing her immediately, and before he could cross, she'd ducked out of sight.

This time she admitted she was running. As far and as fast as she could.

Zack stared out into the street where Tess had disappeared. The woman had the most irritating habit of disappearing at the most puzzling moment. He released a ragged sigh of pent-up frustration.

"Hellfire and damnation," he swore, rubbing a hand across his face.

What had happened?

One moment Tess had been melting against him, the next she'd fled as if her life depended on escaping. He brought his hand around and rubbed the knotted muscles at the back of his neck.

What the hell had happened? To her. And to himself.

The onslaught of fear in her wide eyes hadn't escaped his notice. But he'd done nothing to frighten her. She'd given him inch for inch in their lovemaking; he hadn't forced that kiss on her. Not by a long shot.

He rubbed his neck. She'd had her hands wrapped so tightly at the nape of his neck that she'd even tugged at the hair laying along the back of his neck. That most certainly wasn't the act of an unwilling woman.

There was a lot more to Tess Fontana than what one saw. A whole lot more.

For the life of him, Zack couldn't figure out what had happened to send her running off. He continued to stare at the last spot across the street he'd seen her.

Realization eased upon him and he began to question himself. Whatever on this earth had possessed him to kiss her? Much less continue kissing her?

A smile tugged at the corner of his mouth. He didn't regret that act one bit. Kissing Tess had been like grasping a little piece of heaven all to himself.

He ran his tongue across his lower lip. She'd tasted sweet and all woman. And she'd damn near purred like a contented cat in his arms.

Until that old fear rose up again. Even now, a full five minutes later he could feel it between them like a living thing.

For all the world to see, up on that show's stage, she was self-assured, even a little bit cocky. But here in his arms he'd seen something else entirely. Her gaze held an innocence and a wonder. That was part of the confusing part about her—and part of the attraction.

It had to be an act. No woman who performed onstage in a medicine show that traveled around the country could be an innocent. It had to be an act, a very good one, but an act nonetheless.

A thought struck him with all the force of a gut punch. Tess was no innocent. Hadn't she seduced his brother David? Zack squeezed his eyes shut. Damn.

He'd been holding and kissing the same woman as his brother. A shudder shook his shoulders, and he clenched his hands into fists.

Tess presented a puzzle, and Zack couldn't stand an unsolved puzzle. With one deep, ragged breath of self-control he vowed he'd get to the bottom of what was going on with Tess Fontana if it was the last thing he ever did.

By the time Tess reached the steps to the hotel, she was out of breath, and her ankle hurt like the devil. She paused to lean against the wood railing a moment, sucking in several deep, painful breaths. Her chest felt as if it were on fire.

She hadn't run that hard and fast since the night Joel . . .

Shuddering, she bit down on her trembling lower lip until the stinging taste of blood reached her senses. Releasing her lip, she let her head sag, resting her chin on her chest. Fear, guilt, and remorse washed over her in waves, and she fought them off one by one.

Sudden realization struck her next. She'd behaved like a fool. Zack had done nothing to send her fleeing in the near crazed way she'd run from him. In truth, he hadn't done anything to frighten her. Except his words had been a stark repeat of Joel's jeering remark that horrible night so long ago.

Crossing her arms over her midriff in a self-conscious gesture of protection, she shuddered. The memories came flooding back. . . . his pale eyes glittering down at her as he held her wrists above her head . . . his cruel laughter . . . and then . . . Shaking her head, she forced the past to the back of her mind.

No, she would not let the past control her future. If she stood out here letting the memories possess her, she'd run in fear again. And there was nowhere to run to. Raising her chin, she rubbed her sweating palms down the rumpled fabric of her skirt.

Likely as not, she looked about as rumpled as her wrinkled, dusty skirt. Raising her chin, she smoothed her hair with her hands as best she could, then wiped away a tiny smear of blood from her lower lip where she'd senselessly bit it.

Her upper lip tingled still, but she knew it wasn't from anything she'd done. Well, that wasn't actually the truth, she admitted wryly. Her lips continued to tingle from Zack's kisses. Even the thought of those kisses still had the power to weaken her knees.

She touched her lips with her fingertips, imagining they were Zack's lips on hers. She'd never felt anything like the sensations he'd evoked in her. Why, they were positively sinful. A smile tipped her lips for the faintest of an instant before she sobered.

What she'd been trying to accomplish was to get answers from the lawman. Instead, she gotten every one of her toes curled in the most delicious way imaginable.

Tess shook her head and grabbed hold of her departing senses at the same time. It took some effort to remind herself that he was a lawman. A Texas Ranger, for heaven's sake, she chided herself. And he was trouble, all the way from the crown of his black Stetson to the toes of his leather boots.

Maybe it would be wiser to stay far, far away from Zack Mackinzie.

Focusing her concentration off Zack and on walking into the hotel and through the lobby as if absolutely nothing untoward had happened, she kept her chin up and her spine buckboard straight.

The stairs to the second floor seemed unending. She refused to allow herself to draw an easy breath until she'd reached the stair landing and turned down the hall toward her room. All she wanted was to retreat to the sanctuary of the silent, empty room.

She almost made it, too.

With only three more doors to go, raised angry voices from one ajar door slowed her trip. Absently she noted that it was Uncle Simon's room, and continued walking. However, the sound of her own name halted her in mid-step.

"You know how I feel about Tess."

"Now, my dear—" Simon's voice held a note of cajoling humor.

A shrill laugh cut him off. Tess would recognize that laugh anywhere. Marlene.

The woman had a laugh that sounded like a treed coon. Unable to stop herself from listening, she inched closer to the door to hear better. Through the partially cracked doorway, she spotted the woman. No one could miss the bright jade of her too-snug skirt nor the jade-and-white striped bodice, equally too tightly fitted for her abundant figure.

Marlene dressed like a peacock in full display, attempting to attract a mate While pretty on the feathered male bird, the overbright colors made her look cheap and desperate.

"I'll wire you from San Francisco, my dear," Simon promised, his voice calm and unaffected by the woman's earlier tirade.

The sparkling city by the bay was the next scheduled stop for their traveling medicine show. A smile touched Tess's lips. Papa always liked to winter somewhere warmer, where the show could still perform throughout the cold winter months.

"You're not leaving me behind," Marlene's voice rose to a shriek. "Do you understand me?"

"Now, Marlene—"

"Don't even try it, Sy."

"Calm down, Marlene."

Tess flinched as the argument threatened to rage on between the two. She had no intention of getting caught in the middle of this foray. Perhaps if they were all lucky, Simon would see his lady friend for what she was and get rid of her.

Crossing her fingers in the folds of her skirt, Tess paused to send up a silent prayer for divine intervention. The very thought of Marlene accompanying the show to San Francisco caused her to cringe, then fume in disgust.

Perhaps if she left them alone to their arguing, Marlene would finally say the wrong thing that ended it all between her and Simon. She certainly hoped so. Gathering up her skirt, she tiptoed past the room. With Marlene in such a foul temper, the last thing she wanted was for the other woman to notice her in the hallway, or to suspect that she'd eavesdropped.

Tiptoeing caused her ankle to ache worse. When she felt she was safely far enough past Simon's doorway, she paused to lean against the wall for a moment. Sucking in her breath between her teeth, she heard Ella humming a tuneless song on the other side of the wall.

Consternation. Was everyone staying inside the hotel today?

The thought of a long talk with Ella tempted her a full minute. Then embarrassment at her behavior with Zack washed over her, pushing aside the temptation of stopping at Ella's room.

Right now, all she wanted was to be alone.

Reaching her room at long last, Tess slipped inside and crossed to the bed. In no time, she'd unlaced her shoes and climbed onto the feather mattress. Easing a pillow beneath her foot, she settled back against the other pillow and closed her eyes. For a little while she wanted to shut the world and the disturbing pictures of Zack Mackinzie out of her mind. All she asked for was a little peace and quiet.

* * *

A lone figure paused outside the door to Tess's hotel room. Eyes filled with hatred, then hardened on the wooden door as if attempting to reach beyond the panel.

It wasn't fair. *She* should be the one suffering.

No one suspected that sweet little blue-eyed Tess, all innocence on the outside, hid a murdering heart within. Hatred boiled up. The bitch had lured innocent Joel into her web of trickery.

Then, even worse, far worse, she'd helped her father kill him. She would die for this—in time. Hatred burned in a hot, searing burst.

The silly little fool was so concerned about her precious papa that she never truly saw people for what they were. She assumed a friendly smile meant a friend.

A short burst of laughter echoed in the hall, then was quickly silenced. No sense in rushing things to their ultimate conclusion yet.

All was going according to plan. Time didn't matter. After all, revenge was a dish best savored after a lengthy cooking time.

And this revenge would indeed be savored.

An hour later, a knock on the door awoke Tess. She jerked upright with a start.

"Tess?" a familiar voice called through the wooden door.

Papa.

She sighed in relief, not knowing who she had expected to be at the door. Easing out of bed, she tested her weight on her foot and found it felt better.

"Coming, Papa," she answered, smoothing down her hair and brushing the wrinkles out of her gown.

As soon as she opened the door, her father strode in, filling the room with his presence as he did everywhere he traveled. It was a natural part of him, and it made Tess smile.

"The black scarf's been misplaced," he announced, getting to the point immediately, as always.

It took Tess a moment to catch up with him. She stared at him blankly.

"The scarf from the show," he explained. "Ella came to me a bit ago with the news. It seems that she can't find it anywhere."

"Ella never loses things."

"Tess, dear girl, she is human. That doesn't matter. What matters, though, is that I need that scarf for tonight's show."

"It'll be all right—" Tess attempted to reassure her father, crossing to him.

"Tess . . ." He stared at her as if she'd just materialized in front of him out of thin air. "That scarf is the cornerstone of our show. It's the lead in to the sale of the elixir."

"Yes—"

"Without it, we don't sell the elixir. Without the elixir sales and the money they bring in . . ." He let the rest taper off, knowing full well that she was aware of the consequences.

"So, I'll go out and buy another." The second the offer left her mouth she regretted it.

The last thing she wanted was to venture outside the hotel again today. The very last thing she wanted was to chance an encounter with Zack. That would indeed tempt fate.

"Thank you, Tess." Her father hugged her close. "I just hope to heavens you can find one here."

"Papa, Virginia City is not some unknown burg. It's a booming mining town," she chided him. "Surely its shops have one black scarf for sale."

* * *

Over an hour and a half later, Tess mulled over her earlier assurance as she walked down C Street toward the third store on her continuing search for a black scarf for her father's show. How difficult could it be to locate a filmy thin scarf that also happened to be black? She'd never dreamed how hard the task could turn out to be until now.

She'd headed out on her father's errand less than a quarter of an hour after he left her room to go practice for tonight's performance. She'd only taken time to change out of her rumpled gown into a fresh morning dress of brown the color of sienna and white edged in lace, and brush some semblance of order into her tousled curls. Her unsuccessful search proved to be taking considerably more time than she'd hoped.

More than anything, she wanted to find the blasted scarf and return to the hotel before she encountered Zack again. She didn't feel up to that right now. In fact, her lips still tingled from his kisses. She couldn't believe it. Almost a full two hours had passed since his lips had claimed hers, and she still felt their imprint.

Irritated at the path her thoughts insisted on taking, she shoved open the door to the dry goods store, her third stop. A little bell tinkled overhead announcing her arrival and jarring her nerves.

Maybe the old adage about the number three being the lucky number would turn out to be true. She most assuredly hoped so. She could use some good luck about now. She could . . .

Tess was halfway across the store when her mouth dropped open and not a single sound passed her lips. Across the next aisle, head and shoulders towering over the stack of men's shirts, stood Zack Mackinzie.

Snapping her mouth closed, Tess did the most logical thing under the circumstances. She ducked down behind the closest aisle and practically crawled around the corner of the aisle and out of sight.

She sat back on her haunches and debated her options. She could stand up and greet him over the aisle. She shook her head in vehement denial. She could hide here and look like a fool. While certainly unappealing, it beat her other choice hands down.

Tess smiled at her mental wording. Her hands were flattened against the dusty floor, keeping her balance while she squatted in a most uncomfortable position.

Her skirt inched up, threatening to catch permanently under her chin, and she tugged it down. The bodice of her gown dipped lower, and her bustle ascended to wedge in the small of her back. She seriously doubted if she'd make it out of the store with a shred of dignity left to her name. However, right this instant she was more concerned with escaping without Zack spotting her. She had no intention of facing him again so soon. Not after those kisses.

Cautiously Tess inched upward, pausing to listen for the sound of Zack's deep drawl, but it didn't come. Finally standing upright, she peered through the stack of tins into the next aisle.

Consternation. There Zack stood, the back of his broad shoulders level with her nose.

Tess dove for the floor again. Creeping along on the balls of her feet, she felt like a duckling waddling down the aisle. If anyone walked around the corner she figured she'd just up and die of embarrassment.

"Ma'am?" A woman spoke from behind her.

Tess froze, stiff as a stone statue. She closed her eyes and swallowed, wishing the floor would open up and swallow her whole. This could not be happening to her. She forced her eyes back open.

"Ma'am?" the polite female voice asked again.

Tess swiveled around on the balls of her feet and

looked up at the woman, trying to appear nonchalant when she'd just been caught practically crawling about on the floor of the store, looking for all the world like a demented fool. Or worse.

Forcing a smile to her stiff face, she answered in a voice scarcely above a whisper, "Yes."

Disapproval in her stern countenance, the woman asked, "May I help you find something?"

She thought from the woman's expression she might as well have said, "Such as the door?"

Reaching out, Tess grabbed the closest thing to her hand without even looking at it. Her fingers closed around a thick packet. "Yes, I'd like this," she replied in a low, hoarse voice. "And please wrap it for me."

The woman took the package from her, widened her eyes, then stared down her nose at her.

Tess knew she'd made a mistake the second she saw the woman's expression of horror and disapproval. Forcing herself to glance at the woman's hands, she got her first look at the item she'd given her and barely held back her own groan. The lady held a pair of men's red woolen long johns.

Mustering up a smile and batting her lashes, Tess added in a voice that didn't show a bit of the chagrin or embarrassment she felt reddening her face, "I'd like to keep looking around a little longer."

The woman sniffed and raised her nose in marked disapproval. "If you insist."

Tess swallowed in relief as the lady turned away. Over her shoulder, she heard her mutter in disgust, "Performers, humph."

Tess covered her face with both hands. Then and there, she swore she'd never step foot in this establishment again. That is, if she managed to get outside with a modicum of dignity left intact.

If she encountered Zack Mackinzie right now, she

might just top everything off by slapping the smile right off his face.

Head held high, Tess stood to her feet and adjusted her bustle. When she glanced around the dry goods store, Zack was nowhere to be found. Wondering how long ago he'd left and amazed that she'd likely as not embarrassed herself for nothing, she turned toward the back of the store and the ladies' ready-made clothing.

Minutes later, carrying a packet of men's bright red underwear, wool no less, and still without the needed scarf, she determined that three was most assuredly not a lucky number. She'd never been so humiliated in all her life.

Passing a milliner shop, she stopped dead in front of the glass window. There on display, hanging beside a black-and-red directoire hat, draped a black scarf. Why couldn't she have seen this mere minutes before? Before the debacle in the dry goods store?

Tess spun on her heel, retraced her steps to the doorway and stepped inside the hat shop. It took only minutes to assure herself that the scarf was indeed perfect. Black, gossamer thin, and of the proper length, it was precisely what Papa needed for the show.

Now, two packages in hand, she departed the shop. Turning back toward the hotel, she strolled along the boardwalk, watching for uneven dips in the wooden planks. Intent on watching her step, she scarcely caught sight of Zack in time to duck into the open doorway behind her.

Inside, a loud catcall nearly halted her breathing. Heart in her throat, she slowly turned around, expecting the worst. She got precisely what she'd been anticipating.

She stood in the doorway of a saloon.

Red-faced, she rushed back out the open doorway to a chorus of male propositions. Gulping down her mortification, she pressed her hand against her chest and the pounding heart beneath. Would this embarrassing day never end?

Hurrying away from the saloon as fast as she dared, she rushed past half a dozen storefronts and an alleyway before she stopped to catch her breath. She leaned against the edge of the building, not caring what it might house. She needed a moment or two to steady her breathing and calm her scattered senses. Zack Mackinzie surely had her in a dither. And she had never in her life been in anything remotely resembling this state in her life.

Closing her eyes in sheer mortification, she drew in a deep, calming breath. Why, the man had her crawling around on the floor, ducking into saloons, and . . . hearing his voice?

Tess shook her head, snapping her eyes open. There it came again. Definitely Zack's deep Texas drawl. She'd recognize that voice anywhere.

She looked about her, but he was nowhere in sight. Cocking her head, she distinguished his heart-stopping drawl again. It came from the alley to her left. Inching a little to the left, she peered around the corner of the building. What she saw caused her to jerk back.

Zack Mackinzie stood talking to the sheriff.

One question penetrated the shock that held her immobile. Were they talking about the show and Papa? She had to find out.

Gathering up her courage, she inched back to the edge of the building and pressed herself against the wood. Then she held her breath and shamelessly eavesdropped.

"Sounds like the Fontanas could bear watching," an unfamiliar voice spoke up. Tess assumed it belonged to the sheriff.

"That's what I'm here doing." Zack's words caused her breath to freeze in her lungs.

So the Texas Ranger *was* after Papa and her. She pressed her fist to her mouth.

"What have you found out so far?"

"Murder dogs their show like a hound dog after a fat rabbit," Zack declared, a hard edge to his voice.

Tess shook her head, vehemently denying his false accusation. She pressed her knuckle between her lips to keep her from speaking out loud.

"No," Tess mouthed the denial.

"Definitely one murder is tied to the traveling show and the Fontanas," Zack pronounced, sending Tess's breath skittering away. "And there's likely more."

He was after her and Papa. She felt dizzy and grasped the edge of the building with one hand.

"Are you certain about this?" the sheriff asked.

"Absolutely." Zack's voice took on a hard-bitten edge she'd never heard before. "I knew one of their victims."

Tess's face blanched.

"The killer is hiding in the show—conning and stealing from his or *her* victims. And murdering."

"I'll go back and—"

Zack's next words stopped anything the sheriff had been about to say, as well as Tess's heart from beating. "No. A murder in Texas falls under the Rangers," he declared.

Tess closed her eyes. Murder . . . Joel . . . Zack knew. He knew.

The Texas Ranger was assuredly after her and Papa. What was she going to do? How was she going to protect her father?

The questions died, frozen on her lips, as Zack's voice reached her again.

"The Fontanas are mine."

Eight

The Fontanas are mine.

The words echoed and reechoed in Tess's mind.

She had to get away. She must escape before either Zack or the sheriff spotted her. She desperately needed time to think.

Whirling away from the building, Tess practically ran the distance back to the hotel, unmindful of the slight aching of her ankle. Once there, she slowed enough not to attract undue attention as she crossed the hotel lobby, then holding her two packages tight against her body, she drew in a breath and dashed up the stairs. She didn't stop until she reached the doorway to her room.

There, in relative safety, she tossed her packages down onto the bed and crossed to the window. Glancing out, she shuddered and quickly pulled the curtains closed.

She crossed back to the door, ensuring it was tightly locked. Drawing in a quivering breath, she paced the width of the room.

What was she to do?

Papa's life might well hang in the balance of her decision. She squeezed her eyes tightly closed. She would not give in to the tears that threatened. She hated women who cried at every instance of trouble. She wouldn't cry. She wouldn't.

She'd do something useful instead—like find a solution.

Pacing back and forth across the room, she tapped her lips with the tip of her finger. She searched her mind frantically for an answer, then tossed aside one idea after another. Desperation wore on her, turning her thoughts into a jumble of past and present, and suddenly the old memories threatened to swamp over her. Sucking in a breath between clenched teeth, she curled her hands into fists.

Look forward, not back. Papa's words flowed into her mind, displacing all other thoughts.

That was it! The answer stared right back at her inspired by her father's words. The solution was really quite simple. Send a particular lawman *forward* and onto a different trail—one that didn't include her. One she would set about making by deliberately misleading one Zack Mackinzie.

She'd confess to him the medicine show's continuing plague of problems, but carefully refrain from mentioning that little problems followed along with every traveling show, not only Papa's.

She'd throw Zack's suspicions elsewhere and send him away on a wild chase. Her conscience pricked at the web of lies she concocted, but she assured herself that no one would be hurt by her carefully laid trail of false clues. Those clues would merely take Zack a few days' ride out of his way. The worst that could happen was that Zack would return to Virginia City tired and dusty. And empty-handed.

However, a small chance existed that the web of lies could ensnare herself as well as Zack. The thought made her shiver, and she absently rubbed her arms. She didn't have many other choices—this was the only plan she'd come up with that possessed any possibility of success.

Knowing what she had to do, Tess set about doing it, aware that she dare not give herself the time or chance to reconsider. Spinning about, she crossed to the armoire and threw open the doors. She scanned her small wardrobe, mentally discarding all but one dress.

She carefully drew out the perfect gown—the most enticing gown she owned. Made of cream-colored faille with an overdress of cream-and-white striped India silk, the gown looked like a vision from heaven.

It lent its wearer that same angelic quality, while the bodice managed the amazing feat of having a daringly low cut and giving the illusion of demureness at the same time. The heart-shaped neck exposed a good deal more than she was accustomed to seeing on herself. She'd fallen in love with the gown two years ago when Papa purchased it for her in San Francisco.

Not giving her uneasy conscience the opportunity to deter her, she hastily removed her sienna morning dress and slipped into the cream faille gown. However, she'd filled out a bit more since that trip to San Francisco two years ago, and now the bodice seemed even more enticing than it used to appear.

After several attempts to adjust the neckline, she finally gave up in failure. The delicate-looking material possessed a sturdiness that defied the eye, and it wasn't budging at all—at least not upward.

Tess sighed and smoothed her hands over the lace-trimmed skirt. Doubt plagued her, and she clenched her hands together The gown projected the image she desired; she'd always been told the dress made anyone looking at her tend to believe she couldn't be capable of lying or deceiving. It was perfect. Then why was she ready to turn about and quit the distasteful game now?

Guilt at what she was about to do nagged at her. This time it took longer to shove it aside. Even reminding herself that she was doing this for her papa didn't help salve her now aching conscience.

She surveyed the beautiful but deceptive dress again. The gown guaranteed a gentleman's attention would not be focused solely on the wearer's words. Wasn't that exactly what she needed when confronting Zack? A little voice warned her that he wasn't a gentleman.

Swallowing down the butterflies that arose with a vengeance in her stomach, she placed her hands over her midriff and assured herself everything would go according to her plan. The dress would distract Zack and reassure him of her innocence at the same time. By the time he realized the truth, she and Papa would be long gone from Virginia City and safely out of his reach.

She avoided looking into the room's only mirror, not wanting to see her image. Truth be told, she didn't much like herself right now. Nor what she was about to do, however innocent it might be.

Tess raised her chin in resolute determination. She owed it to her papa to protect him, and she would do anything to keep him safe from the horror she'd caused them both.

The Egans' mountain cabin was a hard five days' ride from Virginia City. That would provide the show a full ten-day head start on the lawman. By the time Zack learned of his mistake and returned to Virginia City, the show would be safely out of town and long gone. He'd have no notion exactly where the show had headed, and likely as not he'd give up and return home to Texas.

She resisted the pang of disappointment this thought brought with it. She told herself it was only because she hated to leave town and not because of anything to do with Zack. That had to be it.

She loved Virginia City, had loved it from the moment she'd first seen the mining town perched so courageously on the side of the mountain. The booming town was a survivor—like her.

Crossing to the window, she dared to peek out at the street below. Her plan would work, and her dear papa would be safe. Most assuredly the Texas Ranger wouldn't return and continue to pursue them past the mountains—even if he tracked them that far. No, he'd turn back to Texas and easier men to hunt down.

Somehow the thought gave her far less pleasure than it should have done.

Tess carefully dropped the curtain back into place and set about arranging her accidental meeting with Zack. She needed a good reason for why she was relaying this information so willingly, and at such an opportune time.

She couldn't very well send him off on a wild chase by revealing that she'd eavesdropped on his conversation with the sheriff. That was the last thing she'd admit to him. She couldn't for the life of her think of any plausible reason to give him as to why she would be simply providing him with this lead. Granted, it was a false lead, but it was for a good cause.

Consternation. How could she do that without revealing that she'd overheard his conversation with the sheriff?

However was she to explain the trail she'd planned for him if she wasn't supposed to know about his search for a killer or his suspicions? This was getting very complicated.

She crossed over to the chair and plopped down onto the seat. Propping her chin in her hands, she stared at the wall.

What if she were to innocently ask for his help? A smile tipped the corners of her mouth. That idea would work—it had to. All it needed was one particular lawman.

Next, she needed to find him. She couldn't very well go walking up and down the steep, hilly streets of Virginia City looking for him. Even if she found him easily, her search would definitely arouse his suspicions. She must avoid that at all costs. No, she had to bring Zack Mackinzie to her.

It took her another full fifteen minutes of careful thought before she had her plan mapped out. Salving her conscience was going to take longer—a lot longer. Like perhaps forever.

She straightened an errant curl, tucking it back into place, then caught up the skirt of her gown and left her room. On the way down the hallway, she crossed her fingers for luck. Something told her she would need every bit she could muster up.

Descending the staircase, she kept a careful eye on the doorway. If Zack entered too soon all would be lost. She didn't release her pent-up breath until she reached the end of the stairs. Smiling for courage, she crossed to the table and chairs where she'd began her faro game—was it only yesterday?

She knew that news of a faro game headed by a woman would flow through the mining town with the speed of a raging fire. It would most assuredly bring Zack in its wake. All she had to do was to wait patiently. And lay her trap.

Once again, the familiar guilt rose up, but she banked it down by reminding herself of the danger her papa was in unless she did something.

Within minutes, the faro game was in full swing. Virginia City possessed an abundance of lonely men more than willing to give a beautiful woman their time and money. Already three such men sat around the table with her.

As before, a small crowd materialized quickly in the hotel lobby, drawn by the tantalizing sight of a lady dealing the cards. Tess played the game by habit, keeping her attention alerted for Zack's arrival.

She knew the instant he walked into the hotel. A sixth sense warned her of his presence. At least that's what she told herself accounted for the way her heart sped up, skipping a beat, as if in a race. It had absolutely nothing to do with the way his broad shoulders and lean body seemed to fill the room, or the way the air suddenly became almost too light to breathe as he strode closer. Absolutely nothing.

Once again a dark Stetson sailed onto the tabletop. This time it dislodged a card, sending it fluttering to the floor. Two men rushed to pick it up and hand it back to her.

Tess's next breath stuck in her throat and she had to swallow twice before it returned to where it belonged. Zack's intense gaze studied her, and she knew with a certainty that she'd pushed him too far. He was surely a man who intended to get his answers, but would he accept her helpful news or would he see straight through it and her?

For all around her, she portrayed nothing more than a startled amazement at his interruption. However, before she could do more than open her mouth to offer a greeting, he stopped her.

"Gentlemen, Miss Fontana regrets an end to the game, but she has an injury to recover from."

He scooped up his hat and her in a move so smooth and precise it silenced the miners around the table.

"If you wish to see her, she'll be performing tonight. Now she needs her rest." With that Zack swung about with Tess in his arms and crossed to the stairs in long, distance-eating strides that brooked no interference.

Halfway up the stairs, Tess regained her voice and her scattered senses. "What—"

That was the only word she got out, before the look

in Zack's eyes silenced her. Now was definitely not the time to speak, she told herself. She'd miscalculated, dangerously so.

She'd correctly assumed news of the card game would bring him to the hotel, but she hadn't bargained on the force of his anger. Or the oh-so-stubborn set to his jaw. Definitely granite, she thought before he unlocked her hotel room door and shoved it open.

All coherent thought fled when he kicked that same door closed.

Zack crossed to the bed and dumped her unceremoniously on it. She bounced twice on the feather mattress before she could grasp the side of the bed to steady herself.

"What in the hell do you think you were doing?" he shouted at her.

Forgetting her plan, she shouted back, "Alleviating my boredom."

"Was that what you were doing earlier today, too? With me?"

Her face blanched, then she felt it heat to a bright red from his cavalier referral to the soul-shattering kiss they'd shared.

"Well?" He glared down at her.

Tess's voice fled her, likely as not taking flight straight out the window for parts unknown. It hadn't been prompted by fear, but by the intense warmth in his dark-gray eyes. That look could singe the hair right off the top of her head.

"No," she answered, unable to give him anything but the truth regarding that shared kiss.

She might be able to lie to him to protect her father, but not herself or her own newly emerging emotions. Her papa had always told her that she exhibited all the self-preservation instincts of a newborn kitten. In other words, where she was concerned they didn't exist.

Right this moment, she tended to agree with him.

However, some small tidbit of instinct told her to get off the bed, and to do it as fast as possible. With only an instant's hesitation, she obeyed.

Sitting up, Tess scooted to the edge of the bed and quickly stood to her feet before Zack could stop her. He crossed his arms and raised one brow at her act of defiance. Her feeling of triumph was short-lived.

Zack took a step forward, his intense gaze never leaving her face. Tess sidestepped to the right. As he took another determined step, she whirled away and crossed to one of the two chairs on the other side of the room. She cautiously kept one chair between her and Zack.

If she allowed him to take her in his arms, she would never be able to lie to him. She knew that without a single whit of a doubt, so she clutched the back of the chair for dear life.

"Tess?" A distrustful frown marred his handsome face.

Gathering up all the courage and determination she could muster, Tess smiled at him. "You know, I think you're right, I do need to rest my ankle." She motioned to the other chair. "Please sit down and join me?" she invited, her voice the perfect pitch of innocence.

Zack crossed to the chair, the suspicion on his face easy to read. It caused Tess's stomach to erupt into a flight of nervous butterflies. Unconsciously placing a hand over her midriff, she faced him. Everything hinged on him listening to what she had to say.

She held her breath, and waited. And waited.

After facing her for what seemed like an eternity, Zack nodded to the chair. Thankfully, she sank onto the cushion, not sure how much longer her shaky limbs would have continued to hold her upright without giving way under his scrutiny. He followed her example and sat down in the chair opposite facing her.

"Once again, it seems you've rescued me," she said, lowering her lashes in an attempt at flattering him. It failed miserably.

"Hardly that," he denied.

His raised brows told her he was having nothing to do with her attempts at flattery. Oh, well, she'd never been any good at that type of thing anyway. She far preferred the honest approach. A sharp twinge pricked her at the poorly worded thought.

Nervous, she blurted out her planned spiel. The words practically tumbled over themselves in her agitated state. "I think perhaps I may be in need of your rescue for real this time."

At his doubting glance, she slowed her words and added, "Zack, I'm serious. And I'm afraid." Her plain statement held the ring of truth.

His expression said she'd struck a nerve.

"The show's been plagued with problems . . ." She paused to glance at him.

Zack's face was a careful mask of mild interest. Her words most assuredly hadn't surprised him in the least, she thought.

"What kind of problems?" he asked her in a low voice.

Tess shrugged, lifting her hands. "Little things at first. A prop missing shortly before a show. A broken wheel." She leaned forward, clasping her hands together. "Then two patrons got sick from Papa's elixir."

Zack's eyes darkened with interest.

"No one's ever gotten sick from it in all our time of selling the elixir."

That was the truth. In fact, most people exclaimed how much better it made them feel, like the miner who'd approached her in the restaurant. Tess drew her thoughts back to the task at hand.

She hated herself for what she was going to do next,

but she had to do it. No one would be hurt, she assured herself, Most assuredly not Zack. Or Bill.

"Then Papa had an argument with one of the men in the show. Bill Egan. He up and quit."

That much of her story was true. However, Bill had left to resettle with his pregnant wife and the argument had been because Papa wanted him and his wife, Molly, to stay. However, Zack didn't need to know that little tidbit of information.

She forced herself to look over at him. "When Bill left, so did our troubles. So—"

"When was this?" Zack interrupted.

Tess nibbled on her lower lip. "Before we reached Virginia City. One of the women from the show went with him. Since then, everything has been fine, but lately I've been feeling uneasy."

That had to be the understatement of her life, she chided herself. Ever since meeting Zack she'd been decidedly uneasy, to say the least.

"Where did he go?"

"To a little town in the mountains." She paused, then hesitantly told him the name.

She hoped Bill would forgive her for what she was doing, but she knew he could take care of himself. And besides, once Zack met him, he'd be assured of Bill's innocence.

"Do you think he could have been at fault? And how do I find out?"

She looked up at him. Tears welled in her eyes and she didn't try to hold them back or blink them away. She was no fool—she'd seen how Uncle Simon responded to Marlene's crying fits.

Perhaps a few tears might help her cause. In spite of how much she hated tears, she'd also heard how much more men hated them.

"I can't help being afraid that trouble is about to

start again." She sniffed delicately and looked around for her lace handkerchief.

That last statement was the truth with a vengeance, she thought, recalling Zack's own statement about her and Papa. Trouble was brewing, and doing so far too fast for her father's safety.

"Ah, hell," Zack swore from his chair as he watched a big tear slide down Tess's cheek. Another one followed in its wake. He was a sucker for a lady's tears. He couldn't stand them and the helpless feeling they caused in him.

Reaching in his pocket, he withdrew his own kerchief and pressed it into Tess's clenched hands. She sent him a watery smile of thanks.

He'd heard rumors of the medicine show's string of bad luck in a saloon weeks back, but he hadn't paid much attention to the drunk's talk of a curse on the traveling show. Maybe there was something to what she was telling him.

He dismissed the niggling voice that warned him that he'd be willing to listen to just about anything that would clear Tess in his mind of any involvement in murder. A part of him already had begun to disbelieve the evidence.

Either way, Bill Egan was a lead he couldn't afford to overlook. He had to at least investigate it.

"I'll head out in the morning and check him out," he assured Tess.

Her radiant smile was all he needed to assure him he was doing the right thing. As another tear trailed her delicate cheek, right or wrong, he couldn't stop himself from drawing her out of the chair and into his arms.

Tilting her chin back with his hand, he lowered his face the distance separating his lips from hers. As his mouth settled on hers, a loud thundering knock at the door jolted him away from her. Instinctively, his hand

reached for his gun. Only Tess's small hand on his arm
stopped him from clearing leather.

"Tess! Tess! Is everything all right?" Frank Larson's
irate voice pierced the wood panel. "Answer the door."

Tess broke out of Zack's hold and crossed to the doorway. Pausing, she glanced back over her shoulder at
him. He couldn't tell if it was in apology or relief at the
interruption. He'd been a fool to even touch her. One
would think he'd know better by now.

Damn.

As her hand closed over the doorknob, the coolness
of the metal penetrated to Tess's heated palm. She
barely stopped herself from sagging against the door.
Whatever had she been doing?

She plastered a smile on her face for Frank's benefit
and swung the door open.

He burst into the room as if he were racing to a fire.
Halfway into the room, he drew to a halt. He looked
from Tess to Zack and back to Tess, then drew himself
up to his full, imposing height.

"I was passing by and heard a man's voice that weren't
your papa's," he explained in a gruff voice of challenge.

Tess didn't know whether to give in to the relief or
the anger his interference drew. She barely restrained
herself from pointing out to Frank that his room was
at the opposite end of the stairs from hers. Obviously
he was being nosy and checking on her again. She
should probably be thankful. No telling where Zack's
kiss would have led. Heaven knew she'd scarcely been
able to draw in a breath, much less tell him no. Even
if she'd wanted to do so.

Tension filled the room, radiating out from each of
the men. Tess resisted the impulse to shake her head.
Why did she have the distressing feeling of being that
single bone between two dogs? Two very large, riled
ones.

As Frank took a menacing step forward, she rushed to cross the room to stand between him and Zack. Frank was going to ruin everything if she didn't intervene.

"Mr. Mackinzie was kind enough to help me up the stairs to my room, and I was thanking him."

"Zack." The single whispered word brushed her ear as he leaned closer.

She glanced at Frank, whose expression held anger and embarrassment. He rubbed the toe of one boot with his other foot.

"If you're certain everything is fine, I'll leave you to rest, Tess," he offered. "Mr. Mackinzie?"

Tess watched Zack stiffen at the barely concealed order. For an instant, she held her breath. Then he sent her a tight, distrustful smile and turned toward the door.

Frank paused at the doorway and called back, "You take care of yourself now, Tess."

Behind him, Zack stopped just short of the door and glanced back at her. "We'll finish this when I get back from my trip," he announced.

Oh, no they wouldn't. She'd be long gone by then.

Why did that thought cause a shaft of pain to course through her chest?

Zack rode out of Virginia City shortly before sunup, eager to finish the job he'd set out on. Bill Egan and his lady friend could be David's killers, but he wasn't convinced yet.

The new evidence definitely pointed in their direction. The two had fled the show before its arrival in Virginia City, and nothing untoward had happened since the show's arrival in that town, but a part of him distrusted information that came too easy. Or at precisely the right time. Tess's lead had the earmarkings of both.

Perhaps he was being too suspicious. If all proceeded well, he'd finish his job and see David's killers brought to justice—all in the space of a week or so.

However, his gut told him not to count on it. His instincts were ringing out loud and clear on this one. He couldn't put his thumb on what was wrong, but the nagging feeling at the back of his neck remained all the same.

This could well be a diversion concocted by Tess to lure him out into the open. Or it could provide the necessary time for Fontana's Fabulous Medicine Show to pull up stakes and disappear. The first concerned him far more than the latter, and he paused to check his holster. No harm in being prepared.

The possible disappearance of the medicine show didn't concern him overmuch. A traveling medicine show wouldn't be too difficult to locate. He'd already found it once before. If Tess were purposely misleading him, he'd find her. Oh, yes, he'd find her. Besides, he knew without a doubt that a woman with her looks, not to mention her charms, performing in a traveling show couldn't go unnoticed for long.

Thinking on her, a memory of the brief kiss they'd shared in her hotel room began to heat his blood. Zack chided himself, swearing aloud, and his horse pranced beneath him at the unexpected sound.

"Easy, boy," he murmured, not certain who he was assuring more. His horse or himself.

Tess managed to keep his body in an almost constant state of arousal, fluctuating between desire, suspicion, and frustration. This time, picturing her in the alluring gown she'd worn yesterday afternoon, desire most assuredly won out over the other two feelings. He spurred his mount on, eager to be done with this mission and ride back to Tess.

After five days and as many unsuccessful attempts at locating Bill Egan, Zack drew his mount to a halt in front of a small cabin high in the mountains. He rubbed his palm across a day's rough growth of whiskers. He felt unkempt, dirty, and tired.

At his knock on the cabin door, a very tall, very pregnant woman greeted him. In her arms she held a small baby.

Zack removed his hat, but kept his other hand close to the butt of his gun. "I'm looking for Bill Egan," he stated in a voice ringing with authority.

A flicker of unease lit the woman's eyes a moment, then she turned and called out over her shoulder, "Bill, a man's here to see you."

Her words confirmed he definitely had the right cabin. Zack glanced from the woman to the baby in her arms and mentally calculated the dates. She couldn't be the woman in David's letter. At the time the traveling medicine show had been in Texas, this lady had been very pregnant.

Something was wrong here.

As the woman stepped aside and a big bear of a man filled the doorway, Zack knew beyond a shadow of a doubt that something was very wrong.

He flashed his badge and watched the man's eyes narrow.

"What do you want, lawman?" Bill Egan asked, moving the woman behind him.

Zack gave him a friendly smile, but kept his hand near his gun. "I'm looking into the trouble with the Fontanas' Traveling Show. I heard you used to work for them."

If possible, the bear of a man stood taller.

"Joined up three months back."

His words jolted Zack. Things weren't adding up at

all. If the man was telling the truth, neither he nor the woman had been with the show in Texas. That left Tess, and she most decidedly hadn't been telling the truth. In fact, he doubted if she'd recognize it if the truth up and bit her on the—

"Something strange going on with that show," Bill cut into his angry thoughts. "And with Molly expecting again, I didn't want no part of it."

"What was wrong?"

"It's like a curse, 'cause it always happened after we were gone from the towns." Bill threw a concerned glance over his shoulder into the cabin. "I don't want to talk about it no more."

An uneasy feeling began to curl in Zack's gut. "What about the Fontanas?" he forced himself to ask the question.

"There's not a finer man anywhere than Mr. Fontana, and you'd be making a mistake to say otherwise." Bill stepped outside the cabin, slamming the door behind him.

Zack had a disturbing feeling he'd definitely made a mistake. And that had been believing Tess.

The man she sent him chasing down was as big as an oak and twice as mean when riled. Right now, it appeared his questions had definitely succeeded in riling Bill Egan.

Without warning, the burly man took the first swing. A single thought crossed Zack's mind.

He'd been had by Tess Fontana.

Bill Egan's first punch missed by mere inches, and Zack moved in, calculating each hit. While the other man had size and weight on him, Zack possessed superior speed, agility, and determination. He used all three to his advantage.

The fight lasted mere minutes, but it seemed like hours as he dodged, parried, and fought. Every one of the burly man's punches that connected took a toll, but Zack refused to surrender. Each hit jolted him all the way to his teeth. A sharp upper cut to Egan's chin hit home, dropping the bigger man to his knees.

The victory did little for Zack's mood. He knew he'd be nursing a battery of bruises for several days. The thought did nothing for his temper.

He owed Tess Fontana one hell of a note of thanks. And he intended to deliver it personally.

Nine

Tess tried to keep her attention on the performance and off her memories and the mental image of a certain too-good-looking lawman, but she failed miserably. No matter how hard she tried, memories of Zack Mackinzie persisted in dogging her thoughts.

She'd done the right thing in sending him away, she argued with her heart. She had. Zack presented too great a danger to her papa. However, while her mind argued the correctness of her decision, her heart fought an entirely different battle. She sighed in disgust and looked down at her hands.

It wasn't as if she missed him or anything. No, absolutely not.

"Tess," her papa whispered under his breath, then smiled for the audience's benefit. "Ladies and gentlemen of San Francisco, the Tempting Tess will now tempt you to concentrate very hard, so that she doesn't disappear from our sight."

He gestured with a grand flourish of his right hand, the mirrors sewn on his crimson cape flickering and shining out prisms of light to the enraptured audience. "Ah, now, ladies and gentlemen, don't dare to even blink, for she can vanish in the blink of an eye or the space of a breath if she so chooses."

Tess gathered her wayward thoughts back and curtsied to the waiting audience. It was time.

Slowly, step by step, she withdrew from the audience, teasing them, daring them not to believe. Her silver cape swirled about her ankles with each practiced movement until she reached precisely the right spot and stood, waiting.

The lamplight flickered across the silver threads in her ice-blue gown, and a hush fell over the audience. As she crossed her ankles and eased down to a seated position on the wooden flooring, the usual creaking sounded from above, signaling the lowering of the cone.

The large paper cone descended slowly, then completely hid her from the view of the audience. With the memory of her previous tumble into Zack's arms still too fresh in her mind, she made sure that she kept her hand far away from the latch to the hidden trapdoor this time.

She reminded herself that Papa would need an extra two minutes to ready the magic trick here in San Francisco, with the tent situated on the uneven ground. She ignored the deep darkness surrounding her beneath the cone and breathed in patterned, even breaths.

Assured no one could see her, she rolled her shoulders back and forth, trying to ease their persistent stiffness. She didn't believe she'd enjoyed a good night's sleep since she'd convinced Papa to pack up the medicine show and flee Virginia City the same morning as Zack.

The ever fitful sleep was beginning to draw on her, not to mention the recurring sense of guilt accompanying it. Her conscience nagged at her repeatedly over sending him off on that false lead.

Even worse, since the show had reached San Francisco Zack seemed to remain on her mind more than ever. The darkness beneath the cone added to her morose thoughts and her tiredness. She felt a yawn coming on, and out of habitual politeness ingrained from her mama, she covered her mouth with her hand, even though she knew no one could see her under the cone.

Suddenly, without any warning, the floor gave way beneath her and she barely covered her scream with the palm of her hand. She tumbled backward through the opening in a flurry of skirts and tangled cape.

Down . . . down . . . down . . . It seemed to go on forever.

Tess had forgotten that the stage in San Francisco had been positioned four feet higher than the one in Virginia City. Now she recalled that fact with sudden clarity and a touch of honest fear.

She instinctively threw out her arms to try to break her fall, but she suspected it wouldn't do any good. She landed with a teeth-jarring jolt against a rock-hard male chest. Tentatively she opened her eyes and met familiar gray eyes.

Zack Mackinzie.

Oh, no.

"Surprised to see me?" he asked in a low voice that held anger barely kept in check.

Shocked and still struggling to catch her breath, all Tess could do was nod her head and stare up at him in open-mouthed amazement.

"I'll just bet you are," Zack bent lower and murmured against her ear.

Ever so slowly, he drew back and eased her down until the tips of her toes touched the dirt. Tess knew for certain that her heart dropped to land right atop her satin slipper-clad toes.

His low drawl held the promise of retribution. He was mad as hell, and she knew it. Her day of reckoning had arrived.

As if to make matters worse, Papa stomped his foot on the platform above her head to order absolute silence from below. Tess raised her gaze up toward the wooden planks in resignation and stared right into the beady eyes of the biggest, ugliest, furriest rat she'd ever seen in her entire life.

Without thinking, she lunged for Zack, grabbed hold of his shoulders as if hanging on for life, and squeezed tightly to him. In fact, she squeezed so hard that he released a startled "oof" against her ear.

As the rat inched forward, she opened her mouth to scream and felt the warmth of Zack's hand over her lips, silencing her. From the corner of her eye, she dared a glance up at him. Less than two inches separated their faces. She saw his eyes trained on the rodent in shocked amazement, mirroring the same look as her own.

Transfixed, Tess stared back at the large rat, unable to move a single muscle of her own. The dreadful thing had to be as big as a tomcat and she'd bet ten times as mean. A second, then a third furry rodent crawled out of the rafters. Three sets of beady eyes fixed on her. She scooted closer in Zack's arms, not minding his presence in the least at this moment.

From above their heads, Papa stomped his foot twice more, giving the signal for her to return to the stage. As if she needed any incentive to get away from the rats, she thought brashly for an instant.

A third loud footfall sent the rats scurrying—right toward her. As the largest one leaped at her, Zack spun around, and grabbing her hand, ran for the side of the platform dragging Tess in his wake.

With scarcely a pause, Zack reached the plank stage platform and swung Tess up ahead of him. She landed hard on her feet and thankfully behind the heavy velvet curtain out of sight of the waiting audience. Before she could do more than blink, Zack swung himself up and landed beside her.

Startled, she stepped back. He took a long stride closer, bringing his body next to hers, his hip brushing against her.

One look at his set face and she did the only sensible thing possible. She turned away and ran straight for Papa's thick, pungent smoke cloud hovering over the center of the stage.

"I present to you the Tempting Tess," her papa's voice rang out, a hint of unease hidden so well that Tess was certain only she recognized it.

Forgetting to hold her breath against the smoke, she was unable to stop her cough as she raced to her father's side. Surely Zack wouldn't pursue her out onto the stage. Would he?

At her assigned spot, she curtsied for the benefit of the audience. Tilting her head slightly, she glanced back to the side of the stage, checking for Zack. There he stood, perfectly still . . . waiting.

Tess gulped and forced herself to face the crowd of spectators again. Her smile felt as stiff as her spine. Her father caught her hand in his and turned away from the audience for a minute to gaze into her face.

"What happened?" he whispered, bowing to her, acting as if it were all part of their performance.

"Rats!" she hissed back, trying not to move her lips from their frozen smile.

"Tess." Her papa's voice held a note of censure for her offhand remark, even as he produced a small bouquet of purple violets and waved them before her with a flourish, then presented them to her.

"Live, furry rats," she whispered back, enunciating each word carefully so he understood her meaning. Then, remembering the watchful audience, she buried her face in the nosegay of delicate purple blossoms to hide her speech. "And one very big human one—waiting for me."

She pulled back from the concealment offered by the bouquet of flowers, stifling her urge to sneeze, and met her father's shocked gaze. He frowned at her, his brows drawing together.

In answer to the unspoken question hanging between them, she jerked her head in the direction of the far left side of the thick velvet curtain. There stood Zack Mackinzie, leaning comfortably against the tent pole, his arms crossed over his broad chest. While scarcely out of the view of the audience, he stood in plain view of both Tess and her father. And quite obviously he intended to stay there.

"Our friendly Texas Ranger," she muttered into the flowers again.

"Damn."

Tess snapped her head up; she'd only heard her father swear one other time in her life.

"What's he waiting for?" he asked.

"Me," Tess whispered in resignation. "Most definitely me."

The remainder of the performance passed in what seemed like slow motion to Tess. She lost count of how many times she'd thrown a seemingly casual glance over her shoulder, only to encounter the all-too-knowing gaze of Zack. He stood in exactly the same place, like a block of the blasted granite she was coming to associate him with so much of late.

He never took his eyes off her, no matter where she moved onstage, his gaze followed her, and it radiated anger and suspicion. It was the most distracting, irritating, unsettling thing he could have done. And it persisted in making her body feel as if she were standing too near a big old stove, its heat constant and more than a bit threatening.

One thing she knew for certain—there would be no escaping Zack Mackinzie tonight. He was here for a showdown.

Zack watched Tess sashay across the stage and marveled at the depth of her duplicity. Her blue eyes portrayed an innocence he knew firsthand to be an illusion while her too-tempting curves dared a man to pay attention to anything but her luscious body, much less to what his own mind might be saying.

She possessed the cold nerve that enabled her to send him off chasing after a guiltless man and his pregnant wife while *she* slipped out of Virginia City to save her own hide.

Damn, but it was a beautiful hide. His own body ached with need, responding to the remembered feel of her in his arms only minutes before under the stage. She'd clung to him in a cross between frightened child and all woman, weakening his own resolve.

He clenched his jaw until his teeth ached. He was attracted to the woman who likely had killed his brother. Attracted, hell. He wanted her in his bed with an intensity that shook him. He tightened his hand into a fist of impotent fury. The knowledge of that desire was tearing him apart.

Worse yet, he didn't trust her one little bit.

Zack directed his anger toward the woman onstage. Damn, but the name fit her as well as the gown outlining each curve of her body. He couldn't seem to be able to take his gaze off her. However, it was time to make his move. This night he'd get his answers.

As the performance ended and the applause thundered, Tess stepped back and curtsied. Glancing sideways, she noticed with surprised relief that Zack had left the edge of the stage. She dared to hope she'd been mistaken about his determination and suspicion. Sighing, she stepped back another step and right into his rock-hard chest. While she'd been woolgathering, he'd moved soundlessly to stand behind her. Waiting.

Grasping her left wrist in a clasp equal to an iron manacle, he led her off the stage. Tess's heart raced right for her toes, and her courage threatened to chase along after it. She reasoned that now, with his anger so close to the surface, this wasn't the time to push him or fight his hold. He didn't release her until they were several feet from the tent. And all alone. She hadn't counted on him taking her so far away from the crowd of spectators from the show.

Fear swamped her for a moment, stealing away her power of speech. She wanted to open her mouth, wanted to order him to release her, but she couldn't do it no matter how hard she tried.

"You set me up." His accusation spoken in harsh condemnation echoed through her mind.

She resisted the sudden impulse to shut her eyes against it. Things most assuredly had not gone well with Bill Egan. The lamplight caught the redness of a recent small scar on Zack's high cheekbone. Her breath froze in her throat at the sight.

No, his meeting with Bill had gone horribly wrong. She hadn't planned on that. She had never dreamed the two men would actually come to blows. She . . .

Hadn't she? Her conscience arose to challenge her, daring her to deny it.

Truth be told, wasn't that exactly what she'd expected to happen when she sent Zack on her wild chase? Tess swallowed down the protest that wanted to break free. She dug the toe of one satin slipper into the soil, plowing up the ground.

He was right. She had set him up.

Anger seethed in him, so close to the surface she could feel it emanating from him. Would he take that anger and frustration out on her? Would he rain blows on her for her part in the deception?

No, from somewhere deep within her came the knowledge that Zack Mackinzie was not a man who made war on women. He'd find some other way to release that anger without striking out at her.

Relief, then shame flooded over her, crashing in waves like the water against the docks.

Raising her chin, she faced him straight on, the only way she knew how to. "What do you want me to do, apologize?" she asked, anger springing forth in an instinct of self-preservation.

"That would be a start, honey." Sarcasm laced the anger in his voice.

His words hit her with the force of a blow, and she jerked back from them.

"I'm tired, angry, and aching for a fight. So I'd recommend that a confession would make things a lot easier." He added, "For both of us."

Tess turned back to face him. "All right. I sent you on a wild chase. There, are you happy now?" She lifted her hands, palms up.

"Not hardly."

She blinked at his answer.

"Honey, I'm nowhere close to happy," he told her in a voice as cold as the wind blowing off the water of the bay in the far distance.

Tess shivered against the chill that began to penetrate her silver cape. She didn't know if it came from Zack or the breeze behind them.

"Would you like to tell me about what you left behind? Again." His voice challenged, daring her to deny his new accusation.

Momentarily confused, she looked back over her shoulder at the show's large tent they'd exited. Whatever on this earth was he talking about?

"Left behind?" she repeated.

He stared down at her, his eyes narrowed. Tess felt a shiver brush across her. Everything about him from the coldness in his eyes to the set of his determined chin told her he was dead serious.

"Don't be coy," he snapped.

Startled, she raised her chin to meet his angry gaze. The anger seemed to radiate out from him, singeing everything in its path. Especially her.

"I'm talking about a body. A very dead, very cold body."

She blanched and staggered backward, shaking her head back and forth. Not a single word passed her numbed lips. Dead? No.

"Oh, yes." Zack leaned closer with the words. "Remember a town called Virginia City?" Sarcasm coated his voice this time, fairly dripping off each word. "The town you and Fontana's Fabulous Show left the same day I rode out to do you a little favor. The same town I returned to only to find you long gone, and him very dead."

"Who?" The question slipped out without her even realizing it.

"An old miner. By the name of Foster. Charlie Foster."

Confusion clouded her mind. Charlie Foster? The name sounded familiar, but she knew practically no one in Virginia City by name. The show had never stayed in the town long enough for her to become acquainted with anyone there.

"Hellfire," Zack swore. "I'd almost buy that innocent act of yours that you perform so well if I didn't know better. But I do. So you can save it for someone else. Like the judge or jury."

"Who the hell is Charlie Foster?" she cried out.

Zack's eyes narrowed on her before he spoke. "An admirer of yours. A rich old miner."

Tess stared up at him in bewilderment. She felt as if the world were crashing down around her. And she hadn't a clue as to why.

"A rich old miner," he repeated. "I remember that day he stopped by our table to tell you how much he enjoyed your show. And your father's tonic."

Tess swayed on her feet at his announcement. The world about her dipped for a second, then righted itself. She recalled their time over pie at Maggie's and the old man who had stopped to talk.

He couldn't be dead, she rebelled against the realization. It couldn't be true.

"No," she whispered, the word barely making it past her lips as nausea rose in her stomach.

The miner had been such a nice man. So polite, even shaking her hand.

"His body was found within hours of when you and your traveling show left town."

"I didn't know."

"He'd been murdered. Poisoned."

"No," Tess whispered the denial.

"And everything of value was gone. His claim had been cleaned out. All that was left was this." Zack clasped her hand, turned it over, and pressed a cold object into her palm. "Yours, I believe."

Tess stared down at the gleaming coin in her hand. She didn't need the flickering lamplight or the moon slipping out from under a cloud for her to recognize the brass token. It was one of Papa's.

Fear seized her, and it took an effort of will not to turn and run. Instead, she forced her chin up until her eyes met Zack's.

"Papa didn't kill him," she stated in a clear, firm voice.

Zack's bark of laughter caught her off guard. "Hellfire, honey, I figure you did."

"No," she cried out in horror.

For the first time in her entire life, Tess fainted dead away.

Tess came to, coughing and gasping for air. She raised her hand to her nose, only to encounter a bottle of smelling salts pressed firmly beneath her nose. Pushing the awful smelling bottle away, she blinked the stinging tears from her eyes.

She struggled to a sitting position and stared into the sea of faces around her. She tried to make sense of the scene of chaos about her. Why ever was she on the ground, the dampness of the sandy soil seeping through her gown and cape?

Ella knelt at her right side with the bottle of smelling salts, trying to position the odious container back under Tess's nose. Papa hovered at her left side and patted her hand, murmuring assurances, a worried frown creasing his face. Uncle Simon kept insisting she take another sip from the glass vial in his hands "for the vapors." Even Frank stood fretting over her like a nervous puppy.

She glanced around, but Zack Mackinzie was nowhere in sight.

All about her people asked her questions until the voices blended together in an unbearable cacophony of noise. She shoved Uncle Simon's bottle away and wrinkled her nose at the bad taste that lingered on her tongue. A warm, fuzzy blur hovered around her, and for a brief, crystal-clear instant she wondered how much of the laudanum he'd eased past her lips. Then the woolly feel of being surrounded by cotton crept over her again.

It seemed to her as if the entire audience from the medicine show stood over her, and each and every one of them had something to say. She wanted to put her hands over her ears to shut them out.

Her father leaned closer, and she focused on him in

an attempt to shut out the noise and the nightmare enveloping her, stifling her very breath. She felt almost as if she were floating on the solid sea of noise.

"Murder," Tess whispered.

"What?"

The din increased, and the faces swirled above her. Then darkness enveloped her again.

Tess awoke the next morning to a cloudy sky, and even more muddled senses. She felt as if she were swimming up from a bank of dark, cloudy water.

Her mouth was so dry she thought she could spit tufts of cotton if she tried. She licked her parched lips.

"Tess, thank heavens you're awake." Her father clasped her hands in his, rubbing them, then dropped a kiss on her palm.

She blinked as the cloud cover broke outside her window and a flicker of sunlight peeked through. Struggling to sit up, she winced at the pain in her head.

"Ouch." She dropped back onto the pillow.

"It's the laudanum," Papa informed her, frowning. "I told Simon you wouldn't want it, but he insisted it would make you feel better after the vapors."

If this was better, she'd hate to feel worse, Tess thought.

"What happened last night?" Her father leaned closer, brushing a curl away from her forehead.

Tess blinked, trying to gather her scattered thoughts. There had been the performance last night, and Zack— She jerked up sharply.

"Zack."

"Who?" Her father eased her back down against the pillow.

"Zack Mackinzie. The Texas Ranger who's been after us. He's here." She sat upright.

"No one's been here," he assured her, plumping the pillow behind her and forcing her back down against it. "Everyone from the show was worried about you, especially Ella. But they're all giving you some time to yourself to recover."

"Papa." She caught his hand, stilling his movements. "He followed us. He is here in San Francisco. He was at the show."

Her father sighed. "I saw him. But—"

"And he thinks I killed someone. A miner."

Her words struck like stones splashing in a mirror-still pond.

"That's preposterous." His voice rose almost to a bellow. "You could never hurt anyone."

"Papa, he had one of your show tokens." She leaned forward in agitation.

"Tess, dear, those are handed out like grain at every town we do a show." He dismissed her worry as if it were nothing at all.

"But, Papa . . ." She paused long enough to be certain she had his full attention. "He said he got it from the dead miner."

"Who could have gotten it from me, or a hundred other places. Don't worry."

"Don't worry?"

"Don't you see? He's not after us; we had nothing to do with a miner's death."

"But, Papa—"

"Tess, dear, don't you see? This means he doesn't know about Joel."

Tess gasped, then stared back at her father. He was right. Zack knew nothing about her husband's death. Or her past. She released her breath in a ragged sigh of relief and leaned back against the pillow.

"Then we're in the clear?" she asked in a barely audible voice. She hoped it wasn't the leftover results of the laudanum giving her the feeling of safety.

"Yes, dear. We have nothing to worry about," he assured her.

Somehow the words didn't give her the surety they intended. In spite of her papa's confidence, a nagging feeling that Zack was only biding his time settled deep in her heart.

Ten

Tess shuffled the cards with practiced ease, resting one elbow casually on the green felt faro table, but she couldn't stop her nervous gaze from straying yet again to the batwing doors. She half expected Zack Mackinzie to stroll into the high-class San Francisco saloon at any moment.

However, that fear hadn't stopped her from leaving the safe but stifling confines of her hotel room for the bustle of the Diamond Lady gambling establishment. While she remained certain that her next encounter with the Texas lawman was only a matter of time, she refused to sit by idly and let the events sweep her along.

The interminable morning had left her unable to stand the forced inactivity and Papa's not-so-discreet mother-henning a moment longer. For heaven's sake, all she'd done was swoon. Granted, it had been the first time in her life, but it had also been the very first time she'd been accused of murdering someone.

By noon her father had already been in to check on her four times in as many hours. He'd hovered and worried and driven her half out of her mind. While she admittedly knew he meant well, she needed something to challenge her and take her mind off a certain Zack Mackinzie.

The Diamond Lady Saloon, only a short walk away

from the hotel, provided all that and more. The bustling establishment was a step above the average drinking establishment and the perfect respite from one's cares. Over the past hour it had fattened her purse with a winning streak at faro.

Tess brushed a loose curl from her cheek and tucked it back into the low Greek coil at the back of her head. She'd dressed too quickly to put her hair up properly. Why, she'd hurried through her toilette as if the devil himself were after her, pausing only long enough to select a promenade gown of sapphire with white striping of India silk. She admitted a fear that someone would stop in to prevent her leaving the too-small room before she managed her escape had propelled her on.

She drew her thoughts back and began to shuffle the deck of cards again when one of the players tapped her hand.

"I'm calling it a day." The gambler by the name of Sterling rose to his feet, giving Tess a wink. "Someone can have my seat."

She returned his smile readily. The sharply-dressed gambler had been the only man to best her this visit. She had admired his skill and enjoyed his easy banter.

Tipping his hat from his blond sunstreaked hair, he held out his arm to his lady. Arm in arm, Sterling and Dahlia strolled from the saloon. Tess envied their loving relationship. In spite of Sterling's teasing words, his heart had never strayed from the auburn-haired woman at his side.

A dark Stetson sailed onto the table and Tess nearly jumped out of her skin. She knew the hat's owner without looking. Zack Mackinzie.

It couldn't be.

It was.

Her heart started for her throat, then took a nosedive

to the pit of her stomach. The showdown she'd feared had arrived.

"Stealing old men's money again?" Zack asked, his hard-edged voice laced with bitterness.

"I don't steal," she informed him with a slight rise in her voice and her temper.

He merely smiled, but it didn't quite reach his eyes.

"I don't steal," she repeated, irritated with herself for being forced to defend her skill at cards and her morals.

"What game are you playing now, Tess?"

She knew he most assuredly wasn't referring to the cards on the green felt-covered table. However, she batted her eyes at him, pretended to misunderstand him, and gestured to the cards.

"The game's faro," she answered. "Are you in or out?"

This time he smiled a long, slow smile of utter confidence. "Oh, I'm in."

Hooking the vacant chair with his booted foot, he drew the chair out and sat down across from her.

That's what she was afraid of, a little voice whispered in the back of her mind. There would be no dissuading him once his mind was set on something. And most assuredly his mind was set on her.

"Then prepare to lose your money, Zack," she warned him in a tight voice.

His harsh laugh disturbed her more than she cared to admit.

Tess dealt the cards without her usual ease. She could feel him watching her every movement, and she faltered, almost dropping a card. She knew he was only biding his time . . . waiting. For what?

She wished he'd finish with his own game, whatever that was, and leave her alone. He didn't have any evidence with which to arrest her, she assured herself in an attempt at serenity.

Zack's presence set her on edge however much she

tried to remain outwardly calm. The handsome lawman presented a new, until now, unknown danger to her, awakening feelings she'd never had before. She reminded herself that while Zack wasn't a danger to her, he posed a very real threat to her father. Not to mention a threat to her peace of mind and her heart.

Thirty minutes later, her stack of winnings sat on Zack's side of the table. Luck had deserted her with a vengeance, right along with that peace of mind she'd hoped to preserve.

"Seems your lucky streak has surrendered?" he asked in a low voice full of meaning.

Did it also hold a threat, or was her imagination merely working overhard?

"Not likely," she responded with a hint of defiance. "But if you will excuse me, I have a performance to get ready for."

Blasted if he hadn't managed to win not only all her winnings, but also the stake she'd brought with her. Consternation. Somehow her usual term of irritation seemed completely inadequate. Her anger simmered, and she knew if she didn't get away from Zack it was only a matter of time before her temper boiled over like a pot of unwatched coffee atop an open fire.

Sweeping up her reticule, she stood and turned away from the table. With her head held high, she walked to the batwing doors of the saloon, leaving him behind in her wake. Right now, she was so angry at him she could just about spit.

As she reached the doors, a hand reached around her and shoved them open. "After you," Zack announced, his breath tickling the fine hairs at her nape.

Looking down at her fair hair and angelic face, a part of him that he refused to acknowledge questioned her guilt. However, all it took was one look into those "eyes as blue as Texas bluebells" to recall David's description.

He wanted to hate her, but that same unacknowledged part of him wouldn't allow it.

He had to remind himself that he didn't trust her, but in spite of that it was getting harder and harder to resist her tempting presence. The unsettling feeling made him even more certain that she had no respect for the law. Wasn't her constant winning at faro, both here and in Virginia City, further proof of that?

No, the lady most definitely wasn't above bending the law to her liking, if not outright breaking the law he had sworn to uphold. And even possibly murder.

Tossing her head in obvious defiance at him, Tess waltzed out the door ahead of him and onto the walk. Taking a deep breath, he followed her. She wasn't getting away from him that easy. In three quick strides, he caught up with her.

"Leave me alone."

Her order caught him off guard, almost making him trip over a clump of dirt. She had nerve, he'd give her that.

"No can do," he answered in a slow drawl guaranteed to irritate.

Her tightly clenched jaw told him he had succeeded. Matching his steps to hers, he kept pace with her down the street. He could last as long as she could.

Tess dared a rapid-fire glance at Zack's face. Determination and downright stubbornness etched each feature. He obviously intended to stay right at her side, no matter what she said or did.

His next shortened stride drew him even with her again, and as she took another step, his elbow brushed against her side, sending a flare of heat and warning up the length of her entire arm. She lengthened her stride in an effort to put more distance between them. He matched it.

She didn't know how much more of this she could

stand. She felt as though she might fly apart into a hundred pieces if he touched her again. Her anger warred with the fascination he presented to her.

If he persisted in keeping pace with her for much longer, she might well end up getting herself arrested—for doing bodily harm to a certain Texas lawman. Darn his arrogant hide.

A millinery shop with its decorative wooden sign advertising MISS MARY'S and with a pert bonnet carved into the wood caught her eye. The perfect answer to any lady's dilemma. Turning on her heel, she flashed Zack a triumphant smile and ducked into the shop's open doorway, leaving him behind.

Certain he would now continue on his way, she crossed to a display of straw bonnets and dared a glimpse back out the store's front window. At the sight of Zack casually standing on the walk outside, her temper rose enough to steal her breath.

Consternation. There he stood outside the shop . . . waiting. Well, he could just wait until a certain place up and froze over.

There were certainly worse places to be stranded. After all, she hadn't visited a bonnet shop in a long time. Yes, she could very well pass *quite* some time in the delightful shop.

A devious smile tugged at her lips. In fact, she had the remainder of the afternoon to do as she chose. And right now, she chose to spend it right here. She might get around to trying on each and every bonnet in the establishment. Eyeing the large assortment of hats, she set about her task with a soft chuckle.

Zack stared at the window before him and its display of colorful bonnets of all shapes and shades. He leaned against the doorway and watched Tess. She swept from one hat stand to another, touching a piece of lace here, brushing a feather plume there. Stalling.

A self-assured smile tugged at his lips in spite of himself. She could only wander around the little shop so long. He'd outwait her. Besides, if he calculated correctly, he'd won about all her funds. It would be interesting to see what happened if she attempted to purchase something.

A full thirty minutes later, he snapped his pocket watch closed with disgust and replaced it in his vest pocket. She'd been in that shop for half an hour. Fortunately the lady proprietor had followed Tess about the shop, too busy to notice his presence outside the door for this long a time.

He tugged his hat lower against the increasing heat of the sun and shifted his weight into a more comfortable position. A little boy of about four dashed past him, his mama in angry pursuit.

Zack shifted position again, moving his booted feet out of the woman's path. He continued to focus his attentions on the little shop as Tess tried on bonnet after bonnet. He'd counted twenty so far, and knew he'd missed some of the blasted things.

His pride demanded that he walk off and leave her, but he staunchly refused. He intended to hound her until he unmasked the truth behind the Fontanas' involvement in murder both in Texas and Virginia City.

Finally, she decided on a hat at long last. It was a tiny thing of straw and trimmed with a fragile-looking blue material and ivory ribbon. He resisted shaking his head at her choice.

He observed while she chatted with the woman at the counter, the owner, he assumed, upon hearing Tess address her as Miss Mary. He glanced up at the sign over the doorway, then his attention was drawn back to Tess. She reached up and settled the little straw hat on her head, tilting her chin to scrutinize the bonnet in the mirror.

It felt to Zack as if the breath had just been knocked out of him by a solid punch to the gut. The damned hat made her look like a vision or a desperate man's dream. Something told him both descriptions fit.

Her hair shimmered in a blend of gold and silver, each nuance trying to outdo the satiny sheen of the ivory ribbons, while the delicate blue fabric tucked around the brim made Tess appear even more fragile and innocent than before. Small wisps of gold had loosened from her coil to frame her face in tempting curls.

She turned, and he caught a sideways view of her womanly curves and immediately discarded the word innocent. She was every inch a woman. A very tempting one.

He tamped down the instant reaction she caused in his body. He concentrated all his attention on the silly bunch of blue feathers atop her bonnet. The plumes bobbed pertly when she ducked her head to search inside her reticle, and the act drew him up. Here came his reward for persistence and patience.

Zack waited for the coming commotion. He didn't have long to wait.

The proprietor frowned and gestured to the hat perched atop Tess's curls. Then with a cry of "thief" the lady grabbed for the bonnet.

"Nothing but a common thief." The owner's sharp accusation reached Zack at the doorway.

He saw Tess raise her chin in the gesture of pride he was quickly beginning to recognize. And dread.

He waited another second, then pushed himself away from the door. It seemed Tess Fontana needed rescuing again.

"I am not a thief," Tess denied, emptying her reticule on the counter and sorting through its contents.

Zack could barely make out her low mutters as she pushed aside each item from her purse.

"Where is it?" she mumbled to herself.

He grinned at the recollection of her winnings safely in his pocket, not her reticule. He patted his pocket and wondered how long it would take for her to recall the same thing.

"Ladies, may I be of assistance?" he offered, presenting his badge to the owner and a knowing smile to Tess.

"Go away," Tess ordered.

He leaned closer to her and whispered, "Is that any way to talk to the man who is going to keep you out of jail? For now."

As Tess reached up to remove the hat, he stopped her. "I don't think the store wants to take back a hat that's already been worn, do you?"

Reaching in his pocket, he withdrew the necessary amount of money and laid it on the counter with a slam of his fist. Tess glared at him, and he knew the instant she realized where his money had come from. Her eyes widened in comprehension, then flared with anger. The blue feathers atop her new bonnet performed a little jig of pure irritation.

"That's *my* money." She said the words in a tight voice.

He calmly answered, "Not any more."

She turned on him, and he was amazed at the suppressed anger written on her face. "You set me up."

His smile was slow and long before he responded, "Yup."

Tess raised her chin a notch in displaced arrogance. "Then I do believe we're even, Mr. Mackinzie."

He leaned closer and answered, "Not by a long shot."

She glared back at his remark and he noted that those blasted feathers were the exact shade of her eyes.

Grabbing her arm, he led her from the store. Once outside, she whirled to confront him. Her full lips pouted while her blue eyes sparkled with anger, daring him, tempting him.

With a supreme effort of will he resisted pulling her into his arms. He found himself wanting nothing more at that moment than to kiss her until her resistance melted away under him.

A little boy dashed away from his mama and careened right into Tess's knees. The impact sent her straight into Zack's arms. Without thinking what he was doing, he closed his arms around her. The feathers bounced as Tess tilted her head back, and her gaze met his.

Damn, did the hat have to match her eyes so perfectly? he wondered, looking down into their depths.

She stared at him in silence, then nervously moistened her lips. Her chest rose with her next breath, and Zack held her tighter. Her eyes widened with a blend of dismay and perhaps pleasure, while sparks of anger still flared at him.

There it was again—that mix of innocent and temptress, and it was daring him. Tempting him beyond belief. He succumbed, and hang the consequences.

Lowering his head, he took her lips in a consuming kiss that heated him right down to his boots. Damn, she wasn't supposed to taste this good. This sweet, he thought, then drew her closer, slanting his mouth more fully over hers. Her body molded against his, fitting his hard planes perfectly.

As she parted her lips ever so slightly to draw in a breath, Zack slid his tongue between her dewy-moist lips. Sighing into her velvet softness, he began a gentle but determined plunder of her mouth and her senses.

The pressure of Zack's firm lips on hers smothered any protest Tess might have been about to make to his kiss. But it no longer mattered. As he cupped her cheek in his palm, her earlier anger melted away like the last patch of snow beneath a spring sun

He tenderly moved his lips back and forth across hers. Tess was unable to stop the sigh of pleasure his kisses brought forth to her own lips. Her mind reeled with a flurry of sensations. Delicious heat . . . breathlessness . . . bewilderment.

Her senses swirled about, refusing to settle, much like a butterfly in a field of freshly bloomed wildflowers. His kisses were opening up an entirely new world to her. She'd never felt this pleasure, this sheer enjoyment, from a kiss. And yes, tenderness, too.

She'd never dreamed it could be so good.

Tess curled her fingers around the edges of his leather vest. The material was buttery smooth to the touch, and she kneaded the vest and the broad chest beneath much like a contented kitten. The tip of one fingernail caught on the corner edge of metal.

The realization penetrated her dulled senses as she drew her hand away from the distasteful reminder of his profession. A lawman. Zack Mackinzie was a lawman.

The pleasurable warmth began to drain from her body, leaving cool reason in its place. Not only was he a lawman, he suspected her of murder. Why, he'd practically accused her of the crime only last night. And now, today, in bright daylight, he was kissing her.

Anger surged up in her, pushing aside her gentler feelings toward him. He was a lawman after all, wasn't he? He'd as much as said he suspected her of murdering the miner, and now here he was kissing her. Was this some new form of interrogation to him? she asked herself in derision.

With a final blaze of anger, she raised her arms and shoved him away from her.

"You can take your suspicions and your kisses and go to the devil, Ranger Mackinzie!"

She whirled away from him and practically stomped off down the walkway.

"Ah, hell," Zack muttered after her.

* * *

Frank Larson unclenched his fists and stepped back into the open doorway of the saloon. He drew in several jerky breaths. If Tess hadn't pushed the fancy lawman away, he didn't know what he would have done. He'd been more than halfway out the door after them before he stopped himself. Even now, he still saw everything around him in a red haze of fury and hot jealousy.

How could she do this to him? How could she let that man touch her, much less kiss her? His sweet, innocent Tess wouldn't even let *him* lay a hand on her. She treated him nice enough and smiled often, but he knew better than to dare touch.

The thought of the lawman doing what he was only allowed to dream of doing enraged him again until everything about him blurred. Tess belonged to him. Surely she knew that.

He'd bided his time, trying to please her, letting her get used to him being around and all. But no more. She was his, and the sooner she realized that the better things would be for all of them.

Frank strode back out the doorway, his movements jerky with still-restrained anger. He had a meeting to go to. Before this, he hadn't been certain whether it was right to go or not, but Tess's unladylike actions and wanton behavior had made up his mind for him.

He'd be at that secret meeting told about in the note all right.

At precisely a quarter past six that evening, Frank Larson pulled back the flap and peered into the shadows enveloping the tent. "Hello?" he called out.

"Over here" came the order. "And close that tent flap."

Not recognizing the muffled voice, Frank stumbled to the kerosene lamp, but the instant he lit the match, it was blown out with a sharp gust of breath.

"Leave it dark."

Frank nodded before he recalled that the other person probably couldn't see his movement. Whoever it was sure liked the dark. "All right with me," he added. "What'd you want to see me for?"

The note with money tucked inside had guaranteed he'd meet with whoever wanted to talk to him. And the other person knew it.

"A favor for a favor," the voice from the darkness stated in an obvious attempt at disguise.

"What do you mean?" Frank sidled closer, his curiosity getting the better of him. However, he forgot that his obvious bulk couldn't be concealed in the near darkness of the tent.

"Stay where you are," the voice snapped. It had the force of a gunshot.

Frank swallowed down the growing unease and shifted from one foot to the other. He didn't like this one bit. If Philip Fontana caught him messing around in here before a show, he'd up and fire him.

What he should do was get out of the show tent while he still could, Frank thought, but he hesitated before taking the first step.

"Leave now and you'll never have her."

The all-knowing statement had the effect of stopping Frank in mid-step. "Who?" he asked tentatively, testing the other person's knowledge.

"Tess Fontana."

A shiver raced along his neck. Whomever the stranger was, he was well informed. Too well. "What about Tess?"

"Like I said, a favor for a favor. You do something for me, and I'll see you get her."

Anticipation roared through him in a surge too powerful to ignore.

"How?"

"Leave that to me. For now, you switch the usual setup for tonight's performance with this."

A bottle was pressed into his hand. Frank curled his fingers around the glass. Unable to stop himself, he pried open the cork stopper. The potent stench of ether filled the air between them. He quickly pressed the cork back on tightly. This wasn't Fontana's usual diluted batch of ether he used in the suspension trick.

Curiosity ate at Frank's gut, and he voiced it. "What for?"

"For me."

Frank frowned at the cryptic remark. "I got to know more than that."

"Let's just say that if Tess's father weren't up and around for a few days, you'd have a better chance with her, wouldn't you? Without her overprotective father to come between you, maybe she'd pay more attention to you?"

The questions had their merit. He never had liked Mr. Fontana much, and the feeling ran the same on both sides.

"Maybe you're right," Frank admitted.

"Of course I'm right. Now go do it."

Holding the bottle close against his chest so no one would see it, Frank crept from the tent.

The figure watched to make certain he didn't return. The fool. A laugh escaped before it was caught back to be replaced by a wide smile.

Philip Fontana had looked tired and old. It didn't take a fool to know that Tess would take his place. After tonight there'd be no more pretty Tess Fontana for anybody to worry about.

* * *

By the time the night's performance began, Tess's nerves were in a state that would have done Uncle Simon's predictions proud. She alternated between embarrassment, a peculiar warmth, and dismay.

Imagine her kissing a lawman and allowing his hands to touch her that way. A lawman! And darn, why did it have to feel so good!

Not only did he have to be a lawman, he was a wanderer, always pursuing. She couldn't give in to a man who was only here today and gone tomorrow, no matter how strong a temptation he presented.

And Zack Mackinzie certainly did present a powerful temptation.

Her heart longed for the security of a real home, with walls and a roof. One that came with a loving husband, and children. She almost scoffed aloud at this—a foolish dream that could never be hers. What man would want her after what she'd done? What she'd allowed?

The piano chords broke into her thoughts, dragging her back. Time for her performance. She'd persuaded her father to allow her to trade places with him for this next illusion. She hated the broom suspension trick and only allowed him to enact it once a month.

However, tonight he'd looked too drawn and pale to her. So, she'd refused to participate unless he allowed her to do the trick herself. Now she wished she'd talked him out of it completely.

A final clang of the piano keys signaled her and told her that it was time for Frank to take a break. From the corner of her eyes she watched him slip away out of sight and off the stage.

She turned her attention back to the show and the waiting crowd. Once again she spotted Zack sitting in the audience, front and center as before. His presence made her decidedly uneasy, and she needed all her wits about her for this trick. If she didn't breathe in enough of the ether, or if she inhaled too deeply, the magic feat would go awry. She tried to ignore him, but could feel his gaze on her every move.

Zack watched the performance, his gaze fixed determinedly on Tess. Anger at himself and his earlier actions ate away at his gut.

He'd foolishly allowed himself to fall under the spell of the woman who might well be the one responsible for his brother's death. He tightened his jaw, clenching his teeth together until his jaw muscles cried out for reprieve.

Hadn't David's last letter told of a woman who'd bewitched him with her golden hair and Texas bluebell eyes? He stared at Tess up on the stage. The lovesick description fit her perfectly.

Her hair hung down her back in thick, luscious curls. As her father placed his hand and some small object over her mouth, her eyes drifted closed. He didn't need to see those beautiful eyes to know their color was exactly the deep shade of the Texas wildflowers his brother had loved.

Unable to tear his own gaze away, Zack watched as Philip Fontana suspended Tess horizontally from a single pole. He had to admire the magic feat, and for a fleeting moment wondered how it was accomplished. Then the pole was lowered until Tess lay on the wood floor of the platform.

"And now, ladies and gentlemen, Tess will awaken." Fontana snapped his fingers in the classic act of a conjurer creating magic.

However, this time nothing happened.

Tess lay on the platform, perfectly still. Her eyes remained closed, her lashes dark crescents against her pale skin under the lamplight.

"Tess, awaken." Another snap of the fingers followed the spoken order.

Zack detected the waver of fear in Philip Fontana's voice as he called for her to awake yet a third time. An answering chill raced up his own back to settle in his neck. He didn't like this trick one bit.

Tess lay too still, her skin too pale. Even from where he sat in the front row, he could see that her cheeks were practically translucent instead of the faint blushing rose he'd grown accustomed to seeing on her silken skin.

Something was wrong.

Eleven

Zack cleared the stage in two leaps, his booted heels hitting the wood platform with a resounding thud. Without a thought for anything except Tess, he shouldered his way past her father.

"Leave her be." Philip Fontana stepped in front of him, taking on a protective stance that Zack would have respected at any other time.

However, now Zack only stopped himself from striking the man by remembering he was Tess's father. He flashed him his badge and knelt at Tess's side. As he stared down at her face, his gut clenched into a tight knot; she was even paler up close than from the first row.

Something had definitely gone very wrong. And it could well end up costing her life.

"What did you give her?" he demanded of Philip Fontana, holding his raging temper at bay with an iron effort of will.

When Philip hesitated, Zack grabbed his arm. "To hell with your magic secrets." He repeated the question. "What did you give her?" His voice left no doubt that he intended to get his answer no matter what he had to do to accomplish it.

"Ether," Philip replied, touching a hand to Tess's cheek.

"You damned fool, you could have killed her."

"But we always use—"

"You gave her too damn much."

"No, I didn't. I gave her much less than usual, because of last night's fainting spell."

"Well, it was too much." Zack tapped down his anger; it wouldn't do Tess any good right now. "We've got to bring her out of it. Now!"

Before it's too late, he added silently. If it wasn't already.

Fear like he'd never faced before confronted him, threatening to rob him of action. He fought the beast, and won. Damn, this was worse than facing down the six-shooter of a desperate outlaw. At least he could see that and knew what to do. Fear arose again like a monster to sap his will.

"Dammit, how do you bring her out?" Without thinking what he was doing, Zack grabbed Tess's father by his voluminous cape. The edge of one mirror cut into his palm, but he ignored the pain and the trickle of blood that ran across his palm.

Philip reached into a concealed pocket of the cape and withdrew a container of smelling salts. "Here, this should help."

The two men worked together, holding the acrid potion beneath her nose, each attempting to bring her back to them by a sheer effort of will. All thought of the waiting, watchful audience was forgotten.

"Tess," Zack called. He bent closer. "Tess, honey. Come on."

Catching her hand in his, he rubbed it between his larger hands, trying to infuse his own warmth and life into her.

Philip Fontana knelt across from him, gently patting her cheeks and calling out to her. Worry and honest fear had drawn his features tight. He stared down at

Tess as if he could draw her back to them by the sole force of his persuasive personality.

When Zack first saw Tess's lashes flutter, he thought perhaps he was imagining it, wishing for it so hard that he dreamed it. The second time her eyelashes brushed her pale skin, he knew the faint movement was real. Thank God it was real and not a figment of his imagination.

She struggled to sit up, but moaned and sank back onto the wood flooring. A rush of conversation came from the spectators still sitting around the stage.

"Hellfire," Zack swore.

Patting Tess's hand, her father stood to his feet with an aura of authority. "Ladies and gentlemen." He waved his arms to capture the audience's attention, but he already had every eye in the place on him.

The conversation before him died to a murmur. Zack had to admire the man's skill with the crowd.

When the crowd fell silent, Philip Fontana continued, "I am happy to tell you that Tess will be fine—"

A flurry of applause erupted from the spectators.

"Thank you, but sadly I must end our show for tonight. My daughter needs her rest," Philip responded in a humble voice. "I apologize for the show and the worry you have been caused. Please make yourselves welcome at our makeup performance in two nights. You will all be my special guests."

Bowing, Philip stepped back to Tess's side. Amongst murmurs and sideways glances at the stage, the audience began departing.

Frank rushed up from the side exit to Tess, fear and disbelief etched on his face. "No, not Tess," he cried out, reaching for her.

Zack pushed him aside, concerned only with Tess's well-being. Right now, she needed fresh air and lots of it. He scooped her up into his arms and carried her outside, but once away from the tent, he sat her gently on her feet. Letting her lean against him, with his arm supporting her, he tilted her chin up until he could look into her dazed eyes.

"Tess, I want you to breathe deeply. We need to get as much fresh air into you as possible."

The glazed look remaining in her dulled eyes told him he needed to repeat his instructions. After the second time, she shook her head slightly as if to clear it, then began to breathe deeply in and out.

Suddenly, Tess stiffened in his supporting arms. He leaned closer, worried at the change.

"I think I'm going to be sick," she whispered, and jerked away from him.

He gave her the privacy she needed, and when she returned to his side a few minutes later, her face was pale and drawn.

"Better?" he asked.

"A little." She gave him a wan smile that scarcely tipped the corners of her lips.

When he reached out to steady her, she didn't push him away. Instead, she almost meekly let him fold his arms around her.

"This is getting to be a habit."

Her soft voice was almost too low for Zack to hear the words.

"What is?" he asked, his own tone equally low, almost hesitant. He wasn't certain he wanted to hear Tess's comments while she was still under the effects of the ether. Would she implicate herself in the miner's murder? In David's? And did he want to hear the answer?

He stiffened, waiting.

"You," she murmured against his throat. "Carrying me." She sighed, a mere breath of sound against his skin. "Rescuing me."

Looking down at her slight form pressed close against

him, the knowledge hit him with the weight of a stone. If someone had tried to kill her tonight, then Tess couldn't be the murderer. Could she?

Zack's heart took a leap in his chest. Tess surely had to be as innocent as she looked, at least innocent of murder. The killer still lurked within the traveling show, not held close within his arms.

It took Zack all of twenty minutes to get Tess to her hotel room. They had walked the short distance at a slow pace; Tess wouldn't hear of him carrying her all the way, so he had to be content with having her lean on him. If she hadn't been so pale, he would have insisted on swinging her slight form up into his arms and carrying her, but he hadn't wanted to upset her unnecessarily.

Worry gnawed at him. She looked weak and quite ill. They'd had to stop walking twice for her to empty her stomach, but each time she'd assured him she felt better. He knew the aftereffects of ether could be quite disturbing.

Once inside the hotel lobby, Zack said a to-hell-with-her-wishes, and lifting her into his arms, he carried her up the stairs and to her room. He gently laid her on the bed, bringing her an extra pillow from the nearby chair.

Hooking his boot on the chair leg, he drew the chair alongside the bed. He heard her sharply indrawn breath at his action.

"Thank you for—"

Zack sank down onto the chair, hopefully putting a stop to her words before she could dismiss him.

"Helping me back. I'll be fine now," she continued, leaning up on her elbow.

He should have known better than to think she'd let him stay without an argument. But an argument she'd get if she attempted to dislodge him from her room right now. She needed someone with her who could be trusted to keep her safe.

"Tess—"

"Thank you." She slid back down against the pillows. "You really should be going. I—"

"I'm staying right here." As she opened her mouth to protest, he cut her off. "And there's not a hell of a lot you can do about it for now. So, just rest. I'll watch over you."

"Don't need anybody to watch over me," she murmured, her words slurring together ever so slightly.

The effect was appealing as all get out. Zack clenched his teeth against the feeling rushing through him. He didn't want to feel this softening toward her. He couldn't afford to allow it. Someone in the traveling show was killing people. If it wasn't Tess, it could be someone close to her. Like her father.

When he didn't immediately answer, she repeated, "Don't need anyone . . ."

Her words drifted off as her eyelids fluttered closed. She sighed and her breathing softened, signaling she'd fallen asleep.

Zack released his own breath in a mixed sigh of irritation and relief. He'd stay all right, with or without her consent.

One thing Tess Fontana definitely needed was someone to watch over her. He tossed his hat onto the other chair and settled in for the duration.

Sunlight peeked through the curtains when Tess next awoke. The sight that greeted her took away all power of speech. Zack Mackinzie sat slumped in a chair drawn so close beside her bed that one of his hands laid atop the coverlet.

She simply stared at him for a full minute. Then the questions rushed in. What was he doing here in her room? How had he gotten here?

Blinking at the apparition before her, she studied him. His lashes rested closed against his tanned skin, his face tipped low. A dark growth of stubble covered his chin and spread across his cheeks making him look dark and forbidding. It also told her he hadn't left her room to shave. In fact, he'd stayed the night.

He stirred under her scrutiny and suddenly she met the intensity in his gray gaze. It was then that she realized he hadn't truly been asleep as she'd assumed. He was as awake and watchful as a mountain lion. And every bit as dangerous against anything that threatened what he considered his.

That realization shook her all the way down to her bare toes. With a start she realized that her toes weren't all that were bare. Her nightgown had ridden upward to mid-thigh, but that reality did little to assure her. Just how in heaven's name had she gotten dressed in her nightclothes? She most assuredly didn't remember doing so.

Her expression must have revealed more than she thought because Zack sat up and rubbed his hand back and forth across his rough chin. Sending her an enticing smile, he leaned toward her. She nearly jumped out of her skin.

"Your father and your friend Ella stopped by last night after the show. She undressed you."

Once again her face must have given her away, for he added, "Pity."

Tess gulped.

"How do you feel?"

"Me?" She knew her voice squeaked, but she couldn't help it.

His expression darkened. "How much do you remember of last night?"

Tess's eyes widened and she felt the heat of a blush

rise from her chin to the roots of her hair. Consternation. What had she done?

Zack laid his hand atop hers, and she jumped back, scooting up in the bed and pulling her hand away. As the coverlet slid down, she grabbed it with both hands, jerking it up to nearly her chin.

"Last night?" she whispered.

She stared at Zack, questions racing across her mind. Her head hurt, and her tongue felt like a big wad of wool had been stuck in its place. A moment later the answers followed in scattered pieces of memory. The show . . . Zack telling her to breathe . . . him putting a pillow under her head . . .

She blinked as the rest of the night fell into place. She hadn't lain with him.

"Tess?"

"I remember most of it, I think." Her answer came out hesitantly, asking him for confirmation of the missing pieces and reassurance that she hadn't forgotten anything important.

Suddenly she recalled his words *I'll watch over you.* Relief washed over her.

"You stayed the night—"

"Yup."

"To watch over me?"

"Yup," he repeated the answer. "Somebody had to." Now nervous, Tess licked her dry lips. "Thank you."

"Then you remember?"

"Most. I—"

"You were given too much ether," he supplied the explanation.

"Papa's always very careful with the ether," she argued back without even thinking. "Because it's dangerous, he keeps it stored away safe. He wouldn't make that kind of a mistake."

Zack raised his eyebrows at her words, then his eyes

narrowed. It happened so quickly, then his expression became shielded. She wondered if she'd imagined it. She still felt as if she were wrapped in wool. Both her thoughts and mind seemed to be running at the speed of a snail. A very slow one.

"Zack?"

"Something went wrong last night. You were nearly killed," he told her in a gentle voice.

"Someone tried to hurt Papa?" she asked, leaning forward. Forgetting all about the coverlet, she let it drop from her fingers.

"No, someone tried to hurt you," Zack corrected.

Fear stole her breath away for a moment. Zack was wrong. Someone had tried to kill her father last night. She had to tell him.

Tess shook her head, then winced as the room spun about in a wide arc. She caught Zack's arm to steady herself.

"You'd better lay back down." He gently clasped her shoulders and eased her back until her head touched the pillow.

As soon as he removed his hands from her shoulders, she sat upright again. She had to tell him before the wooly fog overcame her.

"No, Zack, listen. It was Papa somebody tried to kill."

"Tess—"

"How could anyone want to hurt Papa?" Her voice shook with emotion held tightly in check. She felt if she allowed it free rein, she'd shatter into tiny pieces, the same as the mirrors on Papa's crimson cape.

"They didn't."

Zack's blatant refusal to acknowledge the danger her father was in angered her, temporarily replacing the fear that ate away at her courage.

"That was no accident." Her voice rose with the memory of what had occurred.

"I agree."

"Someone tried to kill Papa." She clasped his hands, desperate to make him listen to her. "You have to believe me."

Zack rubbed her hands between his and shook his head at her.

"Someone did try to kill him," she insisted.

"No, Tess, you're wrong. The intended victim was you. I'm sure of it."

"No, Zack." She sighed and tightened her hold on his hands. "Papa was supposed to perform that trick, but I took his place."

At his disbelieving look, she continued, "Papa looked tired, and I was worried about him doing the trick. So, I insisted that I do it."

"Then I was right. You were the victim."

"But—"

His raised hand cut off whatever she'd been about to say. "Someone did try and kill *you* last night. I'd also noticed how tired and worried your father seemed, and if I noted it, how many other people did, too?"

Tess's eyes widened in dawning comprehension.

"You've substituted for him in the past when he hasn't felt well, haven't you?" It was more of a statement than a question.

"Yes." She nodded, clenching her hands together beneath his palm.

"And if I realized that, how many other people might have, too?" He paused, then added, "People in the show."

"But we're all like family," she protested, her voice taking on a protective edge. "None of them—"

"Trouble has been dogging your traveling show. And if the show moves on and the trouble does, too, that means it's coming from somewhere within the show,"

Zack pointed out patiently. "From someone within the show."

"Who?" Her voice was scarcely above a whisper, but the single word seemed to echo in the room.

Who . . . who . . . who . . .

"That's what I intend to find out." Zack stood and looked down at Tess. "You rest, and I'll be back later to check on you."

She watched him cross the room, half irritated at his words. He'd almost reached the door when he swung around and faced her. Tess's heart dove for her toes. His deep gray eyes held her pinned to the pillows.

Not taking his eyes off her, Zack strode back across the room to stand over Tess. Bending down, he took her lips in a kiss that left her dizzy with need for more.

Tess clasped hold of his wide shoulders to steady herself. This time her very mind seemed to take flight and spin about the room. He planted his hands on the mattress, one hand on either side of her. Slanting his mouth, Zack deepened the kiss, turning it into two, then three kisses, each one more devastating than the one before.

Finally, he drew back, giving her a chance to draw in a shaky breath. She noticed that his own breathing seemed to be almost as ragged and uneven as hers. He drew his thumb ever so gently over her bottom lip. Then he closed the distance separating them for one last joining of their lips.

When he broke the contact, Tess stared up at him in bewilderment. Smiling down at her, he touched her lip again and, stepping back, turned and headed for the door.

This time he turned the handle and walked out into the hallway, carefully ensuring the door was locked behind him. Easing back against the pillows, Tess stared at the wooden door.

She raised her hand to touch her fingers to her lips. They still throbbed from his kisses.

"Oh, my," she whispered to the empty room. "He certainly knows how to say good morning."

Watch over you. His words returned again, this time offering reassurance and comfort. And something else she wasn't ready to face yet.

Zack stepped into his room and closed the door behind him. The action didn't shut out the feel of Tess's lips beneath his, her body under his hands. She had felt so sweet.

What had started out as comfort had turned into so much more. That good-bye kiss had nearly landed him in her bed with no desire to ever leave it.

He shook off the memories that tempted him to turn around and go back to her. He needed a shave and a change of clothes. His own bed beckoned, inviting him with a few minutes' rest, but he resisted. He had things to do. Sleep could wait. It would have to.

Last night he'd stayed awake, watching Tess, worrying over her. He knew he was right—someone had tried to kill her. But why?

That question had run through his mind over and over last night during the long, dark hours of self-imposed guard duty. Now the question returned again. It meant she was most likely innocent of David's death. But who had murdered him? Her father? Someone else in the show?

Zack finally gave in to the lure of David's memory. Crossing to the bureau, he withdrew his brother's last letter to read yet again. He noticed that the paper's creases were becoming worn with the number of times he'd done just this same thing.

He gently smoothed out the folds. By now the words

were committed to memory, etched into his heart. However, this time he read his brother's last words, searching for some clue he'd missed earlier.

Every word remained the same. Unchanged.

They told of the beautiful blond woman David had fallen in love with. Tess? And what of her father? Had Philip Fontana killed David to keep him from Tess? With each word of the missive more questions arose to taunt him. The letter's words told of eyes as blue as Texas bluebells. If not Tess, then who?

Zack faced his obsession with the letter. It was a desperate effort to strengthen his resolve against Tess's lure and remind himself that she and her father were suspects, but instead he found himself aching for the touch of her silken skin and honeyed lips.

Foolishly he told himself he would only continue to see her in order to keep an eye on her father and possibly tie him into David's murder, but he knew it for an outright lie. Heaven help him, he was drawn to her like a firefly to an open flame, and he was certain she posed a danger different than any little firefly ever faced.

Frustrated, Zack tossed the letter atop the bureau and turned away. It was time he began thinking like a lawman and not a grieving kinsman. He'd send a telegram back to Texas and see what he could learn about a certain Philip Fontana and his daughter Tess. A twinge of conscience arose, but he forced it back. He had to do his job.

Scarcely a half hour later, Zack strode out the door, shutting the panel behind him. Freshly shaven and dressed in clean clothes, he felt a great deal more ready to face the day. His boots clicked on the wooden flooring as he strode down the hall.

* * *

A lone figure stepped out of the shadows and stared

at Zack's departing back with hatred. Damned interfering lawman.

Damn him. If the lawman Mackinzie hadn't interfered last night, Tess would be dead by now. Everything had gone wrong.

Philip Fontana still walked free as if by the same magic he practiced so well. Fontana should have been convicted of the miner's death back in Virginia City, but no, he wasn't even in jail at this moment, much less swinging from a rope about his neck. That plan had gone awry. Now this.

Tess should have been dead last night. But no, she still lived. How had she escaped the switched bottle of ether? She should be dead.

Something had to be done soon.

Another one would have to die so that Philip Fontana could go to jail. Then to the hangman's noose. A harsh laugh cut through the silence blanketing the hallway.

Perhaps the lawman's room would relinquish something of value that could be of use.

Checking both directions before moving, the figure crossed the hallway. Within a few moments the door to Zack's room yielded and the figure slipped into the now empty room.

A thorough but cautious search of the sparsely furnished hotel room revealed nothing of any useful interest. Neither the armoire nor the bureau drawers provided anything. The figure resisted the impulse to slam the last bureau drawer shut and instead slid it quietly closed. There was no cause to chance alerting anyone to the presence of an uninvited guest.

About to leave, a keen gaze fell on the letter atop the bureau. Eagerly snatching up the paper, the figure read every word.

"So, pretty Tess snared another one."

Maybe the lawman could use some extra help in

catching the killer. If Philip Fontana were arrested for murder and dragged off to jail, it would destroy both Tess and her beloved father.

A new plan began to form. Once again a short laugh drifted through the silence.

It wouldn't be long now. Revenge beckoned like a waiting lover.

Twelve

Tess rubbed her hands up and down her arms, trying to instill some warmth into her body. It seemed that when Zack left the room he'd taken all the heat along with him. She knew it was a foolish thought, but it remained nonetheless, and now that she was alone, fear had filled the void.

The chilling fear coursed bone deep, and it steadfastly refused to leave her. No matter how hard she tried to push it aside by telling herself it was foolish, it persisted in remaining with her like an unwelcome specter in the close confines of the room.

Unable to stand the imposing silence, where the slightest sound had her jumping, she threw back the coverlet. Residual nausea assailed her at the quick movement, but she tapped it down, breathing in several deep breaths. The ether's aftereffects brought back the hazy memory of last night. She refused to dwell on it and become a skittery mouse afraid of its own shadow. She'd never been one to sit around and wait for things to happen, and she wasn't about to start now.

Determined, Tess left the sickbed, her mind made up. She'd get to the bottom of this situation. It wouldn't defeat her, leaving her a mass of frightful nerves in need of the calming effects of the hated laudanum.

Crossing to the armoire, she threw the door open.

She forced herself to concentrate on the mundane task of choosing a gown and dressing. Bathing and readying herself took up the better part of an hour.

Finished, she stared at her reflection in the mirror, the violet silk of her gown made a comforting splash of color in the room. However, even as she smoothed out a wrinkle in the scalloped flounce of her skirt, the horrible truth of last night arose before her, taunting her. No matter how hard she attempted to shove the fact aside, it reappeared like a determined apparition.

Last night someone had tried to kill her.

Who? Why? The questions chased each other across her mind.

A shiver wracked her, and she trembled under its onslaught. How could anyone hate another person that much? Whatever had she done to provoke that much hatred in someone?

A knock shattered the imposing silence of the small room, seeming to echo and reecho between the four walls. She jumped and clutched her skirt almost as if the silken material could ward off any approaching danger from without.

A bubble of laughter surfaced at the thought, tickling her throat. She fought the outburst down with every ounce of sanity she possessed. Then she stared at the door questioning who could be waiting on the other side. Right now, at this moment, she didn't know who she could trust.

"Tess?"

She groaned aloud as she recognized the voice. Marlene Boudreaux most definitely fit into the untrustworthy category. She toyed with the notion of not answering the door, but the woman obviously knew she was inside. She might well keep knocking until the door collapsed under her blasted determination.

Consternation.

Tess slammed her fist down onto the nearby chair, then pushed herself away. By the time she'd crossed the room and reached the door to unlock it, Marlene had pounded on the wooden panel three more times.

Both irritated and frustrated, Tess wanted to stomp her foot. Why hadn't the greedy whore stayed in Virginia City? Instead, she'd had to accompany Uncle Simon and the traveling show to San Francisco.

Now it seemed as if Marlene and her perky white hair bow had both determined to become a persistent thorn in Tess's side. Not more than a single peace-filled day could pass by without the appearance of the aggravating woman, who seemed to derive immense satisfaction out of needling her.

Obviously Marlene still felt threatened in some way by her. What was it going to take to convince the woman that she wasn't a threat to her? Tess questioned, then wondered if it was worth the effort. She still hoped Simon would see through Marlene and toss her out on her—

The door rattled beneath another overly-loud knock. Tess sucked in a breath between clenched teeth, and unlocking the door, she swung it inward.

"Good morning, Marlene." Tess forced a smile to her face.

Her smile disappeared the moment the other woman barged into the room. Today her visitor wore a gown of emerald green, blue, and white that could practically light up the show's tent without the aid of kerosene lanterns. Tess felt temporarily overwhelmed by the peacock hues proclaimed by the woman's too-tightly-fitted gown. An elaborate trimming of white chenille balls topped off the demi-trained skirt that trailed behind her ample figure.

For the space of an instant, Tess wondered if the

woman got dressed in the dark. Surely no one would choose such an outfit if they could see it clearly.

"Ohhh, I heard about your mishap last night, dear girl." Marlene's voice oozed false concern. "And I came by to see how you are recovering." She batted her lashes. "Sy wanted me to check on you personally."

"I am fine, as you can see," Tess responded in a tight voice.

"You really should be more careful not to inhale too deeply." The smile left her carefully rouged face and her eyes narrowed.

Tess bristled at the woman's unwelcome advice. What was it about Marlene that put her instantly on edge?

She sauntered over to the chair, the bright colors of her gown making the hotel room seem stifling to Tess. Pulling off her gloves, she leaned back in the chair, for all appearances settling in for a long stay. One Tess was far from welcoming. How was she to rid herself of her visitor without being too rude?

"Well, I am fine, so you needn't worry—"

"Ohhh, I wasn't worried, dear girl." Marlene dropped her gloves into her lap. "In fact, I'm truly here on an errand of mercy."

"You?" The word slipped out before Tess could prevent it.

Marlene stood in an angry, sweeping movement, her skirts swishing about her. She pulled on her gloves. "And to think I came here out of concern to offer you a job."

"A job?" Tess blurted in disbelief.

"Yes, well," Marlene paused and brushed at a minuscule speck of lint on the skirt of her bright gown, obviously composing herself. "I'd thought to offer you something safer." She deliberately looked down her nose at Tess.

For an instant Tess thought she saw a hint of a threat

in the other woman, but then Marlene batted her lashes and smiled in the coy way Tess was growing to hate.

"Well, dear girl?"

"No, thank you," Tess enunciated her refusal clearly.

The other woman tossed her head and sniffed at her in disdain. "You'd turn down a job from me? You fool. I could have made you rich."

"No thank you," Tess repeated, barely holding her own anger in check. "Not that way."

"Don't you dare turn your nose up at me." Marlene leaned closer in a posture of intimidation. "Someday I'll own part of your little show, and then we'll see who needs a job. You'll come begging to me someday."

"Never."

"Oh, yes. Wait and see." Marlene patted her perky white hair bow in a gesture of congratulation. "When Sy—"

"He will see through you soon," Tess informed her. He had to, she added silently.

"Never." Marlene threw the word back at her.

Tess raised her chin in a mixture of anger and defiance. "Get out, Marlene."

The woman's narrow brows drew up before she leaned forward and sneered in Tess's face. "Don't try and take Sy away. You can't do it. I won't let you take him from me." Her voice held a thinly veiled threat.

In spite of her normal courage, Tess felt a shiver race down her spine.

"I only wish I could," she responded.

Marlene laughed, her voice high-pitched enough to make Tess's teeth ache. The sound trailed off, and she reached out and stroked a finger down Tess's cheek. "But you can't, can you, dear girl?"

Turning on her heel, Marlene sauntered to the door, her bustle swaying from side to side echoing her self-satisfied smugness. The door clicked shut behind her.

Tess stared at the door in astonishment. If she told anyone what had transpired here, they wouldn't believe it. The Virginia City prostitute, now a transplanted San Francisco brothel owner, she corrected herself, had waltzed into her hotel room, offered her a job, threatened her, and sauntered out full of supreme confidence that Tess would come crawling to her in time.

"Not even when a certain place freezes over," Tess vowed to the empty room.

Dislike was much too tame a word to describe the emotion coursing through her where Marlene Boudreaux was concerned. Somehow, some way, she'd best the witch at her own game.

A short nap revived Tess's spirits after the unpleasant encounter with Marlene. Tea and toast in the hotel's dining room further restored her unsettled stomach. Feeling ready to begin her attempt to uncover the truth behind what happened last night, she decided to check out the medicine show.

She knew Zack would be furious if he knew what she planned. Heavens, he'd be mad enough to learn she'd even left her hotel room, much less gone to the medicine show.

His disapproval dogged her every step, even without his presence to accompany it. Tess didn't need him walking beside her to feel him there. In fact, she could still feel the tender touch of his lips from this morning. The memory stayed with her, refusing to leave her mind. It haunted, comforted, and tantalized her.

She raised her hand to trail her fingertips across her lips. She didn't know what he'd done, but he'd left her wanting more of his kisses. When she saw him again . . . he'd be furious with her.

She didn't look forward to facing his anger when he

learned what she'd done. But by then she'd be finished and back in her hotel room. Maybe, just maybe, Zack need never know she'd even left the safe confines of the hotel room where he'd left her.

He hadn't actually forbidden her to leave her room, hadn't ordered her not to try and find out the answers on her own, she justified. But he might as well have. His softly spoken promise to watch over her had much the same effect as those orders. However, she couldn't simply wait in her room for the would-be killer to make his next move. She'd hurry and maybe return to her room before Zack ever missed her.

The short walk to the area reserved for the show's tents brought a touch of color to her cheeks and she greeted her father with a reassuring smile.

His eyes clouded with worry before he hugged her close, brushing a kiss on her cheek. "What are you doing here?"

"I came—"

"You should be in bed. After last night . . ." His words trailed off, and a cloud of worry drifted across his face. "How do you feel?"

"Fine—"

"Tess, that lawman stayed the night, didn't he?" His voice carried resignation. "He threatened to have me jailed if I interfered. Your own father. He insisted it was the only way to protect you."

Tess recognized her father's true fear behind his questions and remarks. She rushed to reassure him. "That was fine. He did keep me safe. And nothing happened."

Well, almost nothing, she added silently, resisting the impulse to touch her lips again.

"You should still be in bed. What are you doing here?"

"I came to see you. And check on how the show's

doing," she added truthfully, but neglected to tell him what she wanted to check about the show.

"You shouldn't be out of bed—"

"Papa," she laughed, "I'm fine."

At the continued worry evident from the tired lines on his face, she added in reassurance, "Really I am."

"Tess—"

"And I couldn't stand being cooped up in my room a moment longer like a naughty child." She faked a pout at him. It succeeded in bringing a smile to his face as she'd hoped it would.

He leaned forward and kissed her cheek again. When he straightened, his smile widened. "Tess, dear, there's been wonderful news."

All worry seemed to have been wiped from her father's face with his announcement. She smiled back at him, happy with whatever tidings had brought about this change in him.

"What is it?" she asked, making certain to inject eagerness into her question.

"With your accident last night and all, I forgot about telling you."

Tess refrained from letting her father know that last night had been no accident. She didn't want to do or say anything to take away the sheer happiness on his beaming face.

"Mr. Benjamin Thayer wants to discuss selling our elixir."

"Who?"

"He's a prominent businessman here in town. And he's quite interested in selling our elixir in his establishment. Year round."

Tess knew her eyes had widened at the startling news. If this came to pass, they'd never have to worry about money again. No more sleeping in the wagon or tent when show sales were poor in a town.

"He wants to meet at the Palace Hotel."

Tess knew her mouth nearly dropped open at the news. The Palace Hotel on Market Street with its seven stories of luxury towered above the neighboring buildings. Anybody who was anybody wanted to be seen at the Palace Hotel. And her papa was going there for a business meeting.

He pulled out his pocket watch and glanced at it. "Oh, no."

"What's wrong?"

"I'm due to meet with Mr. Thayer in a quarter hour."

"Papa, that's wonderful."

"But we need to leave now if I'm not to arrive too very late."

"Papa, you have plenty of time to reach the Palace Hotel. It's only—"

He shook his head in disagreement. "First I must see you back safely to our hotel."

Tess placed her hands on her hips in defiance. "Consternation. Go on to your meeting. I can take care of myself."

A fleeting memory of Zack's words *someone to watch over you* teased her mind.

"Now, Tess—"

"Don't waste time trying to convince me otherwise, Papa," Tess caught his arm. "This meeting is too important to miss. You go on ahead. I'll visit with Ella a while, and we'll walk back to the hotel together."

"Tess—"

She raised her chin and faced him squarely. "Go," she ordered.

As he still continued to hesitate, she added, "I want to talk to Ella about the new costume she's designing for me anyhow. Now go."

He leaned down and brushed a kiss across her cheek. "If you promise to have Ella accompany you?"

"Yes, Papa," she answered like an obedient child, then shooed him away.

"Impudent." He smiled at her, then added, "You remember your promise."

"Go."

Tess watched him turn away and stride off at a fast pace belying his eagerness. If this meeting of his was successful, then all would change. They could stop moving around quite so much. The sales of the elixir in Mr. Thayer's grand establishment would ensure more than enough funds to live on.

A wide smile of anticipation lit Tess's face. Papa wouldn't have to work so hard. She clasped her hands together and whirled about. A wave of dizziness stopped her and intruded on her exuberance. Maybe she'd better go find Ella, have a short chat, and return to the hotel. Tess turned away and walked toward a small wagon that stored the costumes.

A lone figure stepped out of the shadowed darkness provided by the tent flap. Only the late-afternoon shadows hid the hatred and fury spurred on by the overheard conversation.

So, Philip Fontana thought to get rich, did he? And his sweet innocent Tess was likely as not already plotting how to spend the newfound income.

Something needed to be done now.

The narrow alley in the midst of the Barbary Coast was darker than Hades itself. The only light to penetrate the opening between the buildings came from the nearby deadall that sold vile wine and even worse beer. The lone figure walked deeper into the alley, one hand wrapped around the butt of a loaded pistol watching for cutthroats.

"You're late." A poorly dressed man stepped out from behind a stack of crates. His voice slurred with too much whiskey.

The figure whirled about, gun outstretched. Upon recognizing the other man, the hand holding the gun relaxed. "I had something that had to be done."

"You got the money?" He licked his lips.

"I have it." The figure reached into a coat pocket and withdrew a wrapped packet. "You're certain you know what you're to do?"

"Yeah, I knows." He stared at the gun, then nervously shifted from one foot to the other.

"And?"

"Don't you worry none. She'll die all right, just like I promised you yesterday."

"Make it slow," the figure ordered in a harsh voice filled with hatred.

The man's face crinkled into a grotesque parody of a smile. He slowly withdrew a blade from his waistband and stroked it almost lovingly with his thumb. A small trickle of blood ran over the steel. Grinning now, he wiped it away.

"That'd be my way." He looked back from the knife to stare hard at the other person. Raising his arm in a challenging gesture, he asked, "But I still gets to have her first?"

The figure smiled widely. "Yes, but just make sure she dies after."

Harsh laughter cut through the filth of the alleyway. "You pay me enough and she'll die anyway you wants her to do."

"I just want her dead this time. She should have died before now," the figure shouted, for an instant forgetting the surroundings. The voice lowered to a hate-filled sound that made the hair at the back of the man's neck prickle. "Make sure she dies."

In spite of the knife in his hand, the man stepped back, yielding to the lone figure. "Yeah. I'll make sure."

"You damned well better. And make it today. I'm tired of waiting."

The man watched the figure turn and stride away. A shiver jerked his body. It felt as if somebody had just walked over his grave.

Not *his* grave, he told himself, the girl's. He wiped the blade tenderly and slid it back into his waistband in preparation.

For tonight, Tess Fontana would die.

Thirteen

Tess scanned the area around the gaily painted wagon with the word "Costuming" in bold lettering on the side. She'd been searching for Ella for almost a half an hour. Wherever could she have gone to?

Frustration and a vague sense of unease ate at Tess. Several people remembered seeing Ella today, but Tess couldn't find her at any of the places she'd been directed to check. Uncle Simon had thought he'd last seen her in the show tent, but when Tess looked there, Ella was nowhere inside.

Next, Frank had helpfully offered to lead her back to the costume wagon, but Tess had politely turned down his assistance. He had a tendency to get far too familiar if Papa wasn't close about. Right now, she didn't feel like dealing with the piano player's amorous attentions.

Tess glanced around the show's grounds and frowned with increased unease. It wasn't like Ella to simply up and disappear.

After crisscrossing the area once again, Tess was about ready to give up and return to her hotel when she spotted her friend back beside the costume wagon.

"Ella!" she called across the distance separating them, hoping to catch her before she vanished again.

The tall, blondish woman turned at the sound of her name and faced Tess's approach without the usual welcoming smile. She had both her hands clenched together in the folds of her skirt. One dark-blond curl hung loose from the chignon upsweeping her hair to dangle at her temple.

Tess paused in mid-step for an instant. Ella appeared flustered and rushed, a totally uncommon combination for her.

Continuing on, she crossed the distance to the wagon. "Where ever have you been? I've looked all over for you." Tess caught her friend's arm in concern.

Ella sent her a distracted glance, and a worried frown creased her forehead. A second later it disappeared.

"Are you all right?" Tess asked.

"Of course," Ella responded, her tone a bit sharp, uncharacteristically so.

Tess frowned, staring closely at her friend. It was Ella's turn to touch Tess's arm.

"It's that black scarf. It's disappeared again." Ella plopped her hands on her hips in agitation.

Tess knew her own eyes widened as she watched her in disbelief. Ella never misplaced things. Now this had happened twice.

"Do I need to go buy another one?" Tess asked in resignation.

She hated the very thought of scouring the shops of San Francisco in search of yet another filmy black scarf. She was rapidly coming to hate that scarf and all the trouble it was causing.

"No." Ella shook her head in determination. "I'm certain it will turn up. Don't worry about it."

"Are you certain?"

"Yes." Ella brushed her question aside. "What we need to be concerned about is you. What are you doing here out of bed?"

Tess was getting tired at having that question posed

to her. "I'm fine." She barely stopped herself from snapping the answer out. "I came to see Papa."

"He's left for a meeting," Ella informed her.

"I know. I've already talked to him, but I came to see you, too. I wanted to thank you for . . . ah, taking care of me last night."

"I wasn't the one doing that." Ella's laughter burst forth. "It seemed a certain lawman had the job well in hand to me."

Tess knew her cheeks turned a betraying shade of red; she could feel the heat coloring her face. She didn't need a mirror to know exactly what color she'd turned. Her friend's soft laughter confirmed it.

"So, did you sleep well?" Ella's lips twitched as she voiced her question.

Tess's didn't. "I slept very well, thank you." The words came out crisp and defensive. "Nothing happened," she hastened to add.

"Well, I for one am sorry to hear that," Ella announced.

"What?"

"You need to start living again." She held up a hand to stop anything Tess would say to deny the fact. "I mean, truly living. Remember, not all men are the same." A soft, loving light came into her eyes. "I've learned that for myself."

"Ella?" Tess whispered the question.

Her friend blinked several times and looked away. "There was a man once, not so long back who showed me the truth to that." She inhaled in a long, slow breath, then continued, "But that's in the past. Just a good memory."

"What happened?"

Ella shrugged, and Tess could almost feel her pain. "I was too old. He was too young. I sent him away. I had to. Anyway, by now he's found some sweet young thing to take my place."

Tess reached out her hand, but Ella quickly turned to the wagon. "We need to fit your new costume, if you're feeling up to it."

"Yes," Tess answered, wisely falling silent. She'd known Ella long enough to know when her friend needed to keep her own counsel. But later, they'd talk more. The subject wasn't finished yet.

An hour later, Tess emerged from the wagon to face the near dark outside. She frowned in concern at the rapid approach of dusk. Seated inside the costume wagon talking with Ella, she hadn't noticed the passage of time.

It had taken much longer than anticipated to complete the costume, but she considered it time well spent. The gown of sapphire blue, trimmed with silver to match her cape, was a vision—more beautiful than she'd imagined it could possibly be.

However, now she wished Ella hadn't pleaded an errand that she needed to pursue. Hating to burden her friend, Tess had kept quiet about Zack's concern and her papa's fretting. Now, she'd been left to walk back to the hotel by herself.

The walk didn't worry her over much, but she hated not keeping her promise to her papa. However, if she hurried and reached the hotel before he completed his business, he need never know about her breach. Need he? She quickened her pace.

Only a mere block and a half from the hotel, she passed a darkened alleyway when a hand snaked out and grabbed her. The scream on her lips made it no further as a hand was clasped over her mouth.

Her attacker drew her tighter against him, and the stench from his unwashed body nearly gagged her. A bubble of laughter threatened at this. Here she was being attacked, likely going to be murdered, and all she could think about was how bad the man needed to bathe.

Tess raised her chin and instinctively stiffened her spine. She would not go along meekly like some milk-sop miss. No, she'd fight him all the way.

"Thinkin' of fightin' me, girlie?" he cackled into her ear.

His liquored breath fanned over her cheek, and Tess had to force herself not to retch at his nearness and the terror that engulfed her. He loosened his hold on her mouth and slid his hand down to curl his dirty fingers about her throat.

Tess knew any scream for help would only bring her death with a broken neck from his large, powerful hand.

"Eh, girlie?" he repeated.

"With my last dying breath," she vowed in a hoarse whisper.

"Oh, yeah, fight me, girlie. I likes it when they have some spirit in 'em. Never lasts long, but I likes it." He laughed, the sound a harsh reminder of what he had in store for her.

"I'll die first," she spat back at him.

"Oh, no. But that'll come in time. Never you worry about that, girlie."

Fear washed over her in waves, but she fought it down. She had to keep her head if she was to have any hope of surviving.

Zack stared at the spot where he'd thought he'd seen Tess only moments before. But no one was there. Had he merely imagined it?

The part of him that kept him alive these past years of hunting down killers caused the back of his neck to tingle in an age-old warning of danger. This wasn't a barren desert, and he wasn't a man prone to mirages. Something was wrong.

He'd been crossing the street on his way to check in on Tess when he'd heard a muffled cry, drawing his attention to the boardwalk where he'd thought he'd spotted Tess's blond hair. Surely it couldn't be here? Surely she was safely resting in her hotel room where he'd left her hours ago? Surely . . .

When had Tess ever done what he'd expected and assumed of her?

Turning on his heel, he strode toward the spot where he'd seen *something*. Or someone.

As he neared the darkened alley, the sound of scuffling footsteps baited him on. With his right hand, he released his gun from its holster, easing it into his palm.

Drawing to a halt mere steps before the alley, he slid against the building front, then cautiously peered around the corner. The figure of a man was leaned close over a woman. He sighed in disgust; he'd nearly interrupted a lover's liaison. He was in the process of reholstering his gun when the man glanced up, the movement revealing the woman in his arms.

Tess.

Zack stepped into the alley, gun still in his palm. As the glimmer of reflected light shone off the knife blade at her throat, his breath and heart both stopped for the space of a heartbeat. It was all the time he needed to aim his gun.

But it was too long.

Too late.

The badge on Zack's shirt shone reassuringly in the flicker of lamplight, and as Tess recognized him she scarcely stopped herself from racing to him. The knife pressed against her throat was a cruel reminder to stay where she stood.

She felt the man behind her stiffen, and she knew

he'd seen the badge, too. Then he drew her closer, shielding his own body with hers. The movement brought Zack's gun centered on her chest.

"Get back, lawman. Or I'll kill her now." Her attacker pressed the blade tighter against her neck, proving his intention to both her and Zack.

Desperation and defiance welled up in Tess. She wouldn't remain silent and meek. "He's going to kill me anyway, Zack," she announced in a voice that sounded much calmer than it should to her ears.

The tip of the knife flicked against the slim column of her throat, drawing a drop of blood in its wake. A sharp pain flickered at her neck where the blade pressed against her tender skin. She squelched down the fear that threatened her sanity as much as her attacker threatened her life.

"One more word out of you, girlie, and I'll do it right now," her attacker shouted into her ear.

Tess winced and the blade cut deeper into her skin. She could feel the tickle as warm blood seeped from the cut and ran slowly down her neck to the bodice of her gown. She repressed her instinctive shiver, knowing any movement might well be her last.

"Well, lawman. What's it gonna be? Or you wanting to watch me do it?" he taunted Zack, stroking the handle of the knife with his thumb.

Across from them, a muscle in Zack's jaw flinched. He remained silent, locked in a battle of wills with Tess's attacker, looking for the chance to make his move.

Her attacker leaned closer, brushing his chin against her hair. Revulsion arose in Tess, almost shutting off her breath.

"Ear to ear," the man informed them both. "I'll cut her from one pretty ear to the other." A rumble of laughter choked off his words.

Tess tried to still the tremble that ripped through her

body. If Zack didn't do something, the man was going to kill her, but if Zack so much as moved wrong, the same thing would happen. She'd never felt so powerless in her life. With the knife blade pressing against her throat, she dared not move. It would most assuredly bring about her own death.

She bit down on the terror that threatened to swamp over her, dragging her down. Instead, she concentrated on Zack, watching every flicker of his eyes, every breath he took.

Right now, her life hinged on the Texas Ranger's actions. And she hated that. In almost seven years she'd taken responsibility for everything she did and for keeping both her papa and herself safe and alive. Now her very life rested in someone else's hands. She wanted to scream at the fates, but out of sheer instinctive self-preservation she remained stiff and silent, her every thought damning her attacker.

Zack met Tess's mutinous gaze and knew that if he didn't act soon, she might well take the matter into her own hands. And get her fool self killed in the process, too.

He knew if he surrendered his gun and allowed her attacker to walk free, the man would take Tess with him, then kill her as soon as he had no further use for her. However, he might well rape her before he plunged the knife blade into her soft body.

Tensing, readying his body for whatever was to come, Zack nodded in false acquiescence to the knife-wielding man. He eased the hand holding the gun up in an act of even falser surrender. No way in hell would he allow the man to walk out of there with Tess.

"Don't hurt her!" Zack called across the distance separating them.

"Drop the gun, lawman," the man practically snarled at him.

This was Zack's first clue that the man wasn't as sure of himself and his attack as he'd once been. A nervous edginess emanated from the man.

Zack realized Tess's life hung by a very thin thread, and he was about to cut it. He prayed he could catch her when it gave.

He focused solely on the prospective killer's eyes. Any flicker would give him away, and Zack waited for this. Waited and prayed.

The man's right eye twitched, and it was all Zack needed to alert him. He watched the knife inch away from Tess's throat for the space of a heartbeat. Not much, but it was enough. Before the blade could move again, he aimed and fired. The retort of the pistol echoed and reechoed in the alley.

Tess's scream bounced off the walls of the buildings enclosing them. Her attacker swung to the side and, pivoting, collapsed to the ground.

Zack was at Tess's side almost immediately. After making certain she was not seriously harmed, he left her only long enough to check on her attacker. Justice had reached him first, the man lay dead.

Hastening back to Tess, he drew her up and into his arms. He held her close, feeling the racing of her heartbeat against his chest, and murmured words of reassurance in her ear. Carefully, he blotted away the traces of blood along her neck with his handkerchief, making certain for himself that the small cuts weren't deep or dangerous to her.

The sight of the bright red stains on the cloth tore at him. Never one to be sickened at the sight of blood before, it nearly undid him this time—now that it was Tess's lifeblood.

"Zack?" Tess's voice could scarcely be considered even a whisper of sound.

"I'm right here," he assured her.

She shuddered, turning into his arms, and he forced himself not to crush her slender body to him. What he wanted to do was to pull her tightly against him, enfold her in his arms, and never let anything harm her again. He tamped down on the until-now unknown instincts.

"Zack?"

He stiffened at both his name on her lips and the shaky tone of her usually defiant voice.

"Please? Hold me," she pleaded.

He'd never heard that in her voice before. He'd witnessed anger, defiance, perhaps unease, but never this heart-wrenching weakness and vulnerability. It tore at his own heart.

"I am, honey."

He drew her tighter against his body, their heartbeats so close that they practically merged into one sound. She snuggled even nearer.

"Please don't tell Papa this happened?"

Her voice had gained back a tiny portion of its former strength, but he could still sense the overwhelming fear and shuddering reaction held firmly in check.

When she drew back ever so slightly to gaze up at him, he saw the dampness of tears sparkling on her lashes. His heart nearly turned over in his chest. She looked so fragile and so very innocent.

"He'll worry himself too much if you tell him. Promise?" she pleaded.

Against his better judgment, Zack gave in to her request, murmuring agreement. He could scarcely believe what he'd heard or agreed to. She was more concerned about her father worrying than about her own near brush with death. She snuggled back against his chest once more, distracting his thoughts instantly.

A recollection of yesterday's comment from her after the ether accident tugged at him. She was right. Holding

her was becoming a habit. One he was coming to like—
very much so. He wrapped his arms closer about her.

"Zack?"

Her soft voice shook him, the fear and hesitation that
were back in her tone so completely foreign to the
woman he'd come to know.

"Yes?" he answered, his own voice rough with his
ragged need to protect her.

Tess held to him tightly, and her voice wavered when
she spoke. "Keep me safe. Just for a while."

He'd never wanted anything as much before in his
life as he wanted to take care of her at this moment.
He tenderly brushed a soft kiss across her forehead.

"Don't worry, I'll watch over you," he vowed.

"Zack, don't let go of me." She buried her face
against his shoulder.

"Never," he whispered in a voice too low for anyone
else to hear. Even her.

A small crowd began to gather about the scene. As a
patrolling policeman approached, Zack signaled to
him. A low, brief conversation followed, ending with
him promising to stop in and talk with the captain in
the morning. During it all, Zack never released his protective hold on Tess.

Finished at last, Zack scooped Tess up into his arms,
and without asking her permission this time, he carried
her to the room where he was staying. Nestled in his
comforting embrace and with the reaction of shock settling in, she didn't utter a sound of refusal.

Zack wouldn't have listened if she had anyway. Not
now. Determination to see her safe drove him. Stepping
across the threshold to his small room, he nudged the
door closed behind them with the toe of his boot.

He gently set Tess on her feet, making sure that her
legs would enable her to stand on her own before he

released his hold on her. It took all his willpower to do so, but he knew he had to release her eventually.

Gazing down at her, he regretted his decision. She looked so pale and tiny and vulnerable. He brushed a strand of hair from her cheek. Her faint breath stirred against his fingers. He thanked God she was alive.

His fingers rested a moment on her bare collarbone above the tear in the bodice of her gown. Rage arose in him that her attacker had dared to even touch her, much less attempt to do her harm.

Forcing himself to be tender, to tamp down the rage against the man who'd tried to kill her, he drew her away from the door and into his arms. Her eyes remained closed, her lashes strikingly dark against the worrisome paleness of her cheeks.

Her hair was a tangled cloud around her ashen face. Zack brushed it away with his hand. In the room's soft light, angry red splotches of dried blood marred her neck, standing out in stark contrast to the whiteness of her skin.

"You're safe now," he whispered.

Her eyelids fluttered open and she stared up at Zack. "He . . . he . . ."

Tess bit down on her lower lip. She willed the fear away. If she gave in to it now, she'd be lost. She stepped back, drawing in several deep breaths. Zack watched her, waiting.

Instead of her fear, she focused all her attention on the man who had rescued her. He offered her safety. And strength. And so much more that she wasn't certain she was willing to face it at this moment.

As she continued to meet his gaze, the gentleness she saw there eased beneath her protective shell. For the first time in her life she wanted to reach out to a man. This man.

"Tess." Her name was a ragged whisper on Zack's

parted lips. It drew her like nothing else could have done, reaching to something deep within that she'd kept sheltered and locked away for so long she'd thought it was dead, incapable of responding ever again. But now it blossomed, coming slowly back to life.

Nothing could have stopped her from answering the pull of his voice. When Zack held out his arms, she stepped into his embrace without hesitation.

He wrapped his arms around her, cradling her to his chest. Slowly the warmth from his body flowed into hers, chasing away the chill that had held her so tightly in its terrifying grasp.

She sighed against him. It shouldn't feel so good to be held by him. By any man. But it did. She rested her head on his strong chest. Beneath her ear, his heart beat steady and sure. It shouldn't feel so good—but it did. It offered reassurance, comfort, and invitation.

However, it was too inviting. Reluctantly she drew back. She raised her chin and looked up at him, her gaze meeting the startling intensity and possessiveness in his gun-metal-gray eyes.

Zack lowered his head, and Tess leaned closer. She could no more have stopped herself from doing so than she could have simply and easily stopped herself from breathing. Her lips parted on a silent breath of anticipation. She knew he was going to kiss her.

His breath was moist and warm on her skin. So feather-soft, so gentle, so loving. She raised her head again, unable to resist the pull of the feel of his breath on her face. Their eyes met again and his held hers for several long seconds. He released his gun belt and let it slide to the floor.

Slowly he lowered his head, shutting out the room around them, shutting out the horror in the alley, shutting out everything but his lips on hers.

Lifting his hand, he slipped his fingers through the

hair at the back of her neck. The strands gleamed in the soft light, taking on a shimmer all their own. He raised the curls to his face and inhaled her special scent. Her hair was soft against his knuckles, and he curled his fingers into the lushness, dragging her closer yet.

Tenderness, pleasure, heat all became a part of that kiss. Tess eased her arms upward, around his neck, holding tightly to the corded strength beneath her hands.

His touch was gentle for such a strong man, yet she could feel the additional force of the strength he held back. It offered her the reassurance she needed to meet his kisses and give as well as receive.

Zack drew her closer, their bodies touching intimately, pressing together from chest to knees. Tess gasped at the intimacy, but he swallowed the sound with his next kiss. He ran his hands down her back, molding her body to his, stroking the length of her back.

Tess felt safe, secure, and hot. She returned his kiss, forgetting to breathe or even think. The pressure of his embrace thrilled her, aroused her as she hadn't thought possible.

He swung her up into his arms, his lips never leaving hers. Carrying her to the bed, he eased her down onto the mattress. Then he drew back and brushed his lips against her forehead, giving her the chance to stop him, to say no to his loving.

Zack gazed down at her, wanting her with a desperation he'd never felt before. He wanted to comfort her, to erase the pain and fear from her eyes, and to make love to her.

Tess lay in his bed, looking fragile and so tempting. Her hair fanned out across the pillow like a silken cloud. He leaned closer and ran his fingers through the strands, caressing her.

When she didn't murmur a refusal, he sank onto the bed and drew her into his arms. Whispering words of reassurance in her ear, he laved kisses against her cheek, then trailed his lips from her cheek to her jaw and down to her neck. He feathered kisses along the small cuts on her throat.

He took her fully into his arms, enclosing her in their protective warmth. Tess nestled against him, tilting her head back to gaze up into his eyes. What she saw mirrored there reassured her, wiping away any doubts she might have held. As he lowered his head to take her lips in a kiss sweeter than time, one thought crossed her mind: this felt so right.

"Zack, make me forget," she whispered. "Please."

This time the tenderness in his kiss took her breath away, and a vague anticipation stirred within her. Every place his hand stroked her blazed with heat. That blaze wiped out all fear, past and present.

Time itself ebbed and flowed around them with each movement, wrapping them in a warm cocoon. Zack eased her back downward, and Tess offered no resistance. She met him kiss for kiss.

Her skin tingled under his ministrations, and a sigh escaped her lips. His touch was gentle, yet she could feel that strength held in check again.

As his fingers eased the bodice of her gown downward, she gasped, then stiffened. He rained kisses along her shoulders, and along with them a slow heat began to invade her limbs. It felt wonderful, and she gave in to the pure pleasure of this man's touch on her body.

Zack eased her gown open and slipped the torn fabric down to expose her breasts. He gently circled her nipples with the tip of his tongue, bringing them to life.

Drawing back, he gazed down at her. "Beautiful," he murmured a breath away from her.

Tess's heart stopped for the space of a beat. No one had ever called her beautiful before. She blinked back the burning moisture of the tears that threatened. Now was not the time for crying. It was the time for loving this man, for rebirth.

Her hand trembled as she reached out and touched his shoulder, then slid her hand down his chest along the buttons of his shirt. He caught her hand and held it close.

Easing back, he undid the buttons, and pulling his shirttail out of his trousers, he shrugged out of it. He let the cloth fall to the floor.

Tess stared at his broad chest. He was magnificent. The shirt had hidden so much, such as the way his muscles rippled with the slightest movement, and the way his breath made his chest rise and fall. She couldn't resist the overwhelming desire she had to run her fingertips over the breadth of the skin stretched over his muscles.

She indulged herself, tentatively touching him at first, then growing bolder when he didn't stop her. She ran her fingertips across the faint puckering of an old wound. She couldn't believe someone had tried to harm this perfection. Raising herself up on her elbows, she touched her lips to the scar.

Zack's breath hissed through his teeth. He pulled her head up to take her lips with his, branding her with the heat of his desire. The low groan that slipped past his lips told her more than any words ever could that he desired her. Happiness at this revelation sang through her.

She wrapped her arms around his shoulders, and as she did so, he undid the fastenings of her gown, trailing the roughened pads of his fingers down her spine. She thought the room would spin about her at the feel.

He was making her feel things she'd never felt before, never dreamed she could feel. She moved her lips back and forth over his, giving all she could. As he groaned against her mouth, she increased the pressure of her own lips. The kiss deepened, threatening to sweep her away to a place she knew she'd never been before and never expected to visit.

Tess squeezed her eyes tightly closed and gave herself over to the feelings of pure pleasure that flooded through her. His touch, his loving, was a type of magic she'd never known before, and she reveled in it.

When she didn't stop him, he made short work of her gown and undergarments, gently removing them and dropping them alongside his own clothing on the floor.

Zack paused to lean back and gaze down at her nakedness, and Tess felt herself blossom under the glow in his smoldering eyes. Her breath rushed out in a soft "oh" of awe.

He caught the sound and her lips in a kiss that fired her senses. Cupping her breasts in his palms, he set to loving her the way he'd only dreamed of touching her. He warmed her soft skin with the warmth of his moist breath on her breasts, then worshipped each one with kisses that left her gasping in soft mews of pleasure.

The sound nearly sent him over the edge, but he held on to his desire, wanting to give her every bit of pleasure that he could before he took his own release.

Gradually her shyness fell away under his touch. Not an inch of her body escaped him. He lavished kisses over the gentle swell of her breasts, suckling her nipples until she cried out, grabbing hold of his shoulders as if she never intended to release him.

Slowly, he moved downward, giving attention to the smooth skin covering her ribs and dipping lower to her tiny waist. He spanned it with his hands, drawing her up to suckle her navel.

As Tess moaned beneath him, his own groans of pleasure met hers, blending together as he continued to worship her body with his touch. Finally, when he knew she was ready for him, he eased his legs between hers and gently, slowly, entered her, filling her.

As she gasped in wonder, his murmured endearments filled her ears. Tess felt the sparkle of stars explode around her, enveloping her in liquid heat so intense she cried out his name.

Her own name was a whisper on his lips, and she joined in a release so intense it shattered the stars above them, raining down in brilliant prisms of sparkling light about their joined bodies.

Fourteen

Tess stretched like a contented cat beneath the morning sunbeam shining through the window of her hotel room. She'd awakened with a smile on her lips and it refused to leave. Not that she wished for that.

Closing her eyes, she let her smile widen with delight. She fully recalled Zack returning her to her room sometime in the midst of the night. He'd insisted on her coming back to her own room, saying he didn't want to worry her papa come morning.

Zack had been everything a woman could ever dream of having in the man who made love to her. Tenderness, strength held in check, and so experienced he made her body sing under his hands. The thought described him so perfectly that a soft sigh escaped past her upturned lips. Why had no one ever told her that it could be like this between a man and a woman?

A giggle replaced the sigh, and even in the privacy of her empty, quiet hotel room Tess knew she was blushing. Before their time together had been through, Zack had managed to turn every inch of her body into a heated flush from his touch.

Beneath her closed eyelids a mental picture of him arose. The dark hair she'd tangled her fingers in, the rough stubble at the base of his strong jaw, a very determined jaw she added to the list of his attributes. Eyes that ran the gamut from steely gray the color of gun metal and just as hard to the soft shade of a dove's feather. She'd never seen eyes like his before. Last night they'd shone with tender possessiveness.

The night spent in his arms had been magical. And most assuredly not an illusion conjured up by a master magician, though Zack had been a master all right—a master at making her feel truly wonderful.

Her brief marriage had never allowed her to imagine lovemaking between a man and a woman could be so special. And so precious.

A shiver of premonition traced its ugly finger down her spine. Stiffening, she refused to acknowledge it. Nothing would ruin this memory for her. Nothing.

She wouldn't allow anything to take her back to the woman she'd been before Zack's lovemaking. Not anything, she vowed.

At this moment, Tess had never before in her life felt so loved and safe and protected. She hugged that thought to her like a talisman against anything the future might hold in store for her.

If anyone had told her, she wouldn't have believed this incredible feeling was possible. Zack's tender loving washed away the horror of the past, and the seven-year-old pain eased away, his loving act replacing it with memories of this night and of love given and received.

Even now, this morning, a slow seductive warmth stole through her limbs just recalling the night. She didn't even want to move. She wanted to hold the memories of the wondrous night to her breast in much the same way Zack had held her close.

Tess felt like a flower that had at long last found the sunlight. She was like a beautiful rose, its petals blossoming beneath the sun's warm, gentle rays. That's how being near Zack made her feel now.

She felt wonderful and special and precious. And oh-so-womanly . . .

The scent of roses tickled her nose and she smiled at her earlier comparison of herself to a newly blossoming rosebud. Now it seemed so real that she could smell the petals. She snapped her eyes open, realizing the sensation was real and not imagined.

Laughter tickled her throat. In her enjoyment of last night's memories, she'd managed to forget all about the bath awaiting her. She'd had it delivered after she'd first awakened. The trailing wisps of steam from the water had been cooling these past fifteen minutes while she'd lulled away the time dreaming and recalling the wonders of last night.

The frothy bubbles and softly scented rose water beckoned to her. She knew for certain that the water still retained more than enough heat for her bath. The bubbles and water tantalized her with liquid warmth so reminiscent of the night that she sighed again. To be able to relive that time even in her mind was a miracle to her.

Smiling that self-satisfied smile of wonder that hadn't left her lips this morn, she threw back the coverlet. After she bathed, she'd . . .

A knock on the door sent her scooting back under the coverlet. A blush heated her face at the path her thoughts had been down. She didn't want to share these feelings with anyone else right now.

"Tess?" A soft, familiar drawl called her name through the locked door.

The voice brought the tantalizing warmth back to her body. The smile returned to her face. Zack.

She bounded out of bed and dashed across the room to the door. Turning the lock, she swung it open and he stepped inside, kicking the door closed with his booted foot.

He took her into his arms, enfolding her in his embrace with all the tenderness of a lover holding something dear and precious. His kiss was a combination of gentleness and unassuaged hunger. And once again, it curled every one of her ten bare toes.

He drew back, breaking off the kiss with an obvious reluctance. Gazing down at her, he searched her face carefully for any sign of regrets over their night together.

"How are you this morning?" he asked, his breath stilling in his chest as he waited for her response.

A shy smile tipped the corners of her mouth as she answered, "Wonderful."

Feeling a bravery she'd never experienced, Tess eased away and, turning to the door, flicked the lock. When she turned back around to face him, her face emblazoned the age-old desire of a woman for the man she loved.

Zack opened his arms, and she stepped into his embrace. Burying her face into his shoulder, she couldn't believe her boldness. She'd never in her entire life acted this way. She dared a glimpse at the expression on Zack's face, searching for shock or, even worse, disgust. But she found neither.

Instead, she found pleased surprise, a man's loving possession, and a blatant hunger that stirred something deep within her like never before. Their gazes met and in unspoken communication, he clasped her hand and led her to the enamel tub sitting in the middle of the room.

Tess stared down at the steaming, frothy water, grasping his intention. Why, she'd never in her entire life . . .

"Never?" Zack drawled the word she'd unknowingly whispered to herself.

His chuckle tickled the fine hairs brushing her cheek. She raised a hand and tried to smooth some semblance of order into her tousled curls. She'd planned on being bathed and beautifully dressed with her hair perfectly coiffed when she next saw him. Now she must look a sight.

"I'd wanted so to be beautiful for you." Her words were low and dejected. "Instead—"

As her lower lip trembled so scarcely that only a lover would notice, Zack brushed the pad of his thumb across her lips.

"Don't," he ordered, his soft drawl becoming a tinge harsh. "You look beautiful. Practically the same as when we made love last night."

At her gasp of pleasant surprise, he added, "I don't want you dressed in satin and petticoats." His voice lowered, the huskiness beneath doing strange things to her breathing. "I want you looking just as you do now. Soft and well loved. Loved by me."

Tess gazed up at his face and knew for certain in that instant of time that she loved Zack Mackinzie. With all her heart.

Sliding his hands from her lips along her cheeks, he trailed his fingertips over her jawline and down each side of her neck to her shoulders. The pads of his thumbs were rough against her soft skin, but the friction thrilled her, excited her in a new, yet inexperienced way.

Once at her shoulders he slid his fingers under the straps of her nightgown and eased those straps down her arms. Her soft lawn gown fell away from her, and his hands followed its downward path, skimming her rib cage, pausing at her waist, caressing her hips.

Tess thought she would likely go wild with need if he kept this seductive, wondrous torture up much longer. Finally her nightgown lay in a pool of creamy ivory at her feet.

In return, she ran her hands over his chest, working

the buttons of his shirt free. Spreading the fabric aside, she slipped her fingertips along the dark mat of hair dusting his chest, begging to be touched.

He scooped her up and held her a moment, his lips brushing hers once, twice, and yet again. Ever so slowly, almost as if he didn't want to let her go, he lowered her against his body until the steam from the bathwater rose up around them, enveloping them in a soft cloud of heat and even hotter need.

The need flowed from one to the other. It touched, caressed her shoulders, his chest. Above her, Zack's eyes darkened in responsive passion.

He eased her into the bubbly, frothy water, sliding his hands over every inch of her body before he straightened up and reached for the snap to his pants.

His dark pants hugged his hips and muscular thighs. Tess watched in fascination as he unfastened those pants and slid them down the long length of his legs. Casually, he kicked the clothes aside.

He stood above her, his feet braced shoulder width apart. As he took a step toward her in the tub, the sunbeam from the window glimmered on his naked body. His shoulders were every bit as broad as the vision that had filled her mind before he'd knocked at her door. His hips as lean, his manhood as strong and proud.

Tess couldn't for the life of her pull her eyes away from him. Same as last night, he was magnificent.

And all hers, a little voice whispered in the back of her mind with pride.

The water sloshed up to ripple at her shoulders as Zack stepped into the tub. Drawing her up to him, he half-lifted her out of the water, holding her tightly against his damp chest.

Almost painfully slowly, he sank into the water, taking her down with him, letting the waves rush against her hips. The ebb and flow of the water against their bodies imitated the coming together of a man and a woman. Both of them recognized it, thrilled at it.

Zack's hands tightened about her waist as he drew her closer, lowering her down in the water and down onto his ready, silken shaft.

A groan rolled off his tongue as her velvet warmth took him deeper and deeper inside her. His mouth took hers, this time demanding as well as loving.

Tess gave to him all she had to give of herself. Clinging to his shoulders, her hands slid on the fine sheen of moisture covering his skin. She clung even tighter to him, her world erupting as he pulled her closer, deeper. Ever deeper.

The room encased the only important things in existence, the two lovers and the loving rapture surrounding them.

Tess glanced away from the mirror, embarrassed at the flush still warming her cheeks. After all, it had been more than mere minutes ago she'd dressed and readied herself and still she blushed. However, it had all been done under Zack's attentive gaze.

A movement in the mirror's reflection caught her, and she watched as Zack crossed the room to her. His boots rang out on the wooden floor with each step. Instead of frightening her, the sound promised protection and caring and loving.

As he reached her, he pulled her around and into his arms. Staring down at her, he began to lower his head. He paused, his lips a mere breath away from hers. He couldn't believe she was his. This beautiful child woman. In such a short time she had nearly become his very life blood.

A sharp knock on the door had them drawing apart as if caught stealing candy from the general store. Zack

smiled at her and watched the gentle sway of her bustle
as she crossed to the door. Her fingers gripped her skirt
for a moment in a show of pure nervousness. A grin
tugged at his lips. His beautiful temptress of the enamel
bathtub was shy.

Smoothing her hands down along the deep blue of
her skirt, Tess unlocked the door and eased it open. It
revealed the police captain in uniform.

"Ma'am, sorry to disturb you." He stepped forward
into the room, removing his hat. "I had some questions
about last . . ."

His eyes lit on Zack, and whatever he'd been about
to say slipped away. "I'd wager my officer is on a wasted
trip looking for you, Ranger. But both of you being here
and all will save me some time."

Zack narrowed his eyes on the other man, sensing he
wasn't going to like the news the captain came to im-
part. Everything about the policeman spoke of a problem. A serious one.

Gesturing to the two chairs, Zack invited the captain
inside. Tess preceded them, sitting on the edge of one
chair. The captain took the other chair, and Zack stood
beside Tess, watching the scene with growing suspicion.

"We had a murder last night. I wouldn't normally
even mention it to a visiting Ranger, but the victim was
a prominent businessman here, and this has to do with
the lady and her father's traveling show that's performing here in the city."

Zack's gut tightened into a coil of tension, but none
of it showed on his unreadable face. He merely nodded,
encouraging the man to continue.

"Mr. Benjamin Thayer was found dead late last night,
not far from the Palace Hotel. He'd been poisoned."

Tess gasped, the sound overly loud in the small room.
She covered her mouth with both hands in shock.

"We've been told he met with a Mr. Philip Fontana, the lady's father that same night—"

"They were discussing a business deal," Tess put in, her voice soft and weak.

"Well, it seems your father may have been the last person to see Mr. Thayer alive."

"No!" Tess protested.

Zack clasped her shoulder, keeping her in the chair and effectively silencing her.

"What makes you assume that, Captain?" Zack asked in a low voice of authority.

The officer reached into his pocket and withdrew a black scarf. Tess couldn't stop the gasp as she recognized the thin, filmy scarf from the show. Her father's trademark magic trick.

"A prop from the performance, I presume?" the captain asked her.

Tess nodded her head in answer. "Yes, Papa's scarf," she confirmed without thinking of the consequences. "But he couldn't hurt anyone. Never—" She barely cut off the condemning word "again."

"Ma'am, I'm not accusing your father of anything."

The unspoken word "yet" hung in the stifling air between them as the captain stood to his feet.

"But Mr. Thayer was grasping this in his hand. Along with a show token." The captain's announcement shattered any calm that may have remained in the room. Or in Tess.

"Ranger Mackinzie." He turned his attention to Zack. "I'd like to talk with you some more about this and what happened last night with the lady."

"Of course."

"A telegram also arrived for you early this morning."

Zack's face showed no sign of any emotion at the news he'd been given.

"Ma'am." The captain nodded at her. "Thank you for your time."

Zack gave her shoulder a reassuring squeeze. "I'll be back later to check on you," he said the words softly. "Stay inside and keep your door locked."

Turning away from the stricken look on her face, he followed the police officer out the door, closing it behind them.

Tess stared blankly at the closed wooden door. Waves of disbelief rolled over her. This couldn't be happening. Her papa was innocent. She knew that for a certainty. But someone was going to great pains to make it look otherwise. She could feel their formerly safe world beginning to crumble around them.

How much longer before their true identity became known?

Tess paused outside the tent flap, taking a moment to compose herself. She knew her father would be inside practicing just as he did before each scheduled performance.

She couldn't very well go bursting in and blurt out that he was a murder suspect. He probably hadn't even heard the news of Mr. Thayer's death yet.

As she waited, the further realization of what the businessman's murder meant to them struck her. There would be no sale of the elixir to Mr. Thayer's establishment. No end to their traveling.

In fact, his death might send them fleeing for their own lives.

She bit down on her lip and ordered herself to calm down. She would not give in to the fear that had begun stalking her with the tragic news.

Drawing in a deep breath, she climbed the three

wooden steps to the show platform and stepped into the tent. And into the middle of an argument.

Voices raised in anger reached her even before she saw her father, Uncle Simon, and Frank Larson standing in a semicircle.

"Philip, calm down," Simon suggested, his voice taking on its usual soothing quality, but to no avail.

Uncle Simon rested his hand on her father's shoulder, but she saw her papa brush it off. He'd never done such a thing before.

"Calm? You want me to be calm when I've found this." Her father's voice raised in anger, no longer the master showman charming an audience.

Papa thrust an object at Uncle Simon who turned to stare at Frank. Whatever was going on? she wondered.

Before anyone could stop him, her papa grabbed Frank by the shirtfront and pulled him so that their noses were almost touching. "You tried to kill Tess!" he shouted at the larger man.

Frank shook his head, pulling away.

The accusation hit Tess with the force of a blow. Frank Larson had wanted her dead. She couldn't believe it. Sure he'd hounded her, followed her, checked up on her, but murder?

Simon intervened. "Philip, this is ridiculous. Frank's been with us for years. We all know he wouldn't hurt Tess."

"Wouldn't he?" Her dear father's voice held a chill that she'd only heard in it once before—seven years ago, when he'd confronted Joel that fateful night.

Turning on his long-time partner, her father shoved the object at him. At this angle she had a clear view of the item. The sight of it caused a wave of sickening dizziness to sweep over her.

The ether bottle from the show.

"Then *you* tell me what Frank was doing with this. I

caught him trying to bury it." Her father ran a hand through his hair, sending it into uncharacteristic disarray. "Dammit all, this switched bottle is what almost killed Tess."

He turned back to Frank, and only Simon's intervention kept him from striking out. Tess stood rock-still at the sidelines, frozen in place with shock.

Frank had been a friend. She'd trusted him many times over in the past. Trusted him with her life. Just as she'd done that night he'd now been accused of switching the ether.

Frank surged forward and denied the accusations. "I wouldn't never try to hurt Tess. I love her." He raised his head in defiance. "And she loves me."

His declaration in her stead released Tess from her dazed state. She stepped forward and crossed to where the trio stood.

"No, Frank. You're wrong. I—"

Fury stiffened his stance and turned his eyes to dark pits of coal. "This is your fault, Fontana. You've turned her against me."

"No, he hasn't. I—"

"Liar!" Frank yelled, lunging for her father.

Simon stepped between the two men, but not before Frank's fist glanced off her father's face.

Her father didn't attack in return. He met Frank's furious stare and said in a low voice, "Pack your things. You're through here. I won't have anyone around who is a danger to Tess."

Frank clenched his hands into fists. "But I—"

"Get out. You're fired."

Tess caught her father's hand in hers, and he glanced at her as if just now realizing she stood near.

"Philip," Simon stepped between them, separating Tess from her father. "You can't mean that. Frank's been with us for years. He's—"

"He's endangered Tess." He reached out and clasped her hand again. "I want him out. Now."

Her father turned away from his partner and led Tess out of the tent.

Behind them, Simon faced Frank. "I'll talk to him. He'll see reason soon; he's upset now. Meanwhile, go see Marlene Boudreaux. She'll give you a job at her place playing the piano until I can do something here."

"Philip, you can't do this—" Simon called to their departing backs.

"I already have."

What else could go wrong today? Tess wondered, afraid that she didn't want to hear the answer.

Zack unfolded the dispatch, nearly ripping it in his haste. He scanned the words of the telegram at first, then slowed with each damning word he read.

Tess and her father were impostors. Their name wasn't Fontana at all.

Jackson Philip Colton. Tess Harper.

Zack swallowed down the anger that rose up, nearly choking him with its fury at the length of her betrayal.

Mrs. Tess Harper.

Clenching his jaw until his teeth ached, he read on, each word cutting him like the blade of a knife.

There was also the little detail of the murder, of her husband. And the fact that her father, Jackson Philip Colton, was wanted for that murder, with his daughter Tess as an accomplice.

Zack crushed the paper into a ball with his fist. Just as she'd crushed his trust in her. She'd played him for a fool.

His heart be damned. Now it was time for justice.

Fifteen

Zack examined his reflection in the room's sole mirror in disgust. The image that stared back at him had the look of a beaten man. He looked like he'd been rode hard and put away wet.

Hellfire, here he was bemoaning fate when Tess was likely the daughter of the man who had murdered David. She was herself in some way responsible for his brother's death. What did he think he was doing?

Thinking had little to do with what had gone on between him and Tess Fontana. He curled his hand into a fist and corrected himself with sharp disgust, "Tess Harper. *Mrs.* Tess Harper."

And she was supposed to have been nothing more to him than a job to be done. Justice to be carried out. Vengeance to be earned.

Zack clenched his teeth together until his jaw throbbed with pain. What had happened to his job, to justice, and to the vengeance he owed for David's death?

How could he have so easily forgotten his responsibility, as well as the training he'd learned the hard way through years of fighting and pursuing outlaws? Even his gut instincts had relinquished their precision under Tempting Tess's charm. Zack called himself ten kinds of a fool.

It was time for cool, unemotional thought and logic. It was long past the time for the foolish thought of love. Whatever he'd felt for Tess had all been a ruse. She'd deceived him pure and simple. She'd set him up yet again, and he'd fallen for it.

"Once a mistake. Twice a fool." He narrowed his eyes. "But never a third time, lady," he vowed.

He turned away from the mirror and his reflection with renewed determination and anger barely held in check. He had to face the facts before him. They appeared as clear and as cold as the reflection in the mirror's surface. She'd most certainly played him for a fool.

Tess could easily have planned the little accident with the ether during the show's magic act. *She* could have made it look like a murder attempt. In fact, she'd been the one to insist it was an attempt—but against her dear father, not her.

He, on the other hand, had fallen for her practiced tears and pretense of worry. Her silver-edged tongue was every bit as glib as her father's experienced sales spiel. The pair of them were masters at conjuring up what they wanted a person to see and ensuring that was precisely what the fool concentrated on. Like a prime fool he'd believed that something had gone wrong on that stage.

The only thing that had gone wrong was his own brain. He'd most definitely been thinking with another part of his body.

And what of last night? Had she set up the attack in the alley? In fact, had it truly been an attack, or rather a carefully acted-out performance for his benefit? He recalled that Tess hadn't actually been harmed by the attacker. No, she'd only received a few tiny nicks while the presumed attacker had been silenced forever by a bullet from Zack's gun.

Another killing to add to her growing number of accomplishments? he questioned.

The only thing he knew for certain was that Tess couldn't have killed the San Francisco businessman Benjamin Thayer last night. She'd been with Zack up until the early hours of the morning. However, that didn't mean she didn't play a part in the man's murder.

What was she, some kind of a schemer, like the black widow spider who killed her mate without any remorse? Or did she have her father do the grisly deed for her?

Zack ran his palm over his face, his nerves ragged and torn by these new revelations. She'd been married, for heaven's sakes, he chided his own sense of right and wrong. Married.

Sure, he'd known when she'd lain with him last night that she hadn't been a virgin. But he'd never expected that she would be. Not a woman in her profession. She was a performer, she traveled from town to town. He'd assumed she was experienced, and he'd accepted it. However, last night she'd seemed almost an innocent.

Innocent, hell, he scoffed. She was about as innocent and shy as a diamondback rattlesnake when disturbed. She wouldn't recognize the word innocent if it stared her in her pretty face. She was likely well-versed in the art of telling lies.

And she'd been lying to him ever since the moment they'd met.

Now it was time to put an end to her lies and her charade. He had a job to do, and he'd damned well do it, too.

Zack strode up to the show's tent with its tattered banner proclaiming "Fontana's Fabulous Medicine Show." Even that proclamation was a lie.

Keeping one hand on the butt of his pistol, he entered the tent only to find it disappointedly empty. He left the tent, bitterness eating at his gut. Refusing to give up, he searched the area for the acclaimed Fontanas. With each step his anger grew and his blood chilled to a temperature lower than the afternoon breeze blowing off the bay.

Wisps of fog began to roll into the city, and he knew he'd better find the Fontanas before those filmy wisps turned into a blanket of gray. He would not let them flee the city. He'd pursue Tess to hell and back if he had to do it.

At last, his eyes caught the bright color of Philip Fontana's renowned crimson cape a matter of ten feet away to his left. He stood talking to a shorter person, the identity concealed by Fontana's back. Zack turned toward the two figures, his booted heels thudding ominously in the hard-packed dirt.

Fontana shifted and the sight of Tess clinging to her father's arm hardened Zack's resolve as nothing else could have done. He tightened his fingers over the hardness of his pistol.

"Mr. Jackson Philip Colton," Zack called out. His voice held a deadly coldness to it that rivaled the incoming bank of damp, icy fog carried on the breeze.

The long-unused name sounded a death knell to Tess. Unable to stop her action, she spun around to face the caller. Her throat closed off, and she curled her fingers tightly together until her fingernails cut into the tender skin of her palm.

Zack Mackinzie stood facing her straight and tall, his stance proclaiming him every inch the lawful Texas Ranger. As the sun peeked out from a cloud, it shone for an instant on the Ranger badge on his chest. The shimmer sent a bone-chilling fear racing through her.

She looked up and detected the slight narrowing of his eyes, followed by the tightening of his hand on his pistol. He took a deadly step forward, and in the next second her world shattered, falling around her in pieces much like the small mirrors sewn on her father's cape.

"Jackson Philip Colton," Zack repeated. "I'm placing you under arrest."

"What for?" her father asked with an outward calm that she knew to be false.

Only one word penetrated the horrible realization that had enveloped Tess's brain.

Arrest.

Zack was arresting her father? No, she had to have misunderstood. An undisputable sense of doom warned her, but she refused to acknowledge it. By doing so, she could give it the power to become real.

She forced herself to listen and make sense out of the tumble of words around her. Surely this was all a mistake. A horrible mistake.

No, she'd heard correctly. Zack was arresting her father for murder. She listened in growing horror as he read off the list of charges against her father.

"For the murder of Joel Harper in Texas."

The sound of her husband's name spoken out loud struck her with the force of a cruel blow. She missed part of Zack's next listing.

"For the murder of David . . ."

Tess bit down on her bottom lip, stopping only when she tasted the copper bitterness of her own blood. Horror and a sense of doom that nothing could have stopped or prevented it held her in place. Her world rocked and tumbled down around her, nearly destroying her in the aftermath of its devastation.

"For the murder of Charlie Foster in Virginia City," Zack continued, his voice seeming to come from a long ways off.

Would this nightmare never draw to an end? she wondered.

She'd failed. She hadn't saved her father at all, she'd cost him his very life. Her gaze met his as the last charge was read in Zack's deep Texas drawl.

"The murder of Benjamin Thayer."

As Zack clasped the handcuffs on her father's wrists, Tess broke free from the shock that had held her in place. She shoved between Zack and her father, determined to stop this. She pushed against Zack's broad chest. The tender lover of only this morning had turned into a cold wall of granite.

"No!" she shouted. "He didn't do it. He didn't murder anyone. You're wrong."

When nothing happened, she caught Zack's forearm. It turned to hardened steel beneath her touch. She refused to let go.

"Zack, listen to me."

The look he turned on her could have frozen hell itself.

Zack spoke in a terse voice. "If you interfere again, I'll have you taken in as well, Mrs. Harper."

Tess fell back a step as if she'd been slapped. Hard.

"Tess, let it be," her father ordered.

When she shook her head in refusal, he added, "For now."

Her throat tightened, closing off all speech as well as breath. She'd do as her father asked for now. But she'd find a way to stop him. No matter what.

Refusing to leave her father's side, Tess accompanied her father and Zack to the jail, but all the while she felt as if she were watching a poorly performed play. Everything had a surreal quality, and she sensed an overwhelming finality to it all.

Nothing more could be done. Her father had used those words to reassure her, but they'd had the opposite effect. Unable to be of any help to her father, and ordered away by the uniformed policeman, she'd returned to the show tent in a daze.

How long had she been standing at the open tent flap? she wondered, releasing her hold on the canvas. Ten minutes, twenty minutes? She had no sensation of time. It seemed to have frozen everything in place.

She felt rather than heard Zack's approach. His very presence reached out to her, striking a chord in her. Then anger at his betrayal overrode every other emotion in that instant.

She whirled on him in a burst of fury and condemnation. "What do you want now? Praise for a job well done?" she asked, sarcasm turning her voice into something foreign to the both of them.

"I have a few questions for you, Mrs. Harper," he responded in kind.

"Don't call me that," Tess shouted, something inside her snapping at his use of the name she'd given up seven long years ago. In fact, she'd given it up that horrible night which had led everything to this new horror.

"What should I call you? The Tempting Tess?" he charged.

She faced him, raising her chin in a show of open defiance and determination. "Call me anything but the other."

"If that's the way you want it," he raised his own chin and added, "Honey."

Tess flinched, but remained silent under his intense scrutiny.

"Tell me, what was last night? A diversion to keep me occupied?"

He ran his gaze down the length of her, but this time there was no sign of desire or tenderness in his look. Contempt reached out, almost touching her. Pain flicked across her like the tails of a whip, cutting and drawing blood.

She remained unmoving under the attack. She refused to let him see how his words wounded. To give in would only encourage more strikes to come. She'd learned that in her long-ago past. Learned it so well, she'd never forget the feel of those blows or the contempt.

Her silence seemed to torment Zack. His face tightened and one hand clenched into a fist.

But he didn't strike out at her with blows from his hand. He used words.

"Or did you think to convince me to turn my back on my responsibility? On honor?" he asked her, his harsh voice ragged now. "But you wouldn't know anything about honor, would you?"

"No. What do you know about all this?" The denial slipped past her frozen lips.

Tears burned behind her eyes, begging to be allowed free. She forced the tears down with a rush of bitterness that stole her breath away.

"I know plenty." His eyes darkened as he stared down at her, only this time not a trace of any passion or tenderness shone through.

"My brother loved you," he accused, his voice bitter. "And because of you, he's dead."

Tess stepped back as if he'd struck her with his closed fist. Her own hand slowly raised to cover her mouth. However, not a sound passed her lips.

Zack couldn't be Joel's brother. He couldn't.

Joel had been an only child—he'd told her that. He'd also confided to her that his mother abandoned him years before when her current lover didn't want a young kid around.

She stared hard into Zack's face, searching for any possible similarity to the man she'd married. She found none.

Summoning up her voice, she spoke so low that she

scarcely heard the denial herself. "No, you are not Joel's brother."

Zack's frown deepened, then turned into puzzlement. "Who the hell are you talking about?"

Tess knew her heart stopped beating. The room tilted around her.

"David." Zack's face showed the pain of a deep loss. "His name was David Mackinzie. Can't you even be bothered to remember the names of your victims?"

It was her turn to be puzzled and confused. She didn't know anyone named David. She swallowed and faced Zack head on. "I never heard the name Mackinzie until I met you," she told him in a low, steady voice.

"Liar."

The single word cut through the air like a whip, and to Tess it felt like she'd been struck with one. It had been sharp, cutting, and stinging to her. Involuntarily she stepped back.

"I don't have enough proof yet to get to the bottom of this and prove your involvement. But, trust me, I will."

He stared down at her for the space of a heartbeat.

"And when I do, I'll be back." He nudged his hat back with his thumb. "That's a promise."

Turning on his heel, he strode off away from the tent, leaving Tess to stare after him. He blamed her for murdering a man she'd never even heard of until today. The irony of it nearly buckled her legs. He'd had nothing to say about her husband. No, this had all been about someone she never even knew.

She drew in a deep, cleansing breath and ordered herself to calm down. She had to grip the edge of the tent to remain standing upright. Her legs shook as they'd never done in the past.

As she watched him walk away with distance-eating strides, her heart beat in a rapid staccato.

Why did Zack Mackinzie have to come along and destroy their lives? He'd used her, arrested Papa, and ultimately broken her heart.

She'd given him her heart last night in those late hours. The same heart she'd kept protected and locked away these past seven years, only to have him stomp it into pieces.

She hated him. She did.

Her eyes burned at her lie. If that were so, then why did her heart still persist in racing the way it did whenever he came around?

She was no young girl with a head full of illusions, but what few she'd had, he'd shattered. He'd destroyed everything she held dear.

Dropping her head onto her arms, she let the sobs break free. They shook her shoulders in the dark emptiness of the tent.

"Damn you, Zack Mackinzie," she whispered in a choked voice.

Tess stared out the hotel room window late the next morning, seeing nothing of the bustling crowd outside. A picture of her father sitting in jail, imprisoned behind bars, filled her mind and her thoughts.

My God, she'd helped to put him there.

The knowledge of her own guilt coursed through her. Shame at her own gullibility nearly brought her to her knees in despair.

"Damn you, Zack Mackinzie," she whispered, her voice hoarse with pain.

How many times since yesterday had she uttered those words?

He'd used her. She shook with the harsh, painful realization. He'd brutally used her and her newborn love for him to destroy her father.

At this moment she thought she hated him.

Her breath jarred to a halt. The realization of her true emotions stopped her cold. She was in love with Zack Mackinzie.

No, she denied it, but the truth stared back at her, condemning her. She'd fallen in love with Texas Ranger Zack Mackinzie.

Tess covered her mouth with her hand as if that action could stop the truth from being. Her fingers were icy cold against her lips. Slowly her body took on the same temperature as it coursed up her arms to her shoulders and on. Inch by painful inch, a coldness seeped through her, chasing out any earlier warmth she'd ever experienced from Zack's loving touch.

The wintry chill engulfing her reached outward to her limbs and inward to her heart. It was not content until it had consumed every part of her being.

Love? No, not love.

She couldn't be in love. She *wouldn't* be in love.

Not ever again.

The hand covering her mouth shook with reaction. She lowered her hand and linked her icy fingers together, needing something to hold on to. Her world was crumbling about her. She needed something to hang onto to keep her from being swept away by the maelstrom of emotions and malevolent memories that threatened her.

She'd been in love once. And look where that had gotten her. She'd been beaten and raped by her own husband.

A frown creased her forehead. She reached up to rub it away, and her fingertips brushed over the scar above her temple. Painful memories followed in its wake.

What she felt for Zack was nothing at all like the feelings she'd had for Joel so many years ago. She knew it was more than merely the passage of time. This was different. Completely different.

A question seared her down to her soul. Had she really and truly loved Joel? Or had he been someone to give her attention when she so desperately needed to feel loved? He most assuredly had used her feelings and needs in order to control her. The question haunted her, leaving her troubled and uncertain. Right now she wasn't certain she could trust her own feelings.

The only thing she could trust was her love for her father, and his for her. Because of her, he sat in jail, likely waiting to be hanged.

Tess stood in a surge of anger. She refused to sit idly by wasting one more moment of time. She'd find some way to rescue her father from this no matter what it took. As a last resort, she'd even find a way to break him out of jail.

She had to find answers. And the place to start would be the traveling medicine show. She'd search every inch of the grounds and every single wagon and tent if she had to, but she'd find something to help her father.

Sixteen

For the first time in her life, the medicine show felt foreign to Tess. Did the reason lie in her own motives for walking the grounds this morning? she wondered.

Oddly, it seemed as if the people about her shunned her, afraid to approach. Perhaps it was just her own distraught state of mind, she told herself. She didn't want even to dare believe the former could be true. These people had practically been her substitute family for the past several years.

How could they even consider acting distant now? How could they not instinctivly know her papa was innocent? How could they not believe in him the way he'd believed in them when each of them had needed for him to do so? The questions chased each other around in her mind. Even her friend Ella seemed to be avoiding her—for she was nowhere around.

Tess told herself to take advantage of the troupe's reluctance to spend time with her. As a matter of fact, for now it suited her purposes, for it meant she could search the medicine show to her heart's content without risk of interference or questions.

In spite of this reasoning, she felt like the worst kind of common criminal sneaking around and searching the show for evidence against someone in the show, even to free her father. If she found anything, it would surely point to someone else in the show's troupe as the murderer, wouldn't it?

Did the true killer hide within the traveling show? Was he or she using her papa's show to conceal their own evil acts?

Zack had told her that the trouble lay within the show. Even the thought of the tall, handsome Texas Ranger brought a sharp pain to her breast.

Unbidden memories of the time they'd spent together swept through her, flooding her mind. And her heart. Her eyes burned and threatened to fill with tears, and she angrily blinked them back into the recesses where they couldn't escape.

However, if anything, the memories grew stronger, bringing clear pictures in their wake. Zack swinging her up into his arms and holding her close . . . Zack lowering his mouth to hers, kissing her until her toes curled . . . Zack standing before her, naked and devastatingly handsome to her.

Always Zack. He filled her mind. And her very heart.

He'd made passionate love to her and stole her heart away. He'd made her feel like she was the most beautiful woman on earth, held her tenderly in his arms, then couldn't wait to use this supposed closeness to get even closer and arrest her father.

He'd ruthlessly used her and betrayed her trust. Her heart ached with a pain such as she'd never experienced before. It nearly drove her to her knees with its sheer intensity.

Thankfully she'd never voiced her emotions to him. However, that was little true comfort. She'd obviously been the only one of them to feel love.

Zack Mackinzie had used her. Nothing more. He hadn't felt a thing for her. Not a thing. His heart had never become involved, not in the slightest bit. Unlike hers, which had been broken surely and completely into tiny jagged pieces.

As much as she hated to even allow his name to enter her mind ever again, she had to admit that Zack was probably right. *Someone* in the show was likely using the traveling show for their own means. And destroying her papa in the process.

She could not allow that to continue. She would not permit it. Determined and charged with new resolve, she set about her task.

An hour later, Tess had circled back to the large canvas tent again. Her secretive search had netted her nothing but a few dusty stains on her skirt. She kicked the dirt beside her feet in a vent of frustration.

She hadn't found a single piece of evidence that would help her father. In fact, she hadn't come upon one thing that was out of the ordinary at the traveling medicine show. Nothing.

Suddenly, that fact in of itself struck her as peculiar. The show's grounds, tents, and wagons had been clean and orderly, if a little dusty. But too orderly.

The thought jolted her, taking her breath away for a moment. The medicine show had never been this tidy in all her years of traveling with it. There always remained a bit of disarray about. Realization followed close on the heels of this thought.

Someone had tidied things up, purposely disposing of any evidence that might point to her papa's innocence. And their guilt.

Tess kicked her foot again, dislodging a clump of dry brown weeds. Her toe stung, throbbing through her slipper. Bending down, she rubbed her aching toe, and bit back her cry of pain.

Tenderly she rested her foot beside the displaced weeds and tested her weight on her foot. A twinge of pain remained, but that was all. She'd done no damage in her burst of anger.

She wiggled her bruised toes, inadvertently digging them into the dirt. Once again her toes struck a hard object. This time she leaned closer, brushing the dead vegetation aside.

A glimmer of sunlight glinted off the glass of a bottle. She reached down to scoop up the probable whiskey bottle with the tips of her fingers. Instead, she withdrew a half-empty bottle of her papa's elixir.

She turned the glass bottle over in her hand, and a trickle of the liquid spilled out from around the ill-fitting cork. Wiping her hand on a the edge of her skirt, she took a closer look at the bottle.

Something wasn't quite right.

The label was rippled and uneven. Her father took great pride in anything he did; he would have destroyed this vial rather than allowed it to be sold in this condition.

She knew without a doubt that this was not one of her father's famed bottles of Fontana's Elixirous Waters. It would look the same to most people, but not to her. This clearly wasn't her papa's bottling and preparation. She knew that for an absolute fact.

A memory jolted through her. Yesterday, in her hotel room, the police captain had told her Mr. Thayer had been poisoned.

Poisoned.

The word jogged her memory again, and she gasped. Zack had used the same word to describe the death of the Virginia City miner.

Gingerly prying the cork loose from the suspicious glass vial, she raised the bottle to her nose and sniffed. The liquid smelled different—not quite the same as her papa's, though she couldn't determine exactly what made it different.

But she'd bet her winnings from any faro game that the mysterious mixture contained a poison.

Despite her curiosity, she knew better than to taste the unknown potion; the dead brown weeds on the ground surrounding the area where she'd found the discarded bottle alluded to the deadly effect of the liquid.

Beyond a doubt, the contents in the false elixir bottle were poison.

"Tess, my dear, what are you doing?"

The sharply worded question coming from behind her nearly made her drop the bottle. She clasped it tightly in her hand and spun around.

"Uncle Simon," she sighed in relief, upon seeing his concerned face and balding head.

She'd been so deeply engrossed in her find of the glass bottle that she'd failed to recognize his voice.

"What, in the name of heaven are you doing wandering around here by yourself with your poor papa locked away in that jail?" He patted her shoulder, dropping his customary kiss on her cheek. "You should be resting and have someone caring for you."

His words brought to mind an image of Zack sitting at her bedside "watching over her" as he'd said. Pain at the recollection of how he'd probably been doing that only to use her engulfed her for an instant, and she shoved away the unwanted picture of him at her bedside.

Simon patted her shoulder again in an obvious gesture of comfort. "You really shouldn't be all alone. Perhaps Marlene—"

"No," she cut him off, then added, "No, thank you, Uncle Simon."

He glanced down at her clenched hands, and a frown creased his face as he noted she held something tightly. "What do you have there?"

"A bottle of elixir—"

Simon leaned forward for a closer look, narrowing his eyes. "That doesn't look like one of ours. Where ever did you find it?"

Tess pointed to the ground beside her. Spotting the patch of dampened soil and dead brown weeds, his frown deepened even more.

"Damn, be careful with that, Tess my dear. It could be poison."

"I'm certain it is," she answered with a hint of excitement in her voice.

"Then perhaps your father was right about Frank Larson after all." Simon paused and stroked his hand across the top of his balding head. "First the accident with that ether, and now you finding this right after your father discharged him. It does arouse my suspicions."

She hadn't thought of Frank's involvement until Uncle Simon mentioned it. Was it the possible answer? But what did Frank hope to gain with this? It didn't make any sense, and she said as much to Simon.

"My dear, he could be doing it to get back at your father. Frank was quite angry that day if you remember," he pointed out to her gently.

Perhaps he was right, she thought. It would answer a lot of questions. But not all of them. She couldn't help feeling that while Frank might be jealous and possess a temper, he wasn't a murderer.

"Do you—"

"Here, let me have that, my dear." Simon reached out to take the bottle from her, a handkerchief clasped around his hand.

"No," she refused.

"You really shouldn't be handling it if it turns out to be a danger. I'll check it for you and see if I can find out what it contains."

Without thinking, Tess tightened her fingers on the bottle. "I'll turn it over to the police myself, and tell them about Frank."

"Are you certain?"

"Yes."

"Very well. Only take care," he warned her, dropping another kiss on her cheek.

Smiling her first real smile of the day, Tess clasped the bottle in her hand and set off for the police, and perhaps her papa's freedom.

As Tess left the grounds, hate-filled eyes focused on her. So she'd found one of the damn bottles, had she? She would ruin everything.

Her snooping and ultimate find could force an unplanned departure from the city. Damn. There was no way to gather up all the money earned so far from the killings without any preparation time. More money was needed fast.

Now because of sweet little Tess's interference another one must die to provide the needed funds.

Eyes narrowed, the lone figure thought on who it would be. With a snap of the fingers the perfect victim came to mind. Mr. Miller had been quite solicitous the other day when assisting with a horse. And he was reputed to be quite wealthy.

Yes, the gentleman would provide enough money if it became necessary to leave the city in a hurry. Too bad he had to die to accomplish that end, but it couldn't be helped now.

The plan, the very same one that had worked numerous times in the past, had been to continue selling him the special elixir at an inflated price. Once he became suspicious, and only then, would he have been given the poisoned elixir.

Always before, very specific instructions had been given with the final bottle of elixir so that the victim would drink it at a noted time—that way the person would die *after* the show had left town, and thus leave them free of suspicion from the foolish local law.

Now all that had changed. This time would incur an added risk.

And Tess Fontana would pay for this added inconvenience.

Yes, she'd pay dearly.

Zack spun around, right hand on his pistol as a young man burst through the doors of the police station.

"Did you hear the news? Mr. Miller's been found dead. Murdered." The young officer made the announcement with an aura of importance.

Recognizing the act as one attributed to excitement and poor judgment, not a danger, Zack eased his hand away from his gun.

"Likely as not poisoned the same as Mr. Thayer, that's what the captain is saying." The young man stood taller with the deed of imparting this newest batch of information to those around him.

A bell sounded in the back of Zack's mind. Poisoned? The same as Thayer?

And the same as David had been.

Zack watched as the young officer straightened the collar of his disheveled uniform and added almost as an afterthought, "Wonder what's going to happen to those fancy prize-winning horses that him and his pretty wife Tammy owned?"

Another man joined the conversation, "Heard talk that he might be going to sell a pair of those trotting horses of his to somebody tied up with that medicine show." He leaned forward and asked in a conspiratorial whisper, "Think it could have been the owner sitting in our jail that was the buyer?"

Zack stiffened at the subtle reference to Philip Fontana. Jackson Philip Colton, he corrected himself. No, he was certain Tess's father wasn't a man who knew horse flesh. The telegram had said he used to be a doctor once.

Rubbing his jaw, deep in thought, Zack wondered at this new information. If the livery owner had been killed and someone in the show had wanted those horses bad enough to kill for them—

He jerked up his thoughts. That someone couldn't be Tess's father. At this very moment he was sitting behind bars. Not even a master magician could have accomplished the feat of murdering someone from there. It looked as if he might well be as innocent as Tess had declared.

The thought of her sent a shaft of pain ripping through him. She'd deceived him, hidden her past from him. Hellfire, she'd hidden her marriage from him, for heaven's sake.

That was the part that hurt the most—her deception. A certainty that she'd been winding her way into his heart solely so she could mislead him and protect her father ate at his gut.

He tightened his jaw, thinking of her, picturing her lying in his arms. Hellfire, in spite of everything, he still wanted her with a hunger that shocked him. His mind kept returning to memories of her silken skin and honey-sweet lips.

He called himself ten kinds of a fool. Hadn't the Tempting Tess misled him before in Virginia City? The cuts and bruises earned in that fight hadn't hurt nearly as much as the pain she'd inflicted on him with her lies and duplicity.

A small voice insisted that she was protecting her father, but that didn't lessen the pain a bit. In spite of what she'd tried to do to stop him from doing his job, he had done it. He'd arrested her father.

How she must hate him for that. And she'd hate him even more, in fact never be able to forgive him, if he were as innocent as she dared claim.

Questions coursed through his mind. This latest killing could change everything. With Fontana behind bars, who had poisoned this latest victim?

He owed both himself and Tess answers. Maybe those answers lay silent with the latest murder victim.

"Take me to the murder site," Zack stepped forward and ordered the young officer.

"Sir, I—"

One look at the badge and the set expression on Zack's face stopped any argument the man might have had.

"Yes, sir. This way."

Minutes later, Zack stood in another alley over the body. The man lay flat on his back, his dark Stetson pulled low over his face. Dead.

Bending down, Zack nudged the man's black hat aside with his thumb and recognized the victim immediately. It was a prominent San Francisco businessman, owner of the largest livery in the city and some of the best prize-winning trotting horses in the area—Mr. Denny Miller.

They'd met days ago, he recalled, when he'd stabled his own mount at Mr. Miller's famed establishment. He'd liked the man instantly. Now his gut tightened into a knot at the senseless killing of such a fine man.

Bending down, Zack checked the man's body for any clues. His pockets had been picked clean. However, Zack's instincts told him this had been no simple act of robbery gone wrong.

Sure enough, when he turned the body over, a bright,

shiny token lay on the ground beneath the man's shoulder. He knew what the inscription would read even before he picked up the brass piece. It was identical to the one he carried in his pocket. The one David had died holding tightly in his fist.

Then Zack spotted something else. To the side of the medicine show token, resting on its side, lay an empty bottle of elixir. The slightly crooked label clearly read "Fontana's Elixirous Waters."

He'd be willing to place a bet that the elixir contained a poison. A very deadly one from the looks of Mr. Miller's stiff body.

Hadn't poison been what killed David? That's what the local doctor had proclaimed, and why the law had listed his death as a murder. Slowly, the pieces fell into place. Somehow, Zack knew he held the same murderous potion in his own hand that had killed his brother David.

If the killer hadn't been the beautiful, blond Tess with eyes the color of Texas bluebells, or her charming father, then who did that leave? The question ate at his gut.

He damned well intended to find out.

Excitement coursed through Tess's veins as she walked along the street leaving the medicine show. She wanted to shout for joy. She wanted to sing out the wonderful news. Tightening her fingers around the glass bottle, she smiled widely, not caring who saw it. She had found the evidence needed to free her father.

She took no notice of anyone around her. All her thoughts were caught up with securing her papa's release from the murder charges.

The thud of footfalls nearby failed to give her pause. She hugged her good news to herself much as a child wishing to savor a new and wonderful treat for a time. The sound of a rustling noise close by suddenly gave her cause to glance about her. The area surrounding her looked strangely unfamiliar.

A chill of unease crept up her spine like a finger of fog rolling in from the bay to blanket the city bringing danger. She stopped her steps suddenly and looked around. Where was she?

An appalling realization tugged at her courage, trying to steal it away from her. She was lost.

Too deep in thought about her papa's near release, she hadn't been paying a whit's attention to where her steps had taken her. She'd wandered off her usual path from the grounds surrounding the show. In fact, she was practically certain that the police station was nowhere near where she now stood.

Fear began to lap at her reserve of courage. She tried swallowing down the feeling, but the apprehension continued to grow with each breath she took.

Nervous, and now overly aware of her surroundings, Tess started walking again. She hadn't the slightest idea where she was going, but anything was better than standing frozen in place like a lost little lamb.

She had the horrible premonition that lost little lambs tended to be led away to slaughter. A shiver raced down her back at the thought, and chill bumps broke out on her arms beneath her sleeves.

She might well be lost, but she was far from a little lamb. Why she—

A thud from nearby sent her increasing her pace. Her heart raced right along in time, and she had to forcibly slow herself to keep from running. It would do utterly no good to panic.

Instead, she would continue on this way, and soon she'd—

A sound from behind her caused her to whirl around just in time to see a man reaching out for her. Screaming as loud as her lungs would allow, Tess dodged his outstretched arm. He went down to his knees as he made another grab for her and missed.

Screaming again, hoping for help, she spun around. Right into the second man.

He swore at her and snatched her wrist tightly before she could escape his shackling hold. Yanking her up against his chest, he pinned her arms at her sides. He laughed coarsely at his partner who was only now stumbling to his feet. His sour breath nearly gagged her.

Panic threatened to overwhelm her. This couldn't be happening. But it was, and she knew with absolute certainty that she wasn't a hapless victim.

These two men had been sent after her. They'd likely been stalking her for some time, accounting for the footsteps and rustling sounds that had alerted her too late to the danger.

Well, she wouldn't go down without putting up a fight. A damned good one.

Could she succeed? There was the smallest possibility that she might catch the two men off guard. If so, it would at least give her a chance to escape.

Might she be able to fight her way free? She could well get herself killed if she tried and failed. But she knew these men's plans and those of whomever had sent them after her didn't include an invitation to tea. She had to at least make an attempt to—

Before she could give herself the time or opportunity to change her mind, she sucked in a deep breath, then kicked back with all her might at the man holding her. Her heel struck the shin bone of her kidnapper with a resounding and satisfying thud.

His howl of pain followed, and she didn't even try to hold back her smile. She broke free from the man's weakened hold and, lowering her head, rammed herself into the second man's paunchy stomach. His angry yowl nearly rattled her teeth.

"Get her!" one man yelled the order. "The boss said not to come back without her."

"You get her. I'm not coming within arm's reach of her unless it's to kill her."

Tess caught up her skirts and ran as if for her very life. For she knew it was likely the truth. She'd been correct in assuming that these two men had been sent after her.

A snarl of rage alerted her to their pursuit, and she put all she had into a burst of speed. Footfalls pounded the ground behind her, reechoing the pounding of her own racing heart.

With each step, pain jabbed at her left side, but she forced herself on, pushing for even more speed. She swore she could feel the heat of the man's sour breath on her neck.

Suddenly, she was caught from behind. Her kidnapper slammed against her, shoving her to the ground. She hit the dirt, unable to move for a moment, the wind knocked out of her.

The man sat up, then yanked her to her feet in front of him. This time he held to her so tightly that Tess knew he'd leave bruises. If she lived to see them.

Tess opened her mouth and screamed again, hoping against hope that someone would hear her cries and come to her aid.

"Shut her up, will ya." The other man stepped back, rubbing his stomach.

A thick hand covered her mouth in answer. Tess opened her lips and tried to bite the man's palm, but he shifted his hand. A stream of swearing followed, and he cuffed her against her left ear with his other hand.

Pain shot bright sparks of color behind her eyes, and Tess had to fight off the unconsciousness that threatened to overwhelm her, taking her down into a dark pit. She wouldn't give in. She wouldn't. She'd fight them with her last breath.

"Here. Use this."

A dirty rag with a strong, pungent odor was shoved against her face. She fought not to breathe in the vapors, but eventually she had no choice as her lungs burned for need of air.

The scented vapor penetrated her defiance, enveloping her senses in a hazy fog of blackness. She fought to swim up out of the swirling mist surrounding her, and knew she was losing.

The heavy mist was dragging her down . . . down . . . down. Ever deeper into the terrifying black sea of oblivion.

Seventeen

"Welcome to your new home, my dear girl."

The sound of the familiar, sugar-laced voice spun Tess away from the second-floor, iron-barred window.

"Ohhh, beautiful view, isn't it?" Marlene asked her, gesturing to the bright moonlit night.

Tess clenched her hands into fists. She hated being locked in any place. It always caused chill bumps to break out on her arms.

Facing the other woman, she tried to reason with her. "You have to let me out of here. You cannot keep me a prisoner—"

"Oh, no, you're not a prisoner, my dear girl." Marlene took a step backward, bringing her nearer to the doorway. "You're here for safekeeping. And I could never go against dear Sy's wishes." She batted her eyes in the coy gesture that nearly turned Tess's queasy stomach.

"Why don't you lay down and rest," Marlene advised. "You won't be disturbed." She smiled, then added, "Tonight."

With that parting shot, she stepped back out the door. Tess heard the lock click into place after her.

The old, familiar sound overtook all anger Tess felt. Her mind regressed to a smaller room, seven years ago. Joel had locked her in that last night he'd nearly succeeded in beating her to death. She brushed her fingertip over the scar above her temple.

Memories came flooding back in a rampage. The horror of the past held her firmly rooted in place. Her body refused even the most basic commands. She could not have moved an arm or a leg if her very life depended on that action.

Realization of what the future had planned for her brought back all the old hurts she'd received at the hands of Joel Harper. The haunting of the past warred with the new, stronger Tess, and lost.

Zack's tender lovemaking had set her free. She now refused to take that step backward into the person she'd been before Zack Mackinzie walked into her life. No one could force that upon her, no matter what.

"Thank you, Zack," she whispered to the walls of the empty room.

She absolutely refused to simply stand by and allow herself to be returned to the past where rape and beatings were common occurrences. She'd been set free, and it was her choice now.

In that instant, Tess realized with startling clarity that she had fully escaped Joel's control and the hold he'd retained on her and her emotions over the years. That awareness released her body as well. Alive or dead, she would not surrender to that kind of sick need to control again.

That provided her with the impetus she needed to move into action. It took her a full thirty minutes or more to pry and jiggle and finally release the mechanism holding the door locked.

It seemed that some of her papa's magic feats worked in the world outside the stage as well, she mused, smiling at her accomplishment.

Slipping out the door, Tess cautiously made her way

to the staircase. Perhaps she could manage to sneak out the back door or a window.

No one noticed her as she crept down the stairs. Any of the groping couples climbing the stairs to the locked rooms above had their attentions focused elsewhere. Tess reached the first floor without any hinderance.

Her escape was short-lived. A full-fledged party appeared to be going on in the downstairs rooms. It took Tess scarcely a minute to realize that this was no party she was observing. It was a Friday night at a very accommodating brothel.

She tried to blend in and out of the rooms as much as possible as she made her way to the back of the small, narrow house. Her efforts were for nothing—the back door was barred with thick iron bars that even her papa couldn't escape through with his best magic tricks.

Slowly she learned that escape from the first floor was next to impossible. Iron bars covered each and every glass-paned window, the only exception being the brightly patterned stained-glass window above the front door. And guards were posted at that door and window.

On first glance, they didn't appear to be guards, but Tess recognized them as the two men who had been sent by their "boss" to kidnap her and deliver her here to the inside of the brothel. They were guards all right.

What she wouldn't give for the appearance of a certain Texas Ranger about now, she thought with a wry smile. She'd show Zack and his persistent rescuing a welcome that would likely knock him off his booted feet.

Tess spotted the pristine white of Marlene's hair bow across the room. Consternation. The owner of the brothel was the very last person she wanted to encounter right now.

She quickly turned and slipped into the next room. Velvet-covered sofas sat strategically placed on thinning carpets. She absently noted it was a drawing room at one time. The familiar chords from a piano drew her gaze, and she whirled about and met the bold stare of Frank Larson. Tess knew her mouth hung open, but for the life of her she couldn't seem to stop it. Frank was working here? It certainly appeared so.

Seeing her chance, she made a beeline straight for him. "Frank—"

"You shouldn't be down here," he told her.

"I shouldn't be here at all," she snapped back.

He threw a concerned glance behind him at her raised voice and continued playing his music.

"Frank—"

"Shh," he ordered, a finger to his lips, missing a key.

"Frank," she persisted, "You've got to help me—"

"I can't."

"You mean you won't," she fired back.

"It'll work out, Tess. I'll take care of you." He sent her an embarrassed smile of reassurance.

"You'll what?" She swung her arm in an arc. "Look around you. I'm not here by choice. And I certainly wasn't brought here to be the cook." She pointed out the facts to him. "What does that leave?"

"Tess!" he hissed a warning, nodding his head toward the far corner of the room.

Glancing back over her shoulder, Tess spotted the bright, brassy curls of Marlene.

"Consternation." She caught up her skirts and slipped out of the room.

Ducking down, Tess scurried into the next room. A portly gentleman greeted her with a welcoming smile. Another complication she didn't need right now either, she thought in derision.

Tess batted her eyes at the man, and as he drew nearer, she drew in a breath and faked a large sneeze directly at him. Rubbing her hand across her mouth, she smiled weakly, then screwed up her face again as if another sneeze were coming.

The prospective patron turned and hurried in the opposite direction as fast as his fat little legs and abundant girth could take him.

Tess bit back her giggle. One down. She glanced about the room and stifled the groan that sprang to her lips. One down, she repeated her thought, and twenty to go.

Keeping out of someone's bed this night was not going to be an easy task. Word of a new girl in the house would travel like a wildfire in the dry countryside.

Tess forced herself to remain calm. She needed each and every one of her wits about her tonight. And she intended to use any and every thing she could drag up. The only way she was going back up those stairs to the bedrooms above was by armed force.

That came to pass sooner than Tess ever could have anticipated.

A tall, skinny man with a pockmarked face spotted her from across the room. Grinning, he bore down on her with all the finesse of a Southern Pacific freight train coming down the mountains.

Dodging his determined approach, Tess made her way around the room, keeping to within a few feet of the walls. She eased around furniture and people, not disturbing either. After ten minutes of pursuit, the man either gave up or found an easier and more willing participant, for she could no longer see him behind her.

Tess sighed in relief and turned back around. She was brought up short by a woman standing directly in her path: Marlene Boudreaux.

Dressed in all the splendor she could manage, the brothel owner wore the same gaudy bright pink-and-black gown as she'd flaunted in Virginia City. Her rouged cheeks stood out starkly, even brighter than the pink of her daring bodice, attesting to her fury.

"You!" she hissed at Tess.

Easing her foot back, Tess prepared to turn and attempt an escape, but a large hand on her forearm stopped her. Another hand circled her other arm. She glanced up to see both of the brothel guards flanking her.

Consternation. Damn!

"Please escort the lady to her room, gentlemen," Marlene requested in a haughty tone worthy of the finest drawing room.

Tess opened her mouth, but her hostess's next words stopped her in mid-breath.

"You make one sound and it will be your last, no matter that Sy wants you kept alive." A bitter smile fastened on her painted lips.

Marlene waved her arm in a sweeping gesture encompassing the gaudy room. "Besides, dear girl, no one here would give a damn if you screamed your lungs out. You might as well prepare yourself to 'enjoy' your stay here."

"I'll never work for you," Tess insisted.

"Oh, but dear girl, you won't be receiving pay for any of your . . . efforts, shall we call it. I offered you a job once, and you turned me down. Never again. Now I own you."

"You won't get away—"

"Save your breath pointing out that I won't get away with it. For you see, my dear girl, I already have." She laid her hand on the décolletage of her bodice. "No one cares what happens to any of the girls once they arrive in one of these establishments."

The two men tightened their hold on her arms as if sending her a silent warning.

"Gentlemen." Marlene jerked her head in the direction of the staircase. "Help the dear girl to her room.

And one of you had better stay to see she doesn't get too lonely. Or get into too much trouble."

Tess saw Frank standing at the door. She sent him an imploring look, but he answered with a sad shake of his head, then ducked back out of sight.

The two men hauled Tess up the stairs in spite of the kicks she managed to land on their unprotected legs. It didn't do a bit of good. They didn't stop until they had reached the top of the third floor.

Dragging her down the hallway, one of the men swung open the door of a tiny attic room. Tess balked at entering and tried one more attempt at escape. Kicking out at the first man's legs, she shoved the second man in the opposite direction, then ducked and started to run.

Her feet came up off the flooring, and she shrieked in surprise. Spinning her about, the men shoved her inside the room and slammed the door behind her.

The sound of a chair being dragged across the floor outside the door confirmed her fear that she did indeed have a guard posted to keep her inside the tiny room. She rubbed at her sore, bruised toe.

Furious at Marlene, Uncle Simon, and her own inability to escape, Tess began to pace the room checking for any avenue of escape. The moonlight outside the single window revealed a sheer drop down.

She spun away from the window and circled the room. Within minutes she felt as if the walls were closing in on her. She forced herself to stop and draw in several deep, calming breaths.

Resuming her pacing at an even, practiced step, Tess focused all her energies on devising a way out. She'd be damned if she'd simply lay down and take a nap at this time. No, she'd think this through clearly and then find some way out.

She ran the events of the past day over in her mind, wondering at how she could have been so foolish. She might as well be here by her own hand. It had been through her own refusal to see the truth that she'd gotten herself into this situation.

Simon had been the "boss" her kidnappers had referred to. And he'd done it to keep her quiet. Here, in a common brothel, no one would listen to her preposterous tale of being kidnapped, of having the proof of a murder plot. No, anyone she told this to would merely assume she'd had too much opium and was delirious.

What a fool she'd been not to see Simon, or "Sy" as Marlene called him with endearment in her sugary voice, for what he was sooner. She slammed her fist against the iron bars on the window. A fine layer of powder arose, then resettled.

She'd excused so many odd things Simon had said or done because he was her papa's friend and business partner. He was practically family. She'd assumed Simon would act with the same integrity as her father. Wrong.

At the word integrity, a mental picture of Zack Mackinzie sprang unbidden to mind. She caught hold of the image and held to it for the moment. What she wouldn't give to have his help right now.

However, she didn't have his help or anyone else's. And she had no one to depend on but herself.

Raising her chin, she crossed back to the window. She noted that the bars seemed thinner than those on the second floor. Added to this as a bonus, they were spaced further apart, too. She pressed against the iron bar nearest the right side, and it gave ever so slightly beneath her force. A triumphant smile lit her face. Perhaps her luck was turning around.

Shoving aside the tattered striped curtain, she peered out the cracked glass. It remained a straight drop down, and no trees or branches in sight. Ignoring that, she set to work on the bars.

She'd get out of here if it killed her.

* * *

The lone figure swore and paced the filthy, deserted alley, early for the assigned rendezvous.

Fists were clenched tightly into pockets. Everything was falling apart. All the carefully laid and enacted plans had gone awry.

The Texas Ranger had learned the truth of Philip Fontana's true identity, and even that had failed to make Philip pay. He would surely be set free from jail. He should have hung.

This last killing while netting the necessary funds had fallen far short of the amount hoped to gain.

But there remained one last chance. Tess's mouth had been shut. She would tell no one about what she'd stumbled onto. At least no one worth telling. No one who would have the slightest interest in aiding her or listening.

At this very moment, sweet innocent Tess was spending her time locked in a brothel.

Harsh laughter cut through the silence, sending a startled night creature into a scampered flight.

This time Tess wouldn't be so fortunate. She'd spend the remainder of her days inside that brothel, servicing any man who'd pay for her.

Laughter rang out, gurgling up from the figure's chest.

As an added bonus, her disappearance without a trace would destroy Philip Fontana. Not all was lost.

Revenge did indeed taste sweet.

Zack's mood was far from sweet. It worsened with every barrier he ran into in his attempt to find Tess.

First, he'd tried her hotel room, only to receive a note

telling him that she didn't want to see him ever again under any condition.

Second, he'd tracked her here to the medicine show grounds, only to meet up with a hostile Ella, who insisted that Tess wasn't there. She'd even ordered him off the grounds with all the fury of a mother hen protecting her brood.

The final insult came when Simon White, her father's partner, spotted him. The paunchy balding man bore down on him with pompous indignation.

"Haven't you done enough harm here, Ranger?" Simon sneered.

Zack answered the provoking question with a cool glare. "I've come to speak to Tess."

The other man looked away. "She won't see you."

"I want to hear that from her lips, if you don't mind," Zack told him, anger held in check.

"I do mind. And so does she. Damn, you arrested her father. What do you expect from her?"

The question took Zack aback for a moment.

"I apologize," Simon said with a sigh. "This is hard on all of us. Philip has his faults, of course. But Tess could never see them. She always thought her father could do no wrong. No matter what."

"I—"

Simon shook his head sadly. "She's left orders that she will not see you. Maybe it would be better if you forgot about talking to her."

Like hell. Zack had no such intention, but he refrained from telling the man so. He'd leave all right, but he would talk to Tess. He had some pointed questions for her, and she would have answers.

"Tell her I'll be back," Zack informed him, then turned on his heel and strode away.

Once back in his room, Zack jerked off his hat and tossed it onto the bed. Damn. Tess wouldn't even listen to what he had to say. He'd had his reasons—good ones—for arresting her father. Why wouldn't she even listen to reason? But no, she'd staunchly refused to even give him the chance to speak to her.

"Hellfire," he swore to the empty room.

After all, she'd been the one deceiving him. He'd never hidden who or what he was from her.

He drew his hand over his face and released a ragged breath. Had he really and truthfully expected her to calmly sit down and hear him out?

No, in truth he may have hoped for that outcome, but he hadn't expected things to be that easy with Tess. That didn't sound much like the Tess he knew. And loved.

At the realization of where his thoughts had taken him, he strode to the bed and grabbed up his hat. Settling it on his head, he turned to the door with a determined stride. He knew exactly where he was going.

Tess would listen to what he had to say. One way or another. Even if he had to kiss her into silence first.

Zack's second arrival at the show's grounds was met with open hostility by the troupe. Ignoring their attitude, he headed for the wagon where Tess should be "resting," as one person had told him.

However, once he reached his destination, Tess wasn't there. A rustle from a nearby bush had him reaching for his pistol.

"Hey, lawman," Frank called in a low tone. "I'm not armed."

As Zack turned, one hand on his gun, the former show worker motioned to him. Not trusting the man and keeping his hand on his gun, Zack followed to where the man huddled against the side of the wagon.

"You care about Tess?"

The other man's question caught him off guard, and Zack hesitated in answering.

"Well, do you?"

Zack took note of the man's furtive attitude and unease. "Yes, I care for her," he finally answered, waiting for a reaction.

"Good." Frank nodded his head up and down vigorously. "Then you'll help her."

Zack stiffened at the statement. Every hair at the back of his neck prickled with warning. "Why does Tess need help?" he asked in deliberately measured tones.

"Because she's locked away in a brothel."

Frank fired an uneasy glance over his shoulder and missed the stunned look on Zack's face. Tess? In a brothel?

"It's the one belonging to Simon's friend Marlene Boudreaux." Frank recited the address. He turned away again to glance around the area.

"Simon promised me she'd be mine, but I couldn't go through with it. I couldn't. Even if I could have saved her for myself, I know she'd hate me."

So, Simon White had been lying when he'd said Tess refused to see him. He turned his attention back to the other man.

When he met Zack's gaze, his own was filled with the pain of loss. "I couldn't ever stand having her hate me. Tell her that, will you? I got to get out of here fast or I'm a dead man."

"Why—"

Ducking alongside the wagon, Frank raced for the next shelter of shadows. Zack let him go. If he pursued the man, he'd lose valuable time. And Tess might not have that time.

Zack didn't know if Frank's words had been true or a well-laid trap. His words held the ring of truth, but that could be faked just as well as fact.

An irritating uneasiness nagged at him. Every time he'd rescued Tess in the past, he'd ended up with more bruises than thanks.

Pulling out his pocket watch, he read the time. At this late hour, the night would be in full swing at the local brothels. His best chance would be to find a back door, or a side entrance, and slip in unnoticed.

As a precaution, he took a moment to check over his pistol before he reholstered it. He felt like some knight errant going off to rescue his lady from the tower. He only hoped they both survived the rescue in one piece.

One more twist was all it needed, Tess assured herself for the fifth time. The stubborn bar had refused to give the last bit. Putting all her strength into it, she yanked on the iron bar.

The rod gave way, sending her tumbling over backward onto her backside. The metal piece sailed out of her hands to land against the far wall with a resounding whack.

Pushing herself to her feet, Tess raced for the window. The opening now measured approximately a foot—thankfully enough for her to slip through. Pausing, she grabbed hold of the trail of sheets she'd stripped from the bed and tied together. She tossed them through the opening first.

Wiggling her body through the narrow opening between the side of the window and the remaining bars, she found herself thankful that God hadn't seen fit to overendow her figure.

She kept a tight hold on the makeshift rope of sheets, praying they wouldn't choose this particular moment to rip. As quickly as possible she began to shimmy down the rope.

From above she heard the distinct sound of Marlene's laughter, followed by the jangle of a key in the lock.

"How are you enjoying your . . ." Marlene's voice trailed to a halt.

A scream rent the air, followed by a stream of very colorful phrases that Tess had rarely heard in her life, even from the men working at the show. It gave her added incentive to flee.

Above her, Marlene grabbed the rope with both hands. She yanked on it, trying to pull it back through the window. "No!" she shrieked.

The sheet rope swung haphazardly, and Tess put out a foot against the building to try to steady her descent. Her toe caught on a loose board nailed to the side of the building. As she pulled back, her shoe dislodged, falling free.

"Consternation!" Tess cried out as she continued climbing downward.

The ruckus from above alerted Zack a mere instant before a lightweight object bounced off his shoulder. He drew his gun as he looked up. What he saw nearly scared the breath right out of him.

Tess hung suspended from the building, clinging to a tattered rope of some sort that was about to run out over ten feet from the ground.

An enraged screech jerked his attention up higher. A woman had her head poked out the window and was yanking on the makeshift rope. She was either trying to pull Tess back up or dislodge her.

"Tess!" he called out.

Above him, he could see her stop as if frozen in time for an instant. Then she craned her neck and, looking down, called back, "Zack?"

"Yup. Let go and I'll catch you."

When she didn't move for the space of a heartbeat,

he felt his blood turn cold with fear for her safety. He yelled, "Let go. Now."

She did.

Tess tumbled downward toward the ground and Zack, colliding into him with enough force to knock them both flat on the ground.

"Hellfire," Zack muttered.

"Consternation," Tess responded.

Eighteen

Tess sat up, straightened her skirts, and realized that she was sitting smack in the center of Zack's lap. He let out a derisive groan.

"Honey, don't you have any other way of making an entrance when I'm around?" His low drawl tickled her ear and did strange things to the rest of her body as well.

She resisted the almost overwhelming impulse to throw her arms around him and never let go. Instead, she forced herself to jokingly ask, "Have you ever thought of changing jobs and doing this professionally, say, in a traveling show?" She tossed him a sassy grin.

"Now is not the time or place to get into my opinion of that." This time his voice held no hint of a smile.

He gently eased Tess off his lap, helping push her to her feet, then followed her up. Gazing down at her, his eyes softened, and he gripped her shoulders with both his hands.

"Are you all right?" he asked, concern turning his low drawl to a husky whisper.

"I think so—"

A volley of yells from around the front of the building jerked them away from each other. The sounds alerted them to the fact that Marlene's guards were right on their trail. And getting closer.

"Hellfire," Zack muttered.

"The guards are armed," Tess told him.

Grabbing her hand, he pulled her around the concealing dark of the corner of the building away from the oncoming footsteps. At the same time his other hand slid down toward his gun belt.

"Zack, I—"

"Shh." Releasing her hand, he lightly pressed his fingertips against her lips.

Focusing his energies on the danger that surely lay ahead, he reached to draw his gun. His hand came up empty. The pistol wasn't in his holster. Damn.

He couldn't believe he'd lost his gun. A Ranger never gave up his gun. Well, he hadn't exactly given it up, he reminded himself. It had likely been knocked clear to kingdom come when Tess landed atop him.

Gunfire erupted from behind them, and Zack grabbed Tess and shoved her up against the wall. He covered her body with his own. To hell with his gun; there was no way he could chance searching for his pistol now. He had to get Tess to safety.

"Hellfire, we're going to have to run for it," he told her.

"Why don't you shoot back at them?" She asked the obvious question.

Zack gritted his teeth before he answered in a tight voice, "Because I lost my gun."

"Oh."

He made the mistake of glancing down at her. Her face was pale, her hair a tumble of curls, pure molten gold, rippling over her shoulders. But it was her eyes that held him fast. Fear turned their color to the softest shade of blue he'd ever witnessed, her pupils wide, dark spots of fright.

"We'll be all right."

"But their guns—"

"We'll just have to run faster." He forced himself to

smile down at her in reassurance when smiling was the last thing he felt like doing.

The next instant, he caught hold of her wrist. "Now. Run," he ordered.

He took off at an all-out run, dragging her behind him. The ominous sound of bullets smacking into the wall behind them spurred them on. As soon as they reached the end of the next alleyway, Zack took a sharp left turn to lose their gun-happy pursuers, nearly knocking Tess over in the process.

He could have sworn that he heard her mutter, "Hellfire."

Determined to get them both out of this alive, he forced her onward, alternately encouraging and challenging her to keep up, but never once releasing his unyielding hold on her wrist. The men wouldn't get her without going through him first.

After what seemed an endless zigzag of running and dodging up and down different alleys and streets, at last they reached a safe distance from the brothel and a better area of the city. Only then did Zack slow their race to a fast walk.

"I'll drop you off at the police station," he said in a rush of breath.

Tess jerked to a halt. Turning on him, she asked in disbelief, her voice jerky and interspersed with pants for breath, "You're . . . arresting . . . me?"

Before he could answer her ridiculous question, she rushed on, "For being kidnapped and locked in a brothel. I might add that I wasn't exactly a willing participant in all this." She flung her hands up, her voice rising with each word. "Zack Mackinzie, you have the nerve of a jackass. Why, I—"

Zack could think of only one way to quickly silence her. He ducked his head toward her and covered her lips with his. Encircling her body with his arms, he drew her up against his chest.

Damn, but she felt good in his arms. It was good to hold her again.

Tess sputtered against his mouth a moment before falling silent. Then, surrendering to his embrace, she locked her arms around his neck and held tight. She returned his kiss with a fervor that sent his every sense scattering into the breeze.

Only the disturbing bark of a nearby dog brought Zack back to his senses and stopped him from lowering her to the ground right there. She'd fired his blood like no other woman had ever come close to doing. He shook his head. All she'd done was return his kiss. And it had sent his very senses scattering like a randy cowhand who'd been on the range too long.

Setting her back from him, Zack resisted the impulse to gather her close again. All it took was one glance at the expression of equal desire he saw on Tess's face and his blood was fired again, this time even hotter than before.

He took a step back from her, hoping that the additional distance would help. It didn't. The thought crossed his mind that it might well take the distance of the width of the bay to accomplish that goal.

He dared another glance at her face and finally had his breathing under enough control to speak.

"I was planning to take you there for safety."

"Oh."

A long silence fell between them.

"Did I thank you for rescuing me?" Tess asked, as if suddenly remembering it.

"No." A low chuckle rumbled in the back of Zack's throat.

"Oh." She repeated the single-word response again, clasping her hands in front of her.

Zack grinned at her. "Actually you were doing a darn fine job of rescuing yourself when I arrived. But if you want to, you can thank me later." He winked.

Tess's head snapped up and she stared at him a moment before a soft tinkle of laughter escaped from her lips. The sound reminded him of a beautiful wind chime he'd heard once.

"Come on." He caught her hand in his.

"Where are you taking me?" She pulled back slightly, demanding an answer.

Zack sighed, and it was a ragged sound in the splash of moonlight that lit their way. Why couldn't she just go along with this? But then, when had Tess ever been meek and malleable?

A little question tugged at him. Would he really want her that way?

"I'm not moving another inch until I know," she announced.

Zack faced her. "To my room."

"Not to jail?" she asked, eyeing him closely for any trickery.

A smile pulled at his lips. "Not to jail," he answered. "You'll likely be just as safe in my room. Only don't open the door to anyone while I'm gone."

Tess jerked her hand from his. "You're going to take me there and then leave me?"

Zack ground his teeth together. This woman could try his patience like no one ever had in all his life. Not even any of the outlaws he'd pursued in his career had tested him the way she dared to do.

He took an authoritative step toward her. Tess stood her ground.

Looking down into her face, he explained in low, even tones. "That's exactly what I'm going to do. First, I'll see that you're safe, then I'll do my job and apprehend Simon and Marlene."

He watched a quick flash of pain cross her face. "Simon had me kidnapped." She offered the information in a low, strained voice. "I still find it hard to believe he could do that to me. He'd been Papa's friend and partner for years."

"The desire for money can do strange things to people, honey."

Zack brushed his knuckles across her cheek, and she leaned into his touch for a moment.

"But that doesn't stop betrayal from hurting," she whispered the admission.

He tensed at her words. That's the way he'd felt about her. Once.

Now, he wasn't certain exactly what he felt. Nearly losing her this night had sent everything into a tailspin for him.

"I'll bring them in. Both of them," Zack vowed to her.

"I never did see what Uncle Simon saw in her." Tess shook her head in obvious disbelief. "They seemed so ill-suited."

Clasping Tess's small hand in his again, he added, "Ready?"

"Yes." Her answer was low and held a trace of hesitation.

Zack knew the track her mind had taken without even bothering to ask her. He'd better put a stop to that path right now.

"You're not coming with me after them," he announced.

His softly drawled words stopped her in mid-thought.

"But, I want to—"

"No."

"But—"

"It's either my way or the jail. For your own safety."

He heard her sigh before she grudgingly gave in. "All right."

The remaining distance to his room was walked in terse silence. He could practically feel Tess's rebellion still simmering between them. However, she had given her agreement, and something told him that she was the kind of woman who would honor that.

Once inside the room, he closed the door and crossed to the bureau. Pulling open the second drawer, he withdrew his extra pistol. Checking it, he shoved it into his empty holster.

He turned to find Tess watching him closely.

"Lock the door behind me, and don't let anyone else in. Not anyone. Understand?"

He saw her swallow, then nip at her lower lip before she spoke. "Zack?"

"Yes?" He waited.

"Be careful." Her voice broke on the request.

In two steps he'd swept her into his arms. The parting kiss between them was sweet, sweeter than any they'd shared before.

How he hated to leave her. But she wouldn't be safe until Simon and Marlene were apprehended. Drawing in a ragged breath, he ended the kiss and set her away from him gently.

Staring at him, Tess raised her chin a notch and cleared her throat. As he watched her, he had to give her credit for not letting the tears fall that he could see shimmering so near the surface.

Without any further words, Zack stepped out the door, clicking it closed behind him.

Zack shoved against the door panel to Marlene Boudreaux's private quarters and felt a sense of satisfaction as the wood splintered beneath his weight.

However, his satisfaction was short-lived. Both her bedroom and the attached sitting room were unoccupied. Clothing tossed haphazardly about testified to a rapidly arranged departure.

"Anything?" a uniformed police officer called out from the stairs.

"Empty." Zack circled the room, then strode back out. Slamming his fist in his hand, he stopped at the approach of two more policemen.

They both shook their heads before he could ask what they'd found.

Zack swore and tightened his jaw. When he'd arrived at Marlene's establishment with the accompanying police officers, the front door had stood open, and light had shone out into the street.

They'd found the house hurriedly packed, everything of value and easily transportable gone. The two gunmen who'd pursued him and Tess were nowhere to be found. They'd vanished, as well as most all of the so-called ladies of the evening Marlene employed. Short of two or three of the prostitutes still engaged in amorous activities in bedrooms, the house had yielded nothing.

"Mackinzie?"

Zack spun about at the sound of his name. The police captain climbed the stairs, stopping at the top step. He sighed deeply at Zack's unspoken question.

"Simon White wasn't at the show. Or at the hotel. Or anywhere else as far as my men can tell."

"Hellfire."

If only they'd gotten here sooner. But the only way to have accomplished that would have been to put Tess in more jeopardy than he'd been willing to chance. So, now here he stood, empty-handed. Both Simon and Marlene had fled. Likely as not, by now they'd sailed on a ship out of the bay.

He hated having to relay the news to Tess.

* * *

It was a long three hours before Zack returned. Tess feared she'd wear a path in the narrow runner stretched across the wood flooring of the room, she'd paced its length so many times.

At the sound of a key scraping in the lock, she whirled about. Her heart poised, halfway between its next beat.

The door swung in to reveal the welcome sight of Zack. Tess practically flew across the room toward him, not stopping until she flung her arms around him. Her unexpected greeting nearly knocked Zack over backward. He struggled to regain his balance, and his emotional equilibrium at her act.

"Are you all right?" she asked, pulling back to look him up and down as if confirming it for herself.

Zack smiled at the unexpected note of concern. Had she really been worried over him?

"Yup," he assured her.

Pushing at his shoulders, she stepped back away from him. She planted her hands on her hips. "Then what in hell took you so long?"

Zack stared at her in amazement. He'd scarcely ever heard Tess swear. Practically the only words close to that she'd allowed past her lips had been the occasionally muttered "consternation." Hardly what he'd consider swearing. His lips twitched, but he wisely bit back any outward sign of laughter.

Recalling the reason for his absence, he sobered instantly.

"It took a while to search all the places they might have gone."

"And?"

Her voice was a bare whisper that tore at his heart. He hated revealing what he had to tell her.

"Honey, they're gone. They've escaped."

"Then—"

Zack pressed his fingertips gently against her lips. "They'll be found."

He hated giving the assurance when he feared it wouldn't be so. Simon and Marlene could be halfway up the coast by now. But he wouldn't share that with her. Not yet.

Morning would be soon enough for the harsh reality. For now, she needed assurances and comfort. Both things he intended to provide.

"Come here." He gently tugged on her small hand until she followed him over to the chair. "Let me hold you a minute."

He unfastened his gun belt, making certain he hung it within easy reach. Sitting down on the chair cushion, he tugged off his boots, then held out his arms.

When she came to him, he drew her between his parted legs. Gently, with infinite tenderness, he sat her on his lap and pulled her close against this chest, tucking her head against his shoulder.

Tess snuggled against him, like a small child seeking comfort. In response, Zack's temperature soared like that of water left out under a broiling desert sun too long. What he felt for her at this instant in time wasn't in the least a childlike response.

He'd set out to offer her comfort, not seduction. But damn, his body had other ideas. Desire coursed through him with an intensity that shook him. He clenched his jaw, tightening his muscles into rock hardness to fight off the desire that held him in its relentless grasp.

Inch by agonizing inch, he forced his body to cool, attempting to put out the fire that raged in his blood for her. Now was not the time to make love to Tess. Not after whatever she might have been through earlier tonight in the brothel.

He tightened his hand into a fist. He wished he were

able to tighten it around the neck of those responsible for what had been done to her.

Tess wondered at his restraint. He didn't ask her the obvious questions. And for that she loved him even more. She knew the questions were eating him up inside. It showed in the lines etched on his face. Instead, he'd only given, not asking anything in return.

For just a moment, she welcomed it. She needed the comfort, the gentleness, the trust he offered without her asking. However, she wanted more from him, and she wanted to give as well.

"Zack," she murmured against his shoulder. "Make love to me like before."

"But . . ." he paused. "After tonight? Tess, are you sure?"

She drew back, warmed by his concern. "Nothing happened at that place. I escaped in time." Smiling shyly, she added, "With your help."

He stared at her as if trying to ascertain she told the truth.

"My corset's even still securely tied if you want to check it."

Zack's deep chuckle stroked across her like a feathery caress.

"Or you could just unlace it," she challenged.

He reacted to her invitation like a dying man given a chance at life.

Surging to his feet, he carried her to the bed. Once there, he stopped and slid her body down the full length of his until her toes touched the floor.

Only then did he glance down and notice her one bare foot. At his puzzled look, Tess tapped his shoulder.

When he glanced back into her face, she said, "It fell off when I was climbing out the window." Smiling, she bit her lip to try to contain her laugh. "I think it hit you on the way down."

A deep laugh erupted from Zack, his chest shaking with mirth. "So, that's what that was."

Now that she mentioned it, he did recall something small striking his shoulder. Her shoe. He might have known the object came from her vicinity.

Grinning, he glanced back at her feet, "Would you like for me to remove the other one? It might be safer that way."

"Zack."

His grin widened. He liked the way she said his name. In fact, he liked the sound of his name on her lips. But there was something else he'd rather have on her lips.

Ducking his head, he caught her lips with his, branding her this time with the sheer heat of his kiss. Sighing against his lips in full surrender, Tess kicked her shoe free with the toe of her foot. The slipper landed against the wall with a thud.

Zack's chuckle rumbled against her lips, but he didn't end the kiss, instead only deepening it. As Tess smiled at his reaction, he slipped his tongue into the recess she had unknowingly offered.

His tongue flicked across the roof of her mouth, circled around and under her own tongue. She whimpered against him, completely caught up in his lovemaking.

It was as if by unspoken, mutual agreement they called a truce, each deciding to take what was offered and face the consequences tomorrow when the real world would intrude once again.

Zack ran his hands down her body, and every place he touched seemed to catch fire, to burn for him. He drew her tongue into his mouth, his teeth lightly scraping it. As he began to suckle, Tess moaned and sagged against him, lifting her chin to allow him freer access to her mouth.

Raising up on her bare tiptoes, she wrapped her arms around his neck, burying her fingers in the lush, thick hair covering his nape. Her thumbs rubbed against the stubble at his jaw, and she smoothed the pads of her thumbs back and forth in a repetitive stroking movement that imitated what was yet to come.

He groaned against her lips, never relinquishing her mouth. She flowed toward him, and he had a brief picture of warm, heated honey flowing into his arms and down his body.

He wanted her liquid heat encasing him. Sliding his hands along her back, he paused an instant here and there, dealing away with the fastenings of her gown like a master magician. Within moments, her gown slipped over her shoulders and fell into a puddle of silk around her feet.

"How'd you do that?" she murmured against his lips.

His only answer was a throaty chuckle.

Hooking his fingers under her chemise straps, he slid it off. It landed on the floor. Piece by piece, he slowly, lovingly stripped her.

As he reached for the buttons to his shirt, Tess's fingers pushed his own aside. She unfastened first one button, then a second. Pausing, she slid her fingers between the next two buttons, rubbing and stroking until he groaned against her with need.

Rubbing his hands over hers where they lay splayed across his shirt, he made short work of the remaining buttons of his shirt and shrugged out of it.

Tess leaned forward and slid her chest over his, rubbing back and forth against his bare skin. Her nipples pressed into the soft hair on his chest. His own nipples responded to her seduction, hardening into peaks. Bare skin against bare skin.

Zack groaned, for one second grinding his chest against hers, then he stepped back. Picking her up, he laid her on the bed and, following her down, he came down on top of her, pressing her into the mattress.

Leaning up on one elbow, he rested the fingers of

one hand a moment on her bare collarbone, then began a sensual exploration down over her breast. He circled each peak, touching, gently brushing the pads of his fingers back and forth.

Tess writhed beneath him. She raised her hands and drew his mouth down to hers, her own mouth opening to him. Nipping at his tongue, she drew his tongue inside her mouth, closing her lips tightly around it.

Zack thought his body would explode with need. She was turning him into a raging inferno. He drew back from her, rippling kisses down her neck and over her breasts.

Tess gripped his shoulders, her fingernails biting into his skin. His muscles tightened beneath her hands, coiling and uncoiling against her fingers.

Poised above her, he looked down into the face he loved. Her eyes were almost closed with the heat of passion, and his body burned in response to the look on her face.

He'd come so close to losing her tonight. Forever. Now he wanted to make her his. Completely, totally, forever his.

His upper body tensed with the strain of holding himself back. He didn't know how long he could hold on for her.

"I don't know if I can be gentle tonight, honey," he warned her.

The husky, ragged sound of his need filled his voice, and she responded to it instinctively. Wrapping her arms even more tightly around his wide shoulders, she whispered, "Then don't be."

With this permission, Zack lowered his body, plunging into her. Giving, taking, making them one.

Tess sighed against his mouth, giving herself completely to him.

Nineteen

Once again Tess awoke to the warmth of sunlight streaming through the window. She stretched and felt the solid strength of Zack's body against hers. She smiled and snuggled closer against his side.

It was unbelievably wonderful to wake up next to a man. She'd never felt quite this way before. The morning brought no fears, no regrets.

A little bit of heaven had descended on her earth. She was absolutely certain of that fact.

Memories of the night's lovemaking with Zack warmed her as much as the length of his finely muscled body did against hers. Last night, those muscles had rippled beneath her fingertips. Even now, the thought made her want to run her hands over his wide chest.

She scooted closer to him, shifting her body to conform to his, her waist snug against his hip, her breasts meeting the wide breadth of his chest. She noted how the dark hair on his muscular chest made a sharp contrast to the blond tendril of her hair curled over his nipple.

Last night, he'd rubbed her hair between his fingers, kissing it as well as every inch of her body before they'd finally fallen into an exhausted slumber. She still tingled with just the recollection of being wrapped tightly in his arms.

"Honey, you have one hell of a way of saying good morning." Zack's soft drawl washed over her.

Feeling like a child who just got caught stealing a sweet, Tess answered him back, "Good morning."

"I think I liked the other way you were saying it better."

In spite of herself, Tess smiled.

"Why are you smiling?"

Tess tilted her head back to gaze up at him. Dark stubble covered his cheeks and chin, almost completely hiding the two dimples bracketing his lips. Without realizing she did it, she moistened her own lips. A quick memory of his chin rubbing against her stomach before he—

Tess cut off the rest, her own cheeks heating with a blush. She ducked her head.

"So that's what you're smiling about," Zack observed, a grin covering his own face.

Tess remained silent, her face pressed tightly against the concealment of his bare chest. The heat of her blush warmed his skin.

"I thought maybe we were going to burn the room down a couple of times last night." His soft, seductive chuckle caused her face to redden even more in embarrassment.

"Hum?" He asked for agreement.

Tess threw her head back and meeting his gaze sent him a wicked smile of her own. "But, Ranger, isn't setting a fire against the law?" she asked in pure innocence at the same time her eyes twinkled with amusement and a sweet, seductive invitation.

Zack smoothed back a curl at her temple. Noticing the faint scarring, he traced it with the tip of his finger. "How did you get this?"

A shuttered look came over Tess's face, and she answered quickly, "Not now."

Raising herself up on her elbow, she pressed her body

against his chest and covered his lips with hers almost desperately.

The unexpectedness and intensity of her kiss startled Zack. As he opened his mouth to her invading tongue, a thundering knock sounded on the door.

"Hellfire," he grumbled, pulling back from her. "Is there a sign outside our doors that says 'Lovers within, please disturb'?"

Tess giggled at his remark. "It would seem so," she answered.

Neither of them moved.

"Maybe if we're quiet, they'll go away," Tess whispered.

Another loud knock at the door proved her assumption wrong.

"Hellfire. I'm coming," Zack yelled, tossing back the covers.

He stood at the bedside, tall and proud, and Tess couldn't help but admire him. Turning to her, he bent low and caught her lips in a kiss that spoke of more to come. So much more.

Straightening back up, he pushed himself away from the bed and the temptation Tess offered.

Tess ducked under the coverlet the instant he left her bedside. Once again it seemed as if he took all the heat with him.

A chill rippled down her back and she blamed it on the coolness of the room. However, the nagging sense of something gone terribly wrong gripped her. She tightened her fingers around the edge of the coverlet, hoping she would be proven wrong.

She couldn't help from watching Zack as he walked across the room. Somehow she couldn't seem to keep her eyes off him at all.

He stubbed his toe on her lone shoe, and she had to bite her cheek to keep in her smile.

Grumbling the entire time, Zack located his pants and pulled them over his legs, then fastened them. Another knock came at the door.

"I'm coming," he yelled. His voice rang with obvious irritation.

That deep drawl of his seemed to echo off the walls to her.

Striding to the doorway, he yanked open the door. It swung in to reveal a uniformed police officer. Tess's stomach sank at the sight.

She knew with absolute certainty that her world was about to come crashing down around her. Maybe forever this time.

Zack shifted his body to one side, effectively blocking the other man's view of Tess in the bed. He didn't want any man's eyes on her, except his own. Especially not now. She was his and the sooner everyone realized that, the better everything would be.

"Sorry to disturb you, Ranger." The officer shifted nervously from one foot to the other.

"Yes, what is it?" Zack didn't even try to disguise the impatience he felt.

"A telegram came for you." The young man withdrew a folded piece of paper from his breast pocket. "Thought it'd be best if somebody delivered it to you right away." Quickly, he added, "Sir."

With a growing sense of dread, Zack reached out and took the telegram from the officer. He couldn't help but remember that the last telegram he'd received had sent Tess's father behind bars.

Slowly, Zack unfolded the paper and read the words. Every bit of joy drained out of him, and he drew in a ragged breath filled with dread.

He was about to lose the only thing that meant anything to him. Tess's love.

He forced himself to thank the police officer, all the

while wondering how you set about thanking someone who had just destroyed your entire world with a single act of courtesy.

Acting for all the world as if nothing earth-shaking had occurred, he said his good-byes to the other man and closed the door on his departure.

"Zack?"

He detected the edge of worry in Tess's voice and hated himself for it. How she would hate him when she found out what the message had said. The cold, abrupt wording left no room for doubt or misunderstanding.

Slowly he folded the paper back, stalling for time and searching for words of his own to tell her what the message of doom had revealed.

"What is it?" Tess raised up on her elbow, alerted by the sudden stiffening she'd witnessed in Zack's stance.

Something was wrong. Her stomach tied into a knot while she waited for his answer.

Zack folded the telegram over again, creasing its edges. He closed his fist tightly around the paper before he turned around to face her.

"It's nothing. Business." The lie felt foreign on his tongue, and he nearly choked on it.

He crossed over to the bed and gazed down at her. She looked tousled and rumpled and wonderful. The sharp pain of impending loss tore at his heart.

Hellfire, why now? he thought. Why couldn't this have waited until their love was stronger? Strong enough to withstand this devastating blow.

Tess sat fully up in the bed, holding the coverlet tight against her almost as if it were a shield. He only wished it could protect her from this blow. Hell, he wished he could have protected her.

How was he to tell her that he'd received a telegram instructing him to return her father to Texas to stand trial for murder? A murder they wouldn't even have remembered if he hadn't sent the earlier message of his own making inquiries.

The law never would have looked for Jackson Philip Colton in California if not for him.

Guilt rolled over him. For the first time in his career he wanted to turn his back on the law he worked to uphold. But he knew he couldn't do that. His own sense of honor wouldn't let him. Instead, it would cost him the woman he loved.

"Zack?"

He was about to steal every bit of joy and hope from her life with anything he said.

Tess sat up straighter, the look on her face demanding an honest answer.

He saw her eyes darken, then narrow, but he didn't realize what she was going to do in time to stop her. She snatched the telegram out of his hand. All he was left holding was a small ripped corner of paper gripped between his thumb and forefinger.

As she read the curt message, her other hand tightened on the coverlet until her knuckles turned stark white against the cloth.

"You're not going to do it, are you?" she asked, a tremor in her voice.

"Tess, I have a duty—"

"No," she cut him off.

"I don't have a choice." He made the statement in a firm tone.

"Yes you do." Her eyes filled with tears. "Let him go."

As he stood watching, a single tear drop fell on her cheek and ran down her face. It tore at him, slicing his heart into pieces.

He couldn't do what she asked.

Tess stared up at Zack without blinking. He wouldn't do as she asked. She knew it even though he hadn't yet given her his answer.

"Damn you," she whispered.

"Tess, I'm a lawman. That's what I do."

"Then go do it elsewhere. Why can't you leave my father alone?" Her voice broke on the last word, and she gripped the coverlet even tighter.

"This isn't something that can be wished away, honey. He's been charged with murder—"

"Don't you think I know that. I've known that every day of my life for the last seven years."

The agony in her voice reached out to him, begging him. He tried to embrace her, but she slapped his hands away.

"Don't touch me. He's innocent, and all you care about is your duty."

Sadly he realized it was all he had.

"I'll see to your safety," he told her, attempting to reassure any fears she might have left over from the night before. It was all he had to offer her right now.

"Well, let's not have it take any longer than it has to."

Tess's statement wounded, and he lashed back. "I agree."

She glared at him, no trace of love or caring in her face any longer. "We wouldn't want the law-abiding Ranger to be inconvenienced."

"Honey, you invented the word."

"Damn you, Zack Mackinzie."

"I was damned the day I met you."

And so was David, he thought to himself, guilt rushing over him that he'd forgotten about his brother.

Turning on his heel, he strode to the door where he paused for the space of a heartbeat.

"Stay inside, and lock the door behind me," he ordered.

"Gladly."

The sound of the door being slammed and the lock turned followed him down the hall.

* * *

Tess stared at the closed door, her lower lip trembling with the control it took to keep her from calling him back. It seemed that the door reflected her accusations back at her.

What had she done?

She'd sent away the lawman who had arrested and jailed her father, she told herself.

She'd sent away the man she loved, her heart answered back.

Tears burned her eyes, and she swallowed to hold them at bay. She had truly and fully fallen in love for the first time in her life. Pain wracked her, following on the heels of this discovery. Until now she hadn't realized just how much she loved him.

His betrayal slashed through her defenses. Duty was the only thing that mattered to him.

Her love didn't matter in the least to him. She now knew that her first impression of Zack Mackinzie had sadly been right. He was law and order above all else. Even above love.

But, then he'd never loved her, she reminded herself.

He'd only used her to get to her father, to add one more outlaw's name to his list. She blamed herself for her father's arrest. If only she'd succeeded in ridding them of the Texas Ranger's presence. But no, instead she'd had to go and fall in love with him!

Zack's walk to work off his anger took him to the grounds of the traveling medicine show. He stood on the sidelines, watching.

The memories flowed over him like waves breaking on the beach. The Tempting Tess Fontana looking so beautiful up on the stage that it practically hurt to look at her. The feel of her in his arms beneath the stage when he'd caught her that first night in San Francisco.

As he stood there, image after image crossed his mind. Each one brought on the next, like a floodgate that had been opened.

"Tess isn't here," Ella announced with an edge of anger in her voice. She didn't try to hide it or disguise it in the slightest.

Zack turned and faced her. "I know. She's safe in my room."

Ella gasped in shock.

"Simon had her kidnapped and taken to Marlene's brothel."

The woman's face turned a disturbing shade of paleness, and she swayed on her feet.

Zack caught her before she fell.

"Oh, no, not that." Her voice rose. "Not to Tess." A shudder coursed through her body. "Not after . . ."

Zack tensed instantly alert. "After what?"

Ella shook her head. "If she didn't tell you, it's not up to me to do it."

"Ella?"

She stared at him for a full minute. "You love her, don't you?"

He couldn't lie. "Yes, I do."

"Then take her and her papa away somewhere. Somewhere safe."

"She wouldn't go with me. Not now."

Ella sank down onto a nearby bench and motioned for him to join her. At her gentle, concerned prodding he found himself telling her about the telegram and the upcoming trial.

"Mr. Mackinzie, can't you see?" Ella caught his arm. "Philip was only trying to protect his daughter. Hell, he was trying to keep her alive."

"What?"

"That bastard of a husband of hers nearly killed her that last time—"

"What do you mean that last time?" Zack caught Ella by the shoulder, not noticing that he gripped her tightly.

"I can't tell." She hung her head in defeat.

"Ella, if you care for Tess, talk to me."

She remained silent for several seconds, then sighed a sound that seemed to come from deep within. She met his questioning gaze.

A dread filled his limbs, holding him stock-still in place. One look at Ella's face and he knew he wasn't going to like the answer she was gathering up the courage to give him.

When the silence stretched out, he still waited. Something told him she needed time to put the words together and that it was going to be difficult for her to say what was coming.

He was right. Slowly the words came. She spoke of the beatings, the degrading humiliation, and of the night Tess's husband almost killed her.

"The scar," Zack said softly.

"So you've seen it?" Ella faced him.

"I've seen it," he answered, his mind reeling with what he'd been told.

"So now you know Philip is innocent."

"Ella . . ." he began, trying to explain the law to her.

In one move, she stood, cutting off his words. "And now what are you going to do about it?"

"What I have to do. I'll take him to Texas and tell them what I now know."

Ella caught his forearm. "Mr. Mackinzie, didn't you ever have family you cared about? Cared so much about that you'd do anything to keep them safe?"

His face tightened into a harsh mask of pain, and she stepped back involuntarily.

"Yes." His voice was ragged with anguish laced with

guilt. "My brother died because of Philip's protection over Tess."

"No," Ella denied it hotly, "You're wrong."

"Am I?" He lowered his head to within inches of her face.

This time she refused to withdraw.

"Then you tell me who was the woman David loved so much he died for her? Who was the beautiful blonde with eyes the color of Texas bluebells?" he asked her, harshness etched in his features.

Ella fell back from him, her face so pale it looked almost translucent. Shaking her head, she whispered his words back to him, "The color of Texas bluebells."

Suddenly, she covered her mouth with her hand as she realized what he'd been talking about. "David? Dead? No!"

"Yes, David Mackinzie—my brother."

Ella's blue eyes widened and, looking up at him, she fainted dead away.

Zack caught her the second before she hit the hard ground.

Holding her in his arms, he gently lowered her to the bench they'd been sitting on. He patted her cheeks lightly. Bending over her this way, he got his first real long look at her.

A strand of dark blond hair fell over her cheek, and as he brushed it aside he noticed the color for the first time.

Blond.

Not Tess's shade of silver and gold blended together, but still blond.

Before she'd fainted, her blue eyes had widened in shock.

Blue eyes.

"The color of Texas bluebells," he whispered.

Zack shook his head in disbelief, but he had to face the facts before him.

"I'll be damned," he muttered.

Ella—not Tess—was the woman in David's letter.

He'd heard that beauty was in the eye of the beholder. Now he realized the truth of that statement. To his brother David, Ella had been beautiful. Looking at her now, he could begin to see that beauty, too.

Her eyes opened, and she stared up into his face. "He's really dead?" she whispered.

Swallowing his own pain, Zack closed his eyes for a moment. "Yes."

She sat up, and tilting her head back, stared up at the sky overhead.

Zack's heart went out to her. He lightly took her hand in his. "You cared."

"Yes, I cared for your brother," she paused a moment to wipe away her tears. "But he was too young. I guess I didn't love him enough. If I hadn't sent him away . . ." She sniffed back the gathering tears.

"Ella, it wasn't your fault."

It was the truth, and he meant it.

Looking at her, he could scarcely believe how blind he'd been. Ella was the type of woman his brother would have been drawn to. Not his Tess.

As if sensing that his thoughts had returned to Tess, Ella touched his hand. "Zack, go to her. Tell her you love her before it's too late."

A wry smile pulled his lips. "Did anyone ever tell you you're a smart lady?"

Ella gave him a watery smile. "Tess has, once or twice. Go to her."

Giving her hand a farewell squeeze, and leaving her to her grief in private, he did as she'd suggested.

Tess greeted Zack's return with dry eyes and a cool shoulder of disdain.

When he opened his mouth to speak to her, she stopped him with a startling burst of news.

"I think I know where Simon might be hiding out."

"Where?" he asked.

Zack shoved aside his decision to tell her how he felt at this moment. First, he'd stop Simon and make certain of her safety. Then there'd be time for talking. And loving.

"I recalled that there was a special place he used to like to go to years past. I'll take you there." Her voice was as cool as her attitude toward him.

She turned toward the door, but Zack caught her arm to stop her. "You'll *tell* me where it is."

Tess instantly bristled under the command. "It's an old smugglers' cove. You'll never find it without help. I'll *show* you, or I'll go alone."

As she raised her chin a notch in a too-familiar gesture of defiance, he knew there was no sense in arguing with her. She'd go with or without him. He might as well have her where he knew where she was, instead of risking her sneaking in when his back was turned.

"All right," he gave in.

Tess swept past him, and as she reached the door he noticed she was wearing shoes on both feet. He opened his mouth to question her, then thought better of it and snapped his mouth closed. Did he really want to know how she'd ignored his order to stay in the room with the door locked?

She waited while he rented a buggy for them. He wasn't about to go walking along the docks with Tess in tow without his own transportation. It took several twists and turns as well as a couple of false turns before they came upon the opening to a cave.

Zack realized that she'd been right. He never could have found it without assistance. The opening was practically invisible to the eye, unless one knew exactly where to look.

As Tess started forward, he caught her wrist. "Uh uh." He motioned her back.

There was no way he was letting her go in first. Stepping in front of her, he led the way toward the entrance. Once there, he stopped. Tess was so close on his heels that she careened into his back.

"What are we waiting for?" she whispered.

Zack drew his gun. "This. Now I'm ready. But you do exactly as I say. Understand?"

Sighing, she nodded.

"Promise?" he waited, forcing her to give her word before proceeding.

Together they entered the cave, Tess staying only a breath behind him. The first opening quickly narrowed to a tunnel leading far back into the interior. They continued to follow it, and minutes later heard the low roar of the ocean beyond.

About this time, the tunnel gave way to a larger cavern. Two torches hung against the damp walls, giving off light. The illumination revealed a row of dried herbs hung above a wood table which was partially covered with glass bottles.

Tess recognized them as vials used in the medicine show. She tapped Zack on the shoulder and pointed to the table.

However, his attention was fixed elsewhere. In one corner of the cavern, several objects from Marlene's establishment were stacked together. Beside them were two valises, bulging at the seams.

Tess tapped him on the shoulder again. As Zack turned to her, a figure leaped out from the stack of articles and lunged for him. Tess's scream echoed off the damp, cold walls.

Twenty

Zack whirled around and dodged, recognizing Simon White as he charged again. This time the other man's shoulder caught him in the ribs. Simon hit him hard and both men crashed to the floor, Zack's pistol crushed against their bodies.

Suddenly the steel edge of a knife flashed between the men in the flickering light. Tess's scream of warning froze on its way to her throat. She was held immobile as the horror of another knife fight took her back through the years.

Her palms started to sweat. Recognition of her surroundings faded until she didn't notice the chilling dampness or the flickering torches. She watched the two men fight from her trancelike stupor.

It wasn't until she saw the knife raised over Zack begin to lower that she jerked into action. Racing across the room, she threw herself at the men.

Her shoulder slammed into Simon and sent the knife blade sailing out of his hand. The knife clattered across the uneven floor of the cavern and out of range of the torch lights. Zack jerked his pistol away from the direction of Tess.

She rolled to the other side, trying to get out of Zack's way so that he could fire. A blow from Simon's fist brought tears to her eyes and a trickle of blood to her lip.

Zack drew back his fist and caught the other man with a sharp upper cut to his jaw. Simon reeled back and Zack surged to his feet. Another blow dropped Simon to his knees.

As Zack drew his arm back again, Tess grabbed his arm and held on. "Don't. You'll kill him."

Zack realized that was exactly what he'd wanted to do with his bare hands. Dragging in a shaken breath, he dropped his arm.

Aiming his pistol at Simon, he motioned him to his feet.

"Why?" Tess stepped forward and asked.

Simon glared at her with undisguised hatred. "You really don't suspect, do you?"

A chill skated along her arms, and she forced herself to face his open hostility. "You had me kidnapped," she accused.

"That's less than what you did," he charged.

Tess fell back a step at the vehemence in his voice.

"Always sweet and innocent, weren't you? But you weren't either when you seduced and killed Joel."

Simon advanced on her a step, but Zack stepped forward, gun aimed.

"I arrived too late to stop you. Joel was dead. Because of you." Simon pointed at Tess.

She flinched at the accusation.

"He was my own blood. My nephew."

Tess's gasp clung to the damp walls. She shook her head in denial.

"And you and your father killed him. And nobody was going to do a thing about it. Until I told the law that I'd witnessed his cold-blooded murder at the hands of your father."

"The eyewitness," Tess whispered.

"That didn't work. You two got away. It took me over a year to track you down. By then, I needed a new life, too, so eventually I let it go. Then, last year I met Marlene. And she reminded me of my duty."

Tess bit her lip. She should have guessed the witch was somehow behind all this trouble.

"So we put this operation together and offered our own *special* elixir on the side, with just enough opium mixed in to see that they kept coming back for more." Simon's voice filled with pride.

He waved one arm at the cavern. "My own magic act." Smiling, he bragged, "The fools fell for our scheme so easy. We milked them dry, and once we had all the money we could get out of them, we killed them."

"Poisoned," Tess whispered. "For money."

"Money from those dead fools is what set Marlene up in her new establishment in this city."

Tess gasped at the relayed information. Ever since Simon and Marlene had joined together, he had been using the show to con people out of their savings and then killed them to protect his scheme.

"All for Marlene?" she asked in disbelief.

"Of course not. I took my share, too."

"But Marlene—"

"Don't you dare to speak ill of her. Do you hear me?" He nearly screamed the words at her. Lowering his voice once again, he said in an undisputable statement of fact, "I love her."

Tess had known that without his declaration. It had been evident for all to see. They'd shared a bond that passed beyond murder.

"Your father should have hung for my deeds. We planned it so carefully. It would have been fitting justice."

"I think we've heard enough," Zack announced. He wasn't sure how much more Tess could take. Her face was pale, and her hands were clenched into tight fists. He wanted to go to her and take her in his arms, but now was not the time for that.

As if realizing his mistake in boasting, Simon stepped backward, bumping into the table. The glass vials rattled with the force of the jolt. Before either Tess or Zack could make a move to stop him, he grabbed one of the bottles and pulled out the cork. Tipping the vial, he emptied the contents in two deep swallows.

As they watched helpless to save him, he fell to the floor. His body writhed, and Zack caught Tess and buried her face in his shoulder.

He held her there until it was over. Justice had been meted out in its own way. The poisoner had died by his own potion, in the very same manner he'd taken other lives.

"Zack?" Tess's voice was muffled against his shirt.

"Honey, its over," he told her.

Turning, he led her out of the cave into the dim sunlight outside, keeping one arm tight about her shoulders. He didn't release his hold on her until he had her safely in the buggy. Around them, the fog began to move in.

He flicked the reins and left the nightmare scene behind. He'd send the police captain out after he made his report.

"Oh, Zack," Tess moaned, a sob catching in her throat. "He—"

"Not now." Zack forced himself to keep his eyes trained straight ahead. He'd gotten them both out of this alive so far, he didn't intend to let his guard down until they were past the docks and far away from the dangers offered by the city's famed Barbary Coast.

Tess drew in a deep, calming breath of the damp, cool air. A faint fog had settled in, closing around about them. Shivering against something she wasn't sure of, she laid her hand on Zack's forearm.

He jerked the reins. "Not now."

She snatched her hand away as if it had been burned. However, she knew that wasn't possible, for Zack had been cold enough to freeze steam into ice.

His abrupt rejection silenced her, and Tess huddled down in the seat. She felt like something inside her had just died. She knew it was Zack's love.

"I'll see that the charges are dropped against your father," Zack announced in a tightly leashed tone. Not a hint of his drawl came through the cool tone.

Tess sat back against the seat stiffly. She should at least be thankful for that. Her father was safe. She clenched her hands together in her lap to ward off the pain of Zack's rejection, but it didn't do any good. Pain stabbed through her with each breath she took, each thought, each memory.

Glancing at Zack, she saw that he sat stiff and un-yielding, the reins tight between his fingers.

She'd saved her father, but she'd surely destroyed their chance at love in the process.

The ride to the police station was cloaked in silence.

The next few hours were spent in a flurry of questions and reports. Tess couldn't believe the relief she felt to finally leave the police station. Her father had indeed been released. In fact, even before her.

She inhaled the fresh air outside and walked to the hotel, exulting in the freedom. The fog had lifted. In front of the hotel, she stopped and stared at the distinguished man walking toward her with a mixture of disbelief and hope.

Zack had kept his word to her. Her father was free.

"Papa!"

Her father stepped forward and engulfed her in a hug that tried to shut out the horrors he knew she'd been through while he'd been away.

"It's over, dear." He held her close to his heart.

His voice was as soothing as ever to her ears. Tess let the words of comfort and love wash over her.

"Let's go upstairs, shall we?" he suggested.

Not waiting for her answer, he turned and led her up to her room.

After the door shut behind them, Tess hugged him close again. "You're really here. You're really free." She couldn't resist reaching out and touching his arm as if making certain this wasn't a dream.

"Simon's confession to your lawman cleared me of all charges. Of everything," he assured her.

"Papa, I'm sorry. I know Simon was your friend."

He stepped back and took her hands in his. "He let his bitterness and greed destroy him."

Tess sighed. It had all been such a waste of life.

Her father tugged on her hands and drew her over to the set of chairs. He eased her into one and took the chair facing her. He'd quickly picked up on the sadness in her eyes that coursed soul deep. It came from more than Simon's treachery.

"Tess, tell me the rest," he ordered her in a low, soft voice that encouraged shared confidences.

Tess scarcely noticed he'd used his showman voice, the one that mesmerized, getting him exactly what he wanted. Looking up, she met the love and questions written on his beloved face. She couldn't hold out against both. Giving in, she let the words flow free from her heart and her very soul. In the end, she told him everything.

When at last she'd finished, he caught her hands in both of his. "Well, tell me, do you love him?"

Could she love a lawman? Even more, could she love a Texas Ranger who was always gone, a wanderer?

The questions came too late—her heart had already decided long before, answering with a resounding yes.

Meeting her papa's concerned gaze, she gave her answer, "Yes. More than life itself."

"Well—"

"But he doesn't want me, Papa." Her voice wavered on a choked back sob of grief for a love that died.

"We've made quite a mess of things, haven't we?" He cleared his throat. "Maybe you'd best rest awhile. We'll finish this later. This evening."

Brushing a kiss on the top of her head, he crossed to the door. He sent one more concerned glance back at her before he stepped into the hall.

Maybe he'd go have a talk with a certain Texas lawman about his intentions toward his daughter.

The more he thought about it, the more he liked the idea.

The darkness of evening clothed the hotel hallway in black. It had been a small feat to dispose of the lighting outside Tess's room. The lone figure stepped out of the shadows. Hatred nearly ate a hole from within.

Tess Fontana still lived. It was everyone else who was dead. Hatred for her grew and festered until it coiled through the entire body, becoming the driving force behind every thought and action.

By some miracle, sweet, innocent Tess had escaped everything. Every accident, every murder attempt, every single plot they'd devised for her.

The time for plotting was past. It was time to take matters into one's own hands.

So much pleasure would be derived from squeezing

the life out of Tess with one's own hands, but a gun would ensure death without any more mistakes.

Curling long fingers into angry fists, the figure crossed the hall and eased open the unlocked door. Tess stood across the room, her back to the door. At the sight of her, hatred rose up, nearly blinding in its intensity.

Pushing the door closed, it gave a resounding click that caused Tess to stiffen.

"Bitch." The accusation rang out full of hatred.

Tess whirled around, but the path to the only doorway was blocked by Marlene Boudreaux. The glint of sunlight reflecting off the derringer in Marlene's hand stopped Tess in mid-step.

"What are you doing here?" Tess asked, stalling for time.

"Ohhh, I've come to kill you, of course." Marlene's voice was filled with such hatred that Tess took a step back.

In response, Marlene took a menacing step forward, gun tightly clenched in her fist, and Tess recognized the glint of madness in her eyes for what it was.

The other woman most assuredly intended to see her dead.

"Did you really think you'd go unpunished for murdering Joel?"

Shocked, Tess stared at Marlene. The woman wasn't here for revenge for Simon's death? She repeated the name, "Joel?"

"My baby boy." Marlene practically screamed the words.

Tess's heart raced in shock. "You're Joel's mother?" she whispered.

"Yes. And you killed him!"

Tess reeled from shock. She stared at the woman pointing the gun at her, searching for some resemblance that she'd missed.

"You don't look like him." The statement slipped past Tess's lips without conscious thought. She'd let the first thing that came to mind slip out.

Marlene narrowed her eyes. If anything her hatred of Tess for pointing out that fact increased. "He took after his worthless father."

Tess continued to stare, rooted to the spot with shock. One thought kept repeating itself over and over in her mind: Marlene had been Joel's mother.

Her mind continued on. The next step struck her and she gasped.

"Then Simon—"

"Was my dear brother," Marlene provided.

Brother and sister.

Tess continued to stare at the other woman. Brother and sister?

Tess tried to keep her mouth from dropping open at the news. She'd been so certain they were lovers. Simon's remarks, the little kisses, the loving touches—they'd showed her exactly what Simon and Marlene had wanted her to see.

"Our ploy worked, didn't it?" she sneered at Tess. "You never suspected. You fool."

"But Uncle Simon—"

"Don't you dare call him that," Marlene screamed at her. "Do you know how much I wanted to strike out at you each time you said that foolish name. He wasn't yours. He wasn't."

"We were his only family," Tess said, half to herself, trying to sort it all out.

"No, Joel and I were his family. If not for his stubbornness, we would never have been apart."

Tess recalled Simon telling her that a bitter argument had left him estranged from his sister and her baby.

Marlene waved the gun at her. "But all that was forgotten when we met again in Virginia City. Imagine my surprise when I looked up from my bed to see my little brother waiting to pay for my favors." Harsh laughter cut through the room.

The pieces began to fall into place for Tess. It was shortly after that time when the show began experiencing troubles. She made the mistake of saying this.

"Sy was ready to let Joel lie in his grave. The fool. It took me to make him see you had to pay. Both you and your father."

"Joel's death was self-defense. He—"

Marlene's shriek cut her off. "They were both put in their graves by you." She raised the gun. "And now you'll join them."

As Tess watched in stunned disbelief, Marlene's finger closed over the trigger, and a shot rang out.

Twenty-one

Tess looked up to see Zack standing in the doorway. The gun in his hand trailed a streak of smoke.

She looked from him to where Marlene lay crumpled on the floor. Dead. His shot had rung true, hitting her in the center of the chest, scarcely a moment before she could pull the trigger of her derringer.

Tess gripped the back of the chair to remain upright. It seemed that all the stuffing had gone out of her legs. Zack reached her side just as her legs gave way. He scooped her up into his arms.

"If your father hadn't paid me a visit, I wouldn't have gotten here in time," he whispered against her hair.

Tess noticed his voice was ragged, rough around the edges like she'd never heard before. Gone was all the assurance she'd come to associate with him.

She tipped her head back to look up at him. He groaned low in his throat, then he turned toward the door with her still in his arms. He crossed the room, resolutely keeping her turned away from the body on the floor.

Carrying her tucked close against his chest, Zack strode out the door. Passing the open doorway to an empty room, he shouldered his way inside, kicking the door closed behind them.

He eased her down, testing that her legs would hold

her up before he released her, then stepped back away from her several steps. His eyes held her pinned in place.

"Papa came to see you?" she asked, willing to accept the diversion from what had just occurred with Marlene.

"Your father paid me quite an enlightening visit." He rubbed his jaw in not-so-fond memory of their conversation. "I'd rather not have too many talks with him in the future. For a showman, your father packs one hell of a punch."

Tess knew her mouth dropped open. Her papa wasn't normally a violent man.

"He hit you?" she asked in disbelief.

Zack rubbed his jaw again. "Yup."

"Why?"

"Said he wanted to ensure that my intentions toward his daughter were honorable."

Tess's eyes widened. Oh, no.

"And that's why you're here." She stated it flatly, all life seeping out of her voice. Zack was only here to appease her father.

"No."

Tess swallowed and, meeting his gaze, her heart fluttered. The intensity she saw in those gun-metal-gray depths gave her hope.

"Why are you here, Zack?"

"I came to see if I could change your mind about lawmen. About me." The statement had an edge of challenge in it.

Tess accepted that challenge with a thrill racing through her body. "You do know you're the first lawman I've ever fostered tender feelings toward." She took a step in his direction.

"I don't think those sentiments exactly run in your family," he said in derision. He took one long stride forward, drawing closer.

"Papa will come around. In time he'll accept your career." She took another step, biting her lower lip, hoping she was reading him right.

The corner of Zack's lips turned up in a half-smile at her approach, and the dimples she loved stood out.

"Well, I'm happy to hear that," he drawled. "But I'm not going to be a Ranger much longer."

His words stopped her in mid-step. "What? Why?"

"I have a ranch in Texas that needs taking care of," he paused.

Tess's heart raced, and she was certain he could hear it pound against her chest.

A ranch . . . a house . . . a home . . .

"We could take care of it together, if you'll marry me." His words were so low she had to strain to hear them.

Her dream took substance.

"Well, honey? Can I tempt you into saying yes?"

The slight hesitation in his voice and the look of vulnerability in his eyes assured her of the truth of his love like no mere words could have done.

Tess flung herself the remaining distance into Zack's arms, nearly knocking him over. "Yes! Oh, yes."

She raised her head to kiss him, and the top of her head caught him under the chin with a resounding whack.

He groaned and brushed a kiss on the top of her head. "Honey, do I think maybe you could keep me alive long enough to marry me?"

Laughter bubbled from Tess's lips. "Definitely. Oh, most definitely. Besides, I'm going to need a father for all the children I plan to give you."

Zack caught her close and swung her around in the air. His rich, deep laughter filled the empty places of her heart. Finally coming to a stop, he held her off the ground and planted a resounding kiss full on her mouth.

"Tess, I love you so much it steals my breath," he declared.

"Zack." Tess gazed into the face of the man she loved more than life itself, and told him so.

Zack ran his hand down her back, and Tess snuggled against him, whispering her own declarations. She followed it with a suggestion.

Grinning, Zack eased her down until her toes touched the floor. "Your father definitely gave you the right name."

"What do you mean?" She tilted her head back to look up into his eyes. She could spend a lifetime looking at the love she saw in his gray depths.

"Tempting Tess."

A smile tipped the corners of her lips.

"Could I tempt you into telling me you love me again?" he asked. "Or maybe you could show me?" The soft drawl in his voice was a seductive purr.

"Always," she murmured, pressing her mouth against his lips. She closed her eyes in sheer bliss.

"Always and forever," he answered.

He proceeded to seal that vow with a kiss that curled every one of her ten toes.

Epilogue

Texas, 1880

Tess stepped behind the sprawling ranch house, planting her hands on her hips in mock indignation. "So, here's where you've been hiding."

Her father looked up at her with the grin of a child caught with a forbidden sweet. He held a little blond-haired girl in his lap. In the toddler's hand was a shiny gold piece.

"Guilty. Go show that to your mama, Mary."

Hopping down, the little girl ran up to Tess with the grace only a two-year-old could possess.

"Look, Mama." She held up the coin. "Grandpa made magic."

"I want one, too." The demand signaled the whirlwind approach of a second child, a golden-haired twin brother. David launched himself into his grandfather's lap.

Tess smiled with pure joy.

"I'd tell them to let you rest, but you deserve everything they can throw at you. Whatever gave you the idea to teach them to disappear? I've been pulling David out of closets all morning." Tess tried to fake a frown, but couldn't muster one up. Life was too good to frown anymore.

Instead, she smiled in pure happiness at the scene before her. She had all the people she loved here together on the ranch. How could anyone be so fortunate?

Shading her eyes, she could make out the outline of the small house belonging to Ella and her new husband, the ranch foreman. Her smile widened into a grin.

Ella had balked at coming with them, but both she and Zack had insisted. The same day they arrived, Ben Thompson had taken one look at Ella and swore to marry her. It had taken him two years to accomplish that. And now, Ella was expecting.

Talk about magic. Love was the greatest magic feat of all, Tess decided.

As a rider approached, her smile turned to one of loving tenderness.

Zack. He still caused her heart to race at the mere sight of him.

"Have you told him yet?" her papa asked in a low voice.

Tess whirled on him, openmouthed. "Yesterday. But how did you know I'm expecting?"

A grin was her only answer.

Behind her, Zack swung down from his horse and caught Tess around the waist. Nuzzling her neck with kisses, he whispered, "I told him."

She snuggled into his arms, savoring the feel of his strong, wide chest behind her. She loved him even more today than the day they'd married.

"Care to go make some magic of our own?" he asked, his whisper tickling the fine hairs at her temple.

His soft drawl caused her stomach to turn over. "Definitely," she answered back.

Tiptoeing, they slipped away to the house. Once inside, they dashed up the stairs like naughty children.

Zack swept her into his arms, taking her mouth in a

kiss that she was certain even curled the baby's toes. Slipping her arms about his neck, she clung to him, loving him, giving fully to him.

"Honey, you tempt me beyond control," he growled as he laid her on the bed, then followed her down.

"Always and forever, I hope." She brushed a kiss over his chin.

"Always and forever," he answered.

Author's Note

Every day untold numbers of women in America are abused. Abuse comes in many forms: physical, mental, and emotional.

Abuse is not about love, or mistakes, or anger—it is about control. Sometimes even a short time away from the abuser can allow the woman to see things clearly, and to recognize the control for what it is. If you are being abused, I implore you to call the hotline number. Sometimes all it takes is a chance and a safe environment to start a new life.

Please take that chance.

National Hot Line 1-800-799-SAFE (7233) (toll free)

For hearing-impaired people, the number is 1-800-787-3224

ROMANCE FROM JO BEVERLY